# GENERATION 0

## ALEX VORKOV

PERMUTED
PRESS

A PERMUTED PRESS BOOK

ISBN: 978-1-68261-446-4
ISBN (eBook): 978-1-68261-420-4

Generation 0
© 2017 by Alex Vorkov
All Rights Reserved

Cover art by Christian Bentulan

**PERMUTED**
PRESS

Permuted Press, LLC
New York • Nashville
permutedpress.com

Published in the United States of America

A note on the locations: I've long been fascinated by the subway system in Washington DC, so much so that I set part of this story there. The surreally long escalators sinking deep into the Earth offered a playground for my characters too great to resist. That said, I embellished these locations to suit my needs, borrowing details from train stations and bus terminals in New York City when I desired to expand the fictional landscape.

–Alex

## OCTOBER 9

The one-eyed girl, shin deep in rot, clawed at the knotted mass of green-brown plastic. So far she had only turned over the slime of three-year-old garbage. Nothing close to edible.

Carter climbed onto the dumpster and peered inside. "Come on out. You ain't gonna find anything in there."

The one-eyed girl kept digging. Looking at Carter meant twisting around. He was on her blind side. She yanked an empty Bud Light from the muck and dodged a wad of slop that flew up with it. She tossed the bottle over the side of the dumpster. It shattered on the asphalt.

"Jesus! Are you retarded?"

Josie had been with Carter for a few weeks now, and sometimes that seemed more than plenty. "No one's around. They left."

A gang of kids armed with rifles had come marching down the center of North Avenue an hour earlier shooting at windows and signs, most of which were broken anyway, laughing and acting like clowns. Josie and Carter had hidden in Flamingo Garden Center behind torn-up bags of wood chips until the gang passed.

Hidden for what? She half-wished they would have found her and killed her.

Josie dug out another empty beer bottle, tossed it to the corner of the dumpster where it ricocheted with a clang, and resumed searching. Her hands slid over something hard under a plastic bag. She stood. "Found something."

An upright dumpster was rare after all this time. A few months ago, during the hottest part of summer, she'd found one up by the burned-out Loyola campus. Someone had chucked a can of beans in there. Today she hoped for soup or pear slices. Tomato sauce. Cat food. Anything.

She pulled the garbage bag away. Carter slipped and fell to the pavement.

Two skeletons, adults, lay in the slime, their frozen grins facing skyward. Patches of hair and skin still adhered in places, but they were mostly bones. Their kids must have dumped them. Josie wondered who would put their dead parents in a garbage bin.

"You shouldn't stand in there," Carter said, peering over the lip again.

"They're not exactly fresh." Josie grabbed one by the leg and tried to unstick it from the muck. A can of beans or soup could be under there.

The femur came off in her hand.

Without warning, Carter leaped into the dumpster, sending a spray of slime into her tangled, dirt-caked, once-blonde hair. She glared. "What's wrong with you?"

He crouched in the corner farthest from the skeletons and pulled the revolver from under his belt. "Someone's coming."

Josie stood to inspect, but he tugged her down. "Don't be stupid," he said.

She handed him the femur. "Here. Beat them with this."

"Shhh!"

Josie reached under the muddy frill of her yellow-flower sundress and withdrew her switchblade. "You distract 'em by acting stupid, and I'll sneak up from behind." She thrust the knife at an imaginary foe.

"Would you shut up?"

She stood again and surveyed the desolate lot behind the derelict electronics store. A blue jay picked at something between cracks in the asphalt—a dried up worm, maybe—then gave up and flew away.

The last good rain had come ages ago. The air tasted like dust. She hadn't seen a moving car in a year or someone on a bike or a skateboard in a month. Most of the time, wind pushing old papers or Styrofoam across a parking lot or down an avenue made the only sound. Sometimes, a door would fall open when a hinge rusted through, or a window would pop out of its frame and shatter. Until that gang came through an hour ago, she hadn't even heard that many gunshots lately.

Baltimore was a ghost town.

"No one's there," she said. "Just a bird."

The sun continued its descent, about to slip behind the skyscrapers. It would be dark in an hour. Time to go back to the nest. "Come on," she said, hopping over the side of the dumpster and onto the broken pavement. She scraped the muck from her boots and then slung her canvas bag, empty for the third day in a row, over her shoulder.

Carter scrambled out of the dumpster and dropped beside her. "Don't leave me in there with them."

A cool breeze tore through the alley, chilling Josie's emaciated frame. Normally she would mock Carter for still being creeped out by skeletons. Hadn't he seen millions? But the breeze meant winter was coming, and food would be even scarcer. In a month or two those skeletons would be Carter and her, side by side for eternity. Or until animals came and scattered the bones. In the meantime, it would be slow, agonizing starvation.

***

Too weak and tired to bother zigzagging and sneaking back to their hideout, Josie and Carter ambled south on McCulloh Street.

"What do you miss most, besides food and your mom and comics and obvious stuff?" Carter asked.

"I don't miss my mom."

"Whatever. I mean what *things*? The Internet. Air conditioners. Nintendo."

They'd had this conversation three times already. Josie kicked a bottle cap down the sidewalk. It rolled to a stop near the broken window of the Chinese market.

"Music, I guess. All those CDs lying around, and no way to play them." She wound up to kick the bottle cap again when three gangsters armed with rifles leapt to the sidewalk from inside the Chinese grocery store, blocking their path.

*Shit. Fuck.*

"Run and you die," said the kid in the sleeveless denim jacket. Seven or eight more boys piled out, the tinkle of broken glass about their feet as they formed a semicircle. These were the same gangsters Josie and Carter had hidden from before.

The biggest one, a redhead about seventeen, pointed his rifle at Carter's face.

"Waste him," said the one in the denim jacket. Nobody bothered to target Josie, a scrawny girl. She thought of fleeing and leaving Carter to his fate. She didn't want to end up like Cara.

"Not yet," said the redhead. "I gotta figure out what I want to do with him."

Josie glanced to the right. Maybe if she ran into the Chinese market, she could lose them. She'd cut through there before.

The denim kid speared his rifle at her, and she threw a hand up to protect her eye. He laughed. "Dude, she flinched!"

The redhead laughed too, and most of the other boys played along. The two in the back, the youngest-looking of the bunch, eyed each other. Josie knew what they were thinking: Their leader was a sadist, and they were afraid of him.

The redhead poked Carter's chin with the barrel. "Open your mouth and suck on this," he said. "Do it, or I'll kill you."

"Todd, check it out," the denim-clad kid said to the redhead, thrusting his rifle toward Josie again. "She's only got one eye!"

Todd leaned in close and grabbed her jaw, twisting her head as if inspecting a farm animal for sale. "No shit," he said, staring into the socket. "That is so nasty."

Josie thought of biting his thumb off. Would it be worth it?

Denim grabbed one of the undersized boys by the arm and shoved him toward Josie. "That hole is just your size, Weasel." The other boys laughed. Weasel swallowed.

Todd clutched Josie by the hair and pulled her closer. "How about it, bitch? You going to let Weasel here get a piece of the action?"

Images of Cara played in her mind, like they did a hundred times a day, only now it was going to be her. How could she and Carter have been so stupid as to walk down the main drag like it was a Sunday stroll? How could they have been so careless? Then she envisioned the switchblade strapped to her right thigh. She concentrated on it. Felt it pressing against her and imagined how fast she could get to it.

No. These sadists weren't going to get what they wanted. They might end up killing her outright, but not before she took one of the scumbags with her. She'd been waiting for this.

Her hand was already in motion, swooping for the knife, when Carter whipped the revolver from the back of his pants and aimed it at Todd. "Let her go!"

Todd and the other boys stepped back, their cruel smiles vanished, and raised their rifles at both of them. "Drop it!"

"Leave us alone," Carter said, his voice quavering. The gun wobbled. Josie saw that his finger wasn't on the trigger. The two of them were about to be shot up for target practice.

Maybe it was better this way.

Todd stood straight, snarling for the benefit of his reputation. "Put that gun down, or I'll shoot your kneecaps out and leave you here on the—"

A sharp crack split the air, and the left side of Todd's face vanished in a spray of exploding blood and bone as the noise of the shot reverberated off the storefronts. He crumpled before Josie could grasp what had happened. The other boys all whirled to their right. More shots, blood splashing, bodies falling. Carter stared in shock at the carnage, his revolver unfired. Then Josie got it: Snipers were picking them off from across the street.

The kid in denim fired back into the shadows toward the unseen gunmen, his low-caliber weapon issuing a pathetic pop. He reached into his pocket to fish out another round but was blown back by the sniper, his chest carved out in an instant.

"Come on," Josie said, grabbing Carter by the arm. His gun fell to the sidewalk as they dove into the Chinese grocery, down the center aisle, through the storeroom, and scurried like rats out to the side alley.

They darted right and then into the pawnshop, which had long since lost its back door. The place was empty, no place to hide, so they kept going, bursting onto Tiffany Street, still so many blocks from their nest.

A bullet struck a lamppost fifteen feet away. More shots echoed. The firefight was spilling over to this street. With nowhere to hide, Josie and Carter crouched to the asphalt. "I lost my gun," Carter said.

Josie looked for an escape route. Just then one of the gang members emerged from the alley. Weasel, blood spattered across his jacket, his rifle held in a one-handed grip, saw Josie and froze.

They could use that weapon. "Come with us," she said, extending her arm. Weasel was no sadist.

He stared at her, indecisive for a moment too long. A bullet from the sniper's rifle rocked him forward, his body going limp before his face struck the pavement.

Josie whirled. The lane stretched too wide. Windows and doors were shot out. Only one car in sight, too small, too broken, and too obvious a hiding place. A flattened donut served as a driver's side rear tire. Josie stood to sprint across the street, aiming for the dry cleaner. That's when she spotted the manhole cover.

She bolted for the broken-down vehicle instead, a tan Toyota Corolla, and yanked the door open. She flung out the dusty bones of the driver, held more or less in human shape all these years by a pair of jeans and a dress shirt.

"No way," Carter said. "They'll know we're in there."

Josie crawled into the back and tugged on the seat-release lever while the noise of gunshots filled the air. The seatback dropped forward, given her access to the trunk. "Yes!"

The flat tire the driver had removed on the day of his death still sat in the dark trunk beside a tire iron. Josie clutched the steel implement and snagged the cheap flashlight lying beside it.

She squirmed backward onto the street and crouched before the manhole. "Help me."

The bullet whizzing over Carter's head prompted him into action. Josie pried with the crowbar as he reached under the lip, and the two starving, exhausted kids let out a grunt in unison as they found the strength to move the iron disk enough for their emaciated bodies to squeeze into the hole. Josie went first, tossing in the tire iron and sliding down the ladder into the blackness beneath the street. Carter scurried behind, but his head got stuck between the rim of the hole and the metal cover.

"Turn sideways," Josie said. Carter wriggled and yelped, and he forced his way, barely keeping his grip on the ladder. Once free, he dragged the cover back in place and plopped down beside his companion.

Carter hunched over and gasped for air, rubbing his cheekbone. Josie listened for more gunshots, but her ears caught another sound: Water. Trickling at their feet. Water!

She remembered the flashlight in her hand. She felt for the button and pressed it, but nothing happened. It was too old. She began to smack it against her palm.

"What are you doing?"

"I hear water," she said. On the fifth smack, the light came on, and she aimed the beam toward the floor of the tunnel.

Not water.

Carter gave a parched cry and jumped back onto the ladder. Josie stayed in place as the slithering horde of black rats flowed around and between and over her feet, dragging naked tails across her boots. After a deep breath, she lowered herself to her knee, running her hand up her right leg. Her fingers wrapped around the handle of the switchblade and withdrew it. She pressed the button. The blade shot forth with a snap.

The first flurry of strikes hit stone, but she soon figured out the timing and skewered one of the creatures, pressing down hard until she felt the flesh give way and then lifting the animal into the flashlight beam. Impaled on the steel point, it writhed and whipped its tail and swept the air with its tiny hands. Josie set down the flashlight, opened her canvas bag, and shook the knife handle until the rat slid off the blade and fell in. Then she stabbed again, running another through. And another. With methodical patience, counting beats between thrusts, she impaled a dozen of them, stuffing their twitching bodies into her bag. Carter remained on the ladder, on Josie's blind side, in silence.

When night fell, they climbed up to the street and properly scurried home like rodents.

***

"So what happened to your eye?"

Of the people who had entered and exited her life since that day with Cara, Carter had taken the longest to ask. His goofy awkwardness made him sweet in a way. Most just came right out with it.

"An accident," she said. She picked up one of the rats, turned it over, and laid it back on the grill to cook the other side. Fighting the urgency of her hunger, she had forced herself to skin it and gut it instead of eating it raw.

"What kind of accident?" Carter had already devoured the rump of his rat and began to nibble at the thin layer of meat stretching over its back.

"Just an accident," she said. The fire crackled as bits of fat dripped onto the embers.

Josie had been sleeping in the construction-vehicle depot for months. Nestled twenty-five feet below the block-glass windows and elevated gangway, between rows of dump trucks and diggers, she could light a small fire at night to keep warm and heat food without anyone outside noticing the glow.

"You want some water?" Carter asked. He seemed to have recovered from seeing Todd's face blown apart two hours earlier.

Josie nodded.

He handed her the dirty plastic bottle. They'd found a six-pack of Poland Spring in a construction vehicle at the other end of the hanger the day before. Carter told her the big yellow machine was called a "back hoe." He knew where all the storage compartments were.

She took a sip and handed it back.

He inched closer. "You know what we should do?" he said, offering a sly glance. The orange firelight bounced over his eager face.

"What?"

"You know," he said. "Make out." Carter slid another inch so their shoulders touched. "You're kind of my girl now, I guess."

She laughed. "You wish."

"But wasn't it cool before when I pulled my gun on that asshole? I was like, 'Go ahead, punk. Make my day.'"

She shoved his knee away. "The gun you dropped, you mean? Your finger wasn't even on the trigger. I saved *your* ass, but whatever."

Josie laid another skinned rat on the grilling surface, lifted the cooked one, and chomped into its rump. The juice burst into her mouth as she inhaled the heat and the scent of charred animal. She moaned with pleasure. God, it tasted so good.

Carter, trying a new tack, began to caress her ankle with his index finger. "I'll be soft."

She turned, gnawing at the rat in her left hand, and stared into his eyes. He smiled. Then the click sounded, and his smile drooped. "Feel that sharp thing against your balls?" she said. "That's my switchblade. I will not be soft."

Carter brooded for a good ten minutes, missing his turn for a rat. Josie didn't mind eating his. She turned the half-devoured beast over in her hands, examining the bones, feeling invigorated. "It's almost like cannibalism."

Carter broke away from staring at the flames. "What?"

She meant that she'd survived three years into the apocalypse by living as a rat: scurrying, hiding in the shadows, accepting dirt and grime and death as part of the unavoidable minutiae.

She removed another one from the flame and handed it to her companion, who still acted miffed about her rejection but not so proud that he would starve. As he ate, she observed the muscles of his jaw moving beneath his skin. The way his ears moved up and down as he chewed. The veins and tendons in his wrists and hands as he rolled the rat around in search of his next bite. He seemed so animal-like. She thought she might cook him and eat him someday, if she had to.

"What are you looking at?" he said. "Change your mind about making out?"

"No. Anyway, Williams is watching."

In this vast depot of construction vehicles parked in disciplined rows, one truck sat diagonally, forming a nice little barricade for Josie: A steel pillar on one side, two trucks parallel to each other, and this one angled like a door slightly cracked. It had crashed that morning they'd all died; its mummified driver still hunched over the steering wheel with his head turned. The name stitched on his jumpsuit read WILLIAMS. Josie thought it almost cozy here with flickering firelight reflecting back from the truck's yellow paint and Williams leaning on his steering wheel like he always did, watching over them.

She didn't ever once, in over three years, think how weird it was to dumpster-dive for meals or to eat grilled rats or even to live in a hanger full of trucks with a skeleton and, lately, a stupid boy for company. It just was. She thought of food and water and not getting wet most of the time. And she thought about Cara, always. The only person in the world who ever gave a shit about her.

Though Williams was just one of a million corpses she had seen, she knew one thing about him beyond all doubt: He had dropped dead on Friday, June 10, at 9:27 in the morning, EST, three years and three months ago, give or take a week. So had her mom and her mom's boyfriend and her grandma. And Carter's parents and all her teachers and every other adult in the city and maybe the world. June 10, 9:27 a.m.

The Fall.

# PART ONE

FLICKERING

# CHAPTER 1
## JOSIE

**June 10**
**Baltimore, Maryland**

Cheryl Revelle slipped out of bed, thrusting her pelvis forward to avoid Hector's slap. He took a shot anyway and missed her pale, dimpled behind by an inch. She swiped her bathrobe from the floor and slung it around her naked body. "I'm taking a shower."

"Can't wait to wash off my filth?"

She glanced back at him and his handlebar mustache, the half-assed tribal tats splashed over his muscular chest and shoulders, swastikas inked on his biceps and an iron cross on his sternum, and that White Power icon around his belly button, and thought, *Exactly.* Hector was like a box of frosted donuts: so decadent beforehand, so nauseating after. "Keep it down," she said, gesturing toward the wall. "She's right in the living room."

"Why did you let her stay home? I got better things to do than sneak around."

"She's sick."

Hector said, "Maybe you should find someone else to keep your bed warm, bitch," but Cheryl had already slipped into the hallway.

***

Cheryl locked the bathroom door, tossed the bathrobe, and stepped under the hot spray. She wetted a washcloth and, with abrading strokes, began to scrub away the scent of smoke and booze that Hector managed to leave on everything. *God, Josie must have heard all of it*, she thought. Why couldn't she tell Hector to stay away?

Her skin started to turn red from scrubbing, but she kept going.

***

Hector sat on the red vinyl ottoman in the living room, leaning over Josie and clasping his hands as she rolled her diesel locomotive back and forth along a circle of HO-scale track. Three used tissues sat balled up on the floor next to her.

"So what do you want for your birthday?"

"I don't know," she said. She'd heard Hector doing things to her mom in the bedroom and didn't want to talk to him. She didn't want him at her birthday next week, either.

"You need some dolls? Girls aren't supposed to play with trains." Josie offered no response, so he said, "How old are you gonna be, five?"

She gave him a blank stare. "Ten."

Hector nodded. "Cool. Cool. You really like trains, huh?"

"Are you gonna move in with my mom?"

2

"Can't," he said. "Your mom is still married to your dad, and she won't divorce the bum."

"My dad's not a bum."

Hector sat up straight, fished a cigarette and lighter from his breast pocket, and lit up. "You're right. He's a fuck up."

Josie glared. "Don't say that. If you must know, he's a train engineer."

"A what?"

"He drives a train. He's in Russia." Something like that.

Hector howled. "Is that what your mom said? Darling, your daddy's doing seven years in the state pen for stabbing some dipshit in a bar. He'll be out next year, though. Then I'll be gone, and you'll miss having a real man around."

Josie slumped and went back to sliding her train. Cara told her the same thing about Dad a while ago, but she didn't believe it. "Leave me alone."

"You're a tough little bitch, you know that? Your sister, she's thirteen going on twenty-two and got tits like a stripper already. You, on the other hand, are going to take a guy's balls off one day. You want some advice?"

*Not really.*

"When you see a guy like me coming…fuck, when you see any guy coming, know this: He wants to get in your pants. That's it. Not right now. That's fucking sick. What are you, nine? I mean when you're older and you grow some tits and get an ass like your sister has. Whatever a guy says to you is a lie. He's going to promise you the world and say he's going to make you a queen and that he thinks your friends are great. It's all fucking lies just so he can get you to open your legs. In fact, the only time a guy will ever tell you the truth is me telling you what I'm telling you right now. Your father ever give that kind of sage advice? I doubt it."

Josie slow-motion crashed the train into her tissue box, mimicking the sound of an explosion.

"You getting any of this?"

She already knew men were liars from the way they talked to her mom and from the way Hector called her mom *Baby* while his eyes were all over Cara's chest. "Yes."

"I'll break you yet, kid," Hector said as he mashed out his smoke, stood, and sauntered toward the bathroom.

*\*\*\**

Cheryl stood under the hot stream, building the nerve to tell Hector he had to leave. For good. It wasn't fair to Josie to have an ex-con around. At least not one she wasn't married to. His fist pounded on the door, and she heard a muffled, "Hurry up!"

Shaking her head in disgust—mostly with herself—she turned off the water, slid the pink plastic curtain aside, and stepped one foot out of the tub to reach for the towel. She glanced through the steam at the battery-powered clock on the sink and saw it change from 9:26 to 9:27. Then the readout fluttered.

Even as she began to puzzle what she had just witnessed, she knew something was wrong. A shiver crawled up her naked skin, and then a savage, cruel pain exploded in her head. "Oh no," she said, her legs buckling.

She was dead before she hit the floor.

*\*\*\**

Hector found the bathroom door locked and rapped on it. "Hurry up!" he said. The shower noise stopped. He waited a moment and then craned his neck toward Josie. "Hey kid, what time is it?

4

Josie rolled her eyes and glanced at the cable box. "9:27." Then the clock display flickered, and Hector made a weird grunt.

Clutching the doorframe for balance, he reached to her with his free hand. His eyes looked so sad for a second, she thought. Then they went blank, and he fell face-first onto the wood-laminate floor. The thump reverberated through the apartment. Hector's tongue rolled out and dangled into the pool of blood that began to seep away from his head.

"Mom?" Josie said, panic rising in her voice.

Outside, cars began colliding, and then the building shook when a delivery truck jumped the curb and rammed the apartment downstairs.

***

Andre Williams maneuvered the dump truck out of the line, in low gear, steering with one hand and feeding himself a McDonald's hash brown with the other. Bits of greasy potato landed on a belly that never used to be there. His cell rang.

"Dang it."

He tossed his breakfast on the passenger seat and answered. Bernice, calling from the diner. He knew what was coming.

"What the hell do you think you're doing?"

Andre pinched the phone between his ear and shoulder and let off the accelerator. "I'm working. You know. For money." Bernice's waitress salary wasn't getting them out of the poorhouse in a hurry.

"Didn't we just talk about this yesterday?" Bernice said.

"Jesus Christ, Bernice. They called me in. It's money. You're the only woman I know who bitches at her man for working." He steered the truck around the big wheel loader parked at the end of the hanger and turned up the lane toward the exit. "Shawnika can let herself in. Eleven ain't a baby. My mom worked when I was eleven, and I managed fine."

"Yeah, and Tre gets home a half hour before she does. He's nine, in case you forgot. You need to be there for those kids, Andre. And don't blaspheme."

*Oh yeah. Tre got home from school at 2:55, Shawnika at 3:20.*

Andre held the phone out to check the time. 9:26. No way he was going to be off the job site and back from Baltimore before eight o'clock tonight. Not even close. "I gotta do the work when it comes up. Working for Barzán ain't what it used to be. Anyway, it's not cold out. Tre can wait on the stoop for a time."

"Oh, that's great. In case you didn't notice, we aren't living like we used to. You want him to turn out like his cous—"

The message garbled. Andre looked at his phone, shook it, and put it back to his ear. "Bernice?"

*"Oh my G—"*

Andre Williams's head swooned as a creeping sensation ran up his spine. He looked at the phone again.

The last thing he ever saw was the clock on his cell reading 9:27.

# SHAWNIKA

### Washington, D.C.

"Would you hurry up and pick something?"

Shawnika Williams tilted her head and read the words on the ratty, taped spine. *George Washington: America's First President.* At least the parts that weren't torn off suggested that was the title. "Relax. We just got here."

Friday was library day. This, the last one of a school year already dragged out by floods that had shut everything down for two weeks in April.

Michele Cowart leaned closer. "What's wrong with that one? *George Washington.* Just get it."

Shawnika continued to scan the gray metal shelf. "Because it's for two-year-olds."

The library at Liberty Middle School on the east side of DC was stocked with leftovers from the Dark Ages. One identified Richard Nixon as sitting president. Shawnika found a biography of Mahatma Gandhi and hooked it down with her index finger.

Michele took one look. "You gotta be kidding."

"What are you getting?"

Michele showed the cover. "*Goblet of Fire,*" she said. This copy was half book, half Scotch tape.

Shawnika shook her head. "Girl, you read that, like, five times."

Just then, Tamara Toomey passed behind them and muttered, "Bitch" to Shawnika. Tamara had ignored Shawnika up until a week ago, and then, for whatever reason, decided to target her. Shawnika paid no mind to the older girl.

Michele leaned against Shawnika. "What's her fucking problem?"

Shawnika shrugged and put the Gandhi book back, rattling the oxidized bolts that kept the whole shelving unit from collapsing. "She's been stuck in middle school for ten years? Who cares. Let's go look at the art books." The two girls walked to the end of the aisle and came around the other side to the last section of books along the wall.

Tamara waited there with her henchwoman TaKisha, that girl with the too-small head who hardly ever talked. "I heard what you just said, you skinny bitch."

"I'm just trying to look for a book," Shawnika said. Tamara put her arms on her hips and blocked the lane. Shawnika had only been in the school for four months and didn't know or care about its politics. She gave a bored glance. "Can you move your fat fucking ass please?"

Everyone but Shawnika gasped. Tamara Toomey was two years older, forty pounds heavier, and could beat up most of the boys.

"Let's just go," Michele whispered to Shawnika. Michele and most of the other girls had been taking shit from Tamara since first grade and knew to keep their heads down.

Shawnika turned to browse the bookshelf. "I'm just trying to look for a book," she said again. She spotted the one on Paul Gauguin she'd almost borrowed last time. He was the guy who painted all the pretty black island girls against colorful backgrounds. "This'll do," she said to no one in particular.

Before she could tuck the book under her arm and turn away, Tamara smacked it loose. The pages ripped from the binding when it hit the floor, fanning out across the carpet.

"Oops."

Michele took a step back as Shawnika stood with her palms out. "It's 9:30 in the morning," Shawnika said. "Can't we do this some other time?"

TaKisha said, "It's 9:25."

That was about enough. Shawnika, staring at Tamara, slowly unrolled a middle finger at TaKisha. "I didn't know pinheads could tell time."

8

Tamara stuck her chin out. "Check it out. From now on this is my library. And the toilets in the girls' room are my toilets. And the desks are my desks. If I catch you using any of that shit, I'll fuck you up. You get it? I ain't friends with you."

Michele tugged at Shawnika's shoulder. "Let's go."

Shawnika shrugged her friend off and remained fixed on Tamara Toomey. "I know you don't know me that well, and I can tell you're mad 'cause I'm not scared of you. The thing is, I'm just trying to pick out a book, and you're getting on my nerves. So, for the last time, get your pinhead friend and your fat fucking ass away from me."

Tamara looked over her shoulder to confirm they were unseen by the librarian and then glared at Shawnika. "You're dead, bitch."

She lunged forward and grabbed Shawnika by the hair, slipping on the loose clump of pages. Shawnika took advantage of Tamara's imbalance, grabbed the bigger girl's wrist, and blasted her with a roundhouse right that snapped her head back. As Tamara staggered backward, Shawnika hurdled the scattered pages, caught her by the collar of her T-shirt, and drilled her with a straight right to the nose.

Tamara would have hit the floor if not held up by the book shelf along the back wall. Shawnika came down with an overhand right and then a second one, knocking Tamara out on her feet. TaKisha stepped in and made a heartless attempt to put Shawnika in a headlock, but Shawnika threw an elbow into her mouth, spun, and bloodied her nose with a left jab. She wound up to blast Tamara with another right when someone yanked her backward and threw her to the floor. She looked up to see the school security guard, a no-necked white dude named Wally, standing over her. "You done?" he said.

Shawnika nodded and stood as Tamara moaned and TaKisha, face awash in blood, sat on the floor and stared with saucer eyes of terror. She checked out her hands. The right one was cut up, probably from Tamara's teeth. "My dad was a heavyweight boxer," she said, somehow feeling she had to justify all the carnage to Wally.

"Oh, look at this mess!" Ms. Harriet said as she burst on the scene, her short legs struggling to navigate the turn in those clunky grandma heels. "You're going to pay for that book, young lady," she said, pointing at Shawnika. The librarian offered a disgusted grimace toward a crumpled Tamara, whose left eye was already puffing shut.

Shawnika threw her hands up. "I didn't wreck the book, she did! Why do you think I hit her?"

Ms. Harriet pointed again. "Don't think I don't see you back here snooping around all the time."

More outraged gestures from Shawnika. "Duh. Because I like books?"

"She didn't do anything," Michele said, now gesturing along with her friend.

Ms. Harriet retargeted her index finger. "You'll be quiet until I ask you a question."

By then, other kids were gathered at the end of the aisle. Wally raised his palms. "All right. Why don't we all calm down and sort this out. Now how did—"

Shawnika stared, waiting for him to finish. Instead, he looked at the ceiling and moaned. Ms. Harriet clutched her head and tumbled forward, plowing into the floor. Wally fell across her.

None of the kids moved. At last, Michele crouched beside the two fallen adults. "Ms. Harriet?"

The thunder of metal slamming metal sounded outside. Everyone ran to the window and gazed toward the street below. An eighteen-wheeler had jackknifed with two cars wedged underneath, their sheet-metal exteriors crumpled like paper. Pedestrians lay scattered and motionless across the sidewalks. Even the cop on the corner was face-down in the street, a dark red patch radiating from his head.

"Oh my God," Michele said. "Oh my God!"

Shawnika forgot all about Tamara Toomey and being blamed for the torn book. She only thought of one thing: Tre.

# GRACE

## Charleston, West Virginia

"Is *that* Dad's jet?"

Judy Cavanaugh began to regret bringing Grace to the airport. "I already said I don't know, honey." They were watching the puddle jumpers land, one about every five minutes, through a big window in the arrivals bay. Commuter flights from exotic places like Cincinnati and Charlotte.

Grace hadn't seen her dad in eight months. "Are you guys going to sleep in the same bed?"

"Grace!"

Her daughter stared up at her, and Judy felt stupid for over-reacting. Kids have a way of drawing attention to things adults don't want anyone to notice. "I'm sorry. I don't know what's going to happen. We already talked about it. We're going to try."

The jet rolled past the window on its way to the terminal. On the side of the fuselage, a green arrow pointed toward the cockpit and framed the words COASTAL AIR. Grace leaned her face on the glass. "Is that him?"

Judy pulled her back and rubbed the face print away with a tissue. "No, Daddy is flying a charter jet today. That means someone rented a plane, and he's flying it. It's yellow and white, he said."

"One person rented a whole jet?"

"Yeah. Some rich guy."

"Is he famous?"

"I doubt it. I think he owns a construction company."

Grace checked the arrivals board. "Is Daddy's jet on here? I can't wait to see him. Don't give him a hard time, Mom. I don't want him to leave again." Her words carried an admonishing tone.

Judy felt like saying, *Tell your dad not to fuck any more flight attendants.* No, the same-bed thing would have to wait for a while. She felt that anger start to well again—Grace was here to help her keep that in check—and then her daughter mercifully changed the subject.

"Can I get a Coke?"

Tempting to say yes, but what would Greg think? "I'm sorry, but not at nine in the morning. How about an orange juice?"

Grace exhaled and glanced at the arrivals board again. "It's almost 9:30. Can I?"

Her turn to change the subject. "Look. Another one coming in. I bet that's him."

The glint in the sky began to take shape as it drew closer, gliding toward the runway but still a mile and a half distant. Grace took her mother by the hand. "Please be nice to him."

If Grace didn't stop with the peacemaker act, Judy was going to punch something. Somehow people expected her to wear a smile and glue the family together while Greg was off tapping the ass of a twenty-three-year-old bimbo in a powder-blue uniform. *It only happened once*, he said. *For Christ's sake, Greg*, she said back to him, *you're fifty! Your oldest son is eighteen.*

She spied her wristwatch. 9:27. Keep it together for Grace.

Grace's face lit up. "It's yellow and white! It's Dad!" Then her mother's hand yanked away from hers.

Grace turned as Judy Cavanaugh collapsed onto the industrial-grade carpet with finality, limbs overlapping like those of a rag doll tossed to the floor.

"Mom?"

Grace extended an arm toward her fallen mother and then recoiled with a shriek as the yellow and white jet cart-wheeled past the window in a roar of flame, debris flying in every direction and exploding into ever smaller pieces. The fuselage rammed into the terminal extension and disappeared in a ball of fire.

Grace whirled, screaming for help, and discovered the floor of the airport littered with crumpled bodies. Babies and toddlers began to wail, but no one responded.

She dropped to her mom's side, shaking her and then rocking her back and forth. "Mommy. Wake up!"

Another explosion quaked the building. Grace dove onto her mother's lifeless body.

The cell phone in Mom's handbag began to chime. It took three cycles for the sound to register in her brain, but at last Grace snapped to life and began digging frantically in Mom's purse. She withdrew the phone. The caller ID read ANDREW. Her fifteen-year-old brother. "Andy?" she said, her voice warbled by tears.

"Grace, put Mom on," he said. "People are just...dropping everywhere."

Grace began to bawl into the phone. "Help me..."

# ZANE

## Alexandria, Virginia

Bart Barzán, whom everyone called Zane and who was the son of Gareth Barzán, president of multimillion-dollar Barzán Industries, couldn't locate the willpower to go to school today. Stealing money from his dad's petty cash box? That he had willpower for. The cash was to pay off Old Charlie, his driver. For a hundred bucks, Charlie would look Zane's dad in the eye and say, "Sure, Mr. B. I dropped Bart off at 9:10 on the dot." For another hundred, Charlie would call the school, pretend to be Dad, and report Zane absent for the day.

Both happened this morning.

Dad was flying into West Virginia to look at property with the idiot brigade, aka his management team, and wouldn't be back until whenever. Dad treated Charlie like a trained monkey most of the time and, therefore, underestimated Charlie's willingness to sell him out for two hundred dollars. Besides, who wants to be in school on a Friday? A blast-it-all-to-hell private school in session ten goddamn months of the year.

Destiny demanded that Zane stay home.

Zane sat on the couch with his feet on the Bubinga coffee table, watching the financial news on an eighty-inch TV in the family room. The stock ticker scrolled across the bottom while the jokers blabbed about investing, as if they had a clue.

He saw the oak door swing inward from the corner of his eye.

"What are you doing not in school?"

Zane rolled his eyes. He'd totally forgotten Rosalita was coming to clean. She walked into the family room and stood at the edge of the throw rug, hands on her substantial hips. "Why

14

you not in school," she said again. "Oh, Zany. What would your mother say?"

He motioned for her to sit. "My mother would say nothing because she doesn't exist anymore. She dead."

Rosalita dropped into the plush sofa, folding her hands over her lap. "Your mother is in God's house, watching you."

He looked away from the TV. "God is for poor people, Rosie. Rich people invented him to control you. I mean, there's a lot more of you than there are of us. If you had any sense you'd band together and kill us. But then, if you had sense, you wouldn't be stuck cleaning toilets for a living." He withdrew the forty dollars he'd stolen from his dad's dresser and placed it in her lap. "Now *this* you can believe in. Don't say anything to my father."

She threw the pair of twenties back at him. They fluttered on crisscrossing air currents and landed like magic carpets. "I'm not taking no money."

Zane sighed. "Then I'll plant something shiny in your van that belongs to my dad and make sure he knows you robbed him."

She crossed her arms.

"We can do this the easy way or the hard way," Zane said. He got that line from his father. He was preparing to stare her down when he became aware of a sudden lack of chatter emanating from the TV. He turned back to the screen just in time to see the three yappers on the financial channel, eyes wide, drop like potato sacks onto the news desk. Then the image jerked, and the camera began to drift to the side, as if unmanned and loose on its dolly. Moments later, the stock ticker went blank.

Zane pointed at the screen, jaw hanging open. Then he started laughing. "Did you see that?" he said to Rosalita, but she didn't answer. She was lying back, her arms at her sides, face to

the heavens, real or imagined, with her tongue dangling stupidly
from the side of her mouth.

"Huh," Zane said.

# CHAPTER 2

**June 10**
**Washington, D.C.**

Shawnika and Michele sped from room to room, dodging panicked classmates and scattered notebooks and papers as they looked as for a teacher. In each classroom, an adult lay on the linoleum floor. One was being shaken by a student calling, "Mr. Tobin. Mr. Tobin." Another, having fallen in a grotesque pose with her legs spread and arm snagged on a cabinet, stared at nothing while kids cowered and cried.

"They're all dead," Michele said, her voice thickened with tears and snot. "They're all dead." Overwhelmed, she collapsed, but Shawnika hoisted her back to her feet. More kids ran past them shouting and crying. Some sat in front of lockers, shivering in the humid June weather. Others pleaded into their cell phones for someone to answer.

Abandoning the hopeless search, the girls sprinted for the exit. They burst through the school's front doors into the sunny morning and into madness: overturned and smashed cars, bodies strewn, a toddler bawling and wandering into the street calling "Mommy." No police cars. No sirens. No help.

The girls stood on the sidewalk, holding each other up, unable to comprehend. But for the crying child and the distant whoop of a car alarm, they inhabited a world without life. The motionless bodies made Shawnika think of preschool, when it was naptime and all the kids had to lie there unmoving. Chattering and doing projects one minute, then playacting at sleep the next in a weird, noiseless performance.

The near silence was shattered and the girls almost trampled by the flood of kids racing onto the sidewalk and scattering. Someone, maybe Tamara Toomey, knocked Michele from her grip for a moment, but Shawnika grabbed her friend's arm and pulled her close. Their noses almost touched. "We have to find my brother."

Michele's tears started anew. "My mom," she said. "She's home with the baby. She can drive us to pick up Tre."

Shawnika didn't have time to run eight blocks in the wrong direction. Much later, she realized she could have taken a cell phone from one of the bodies, but she also realized it wouldn't have mattered.

She held Michele by the shoulders. "Listen. You go back to your house and wait there. I'm going to find Tre and then go get my mom. I'll call you later."

Michele was frozen.

"Hey," Shawnika said. "I said go to your house, okay? I will call you when I get to the diner."

Michele nodded, and Shawnika gave her a small shove to get her moving. As she watched her best friend jog away, she fought the urge to run up and hug her. She had an eerie feeling she was never going to see Michele again. *That's stupid*, she thought, but the feeling turned out to be right.


## Charleston, West Virginia

Grace hyperventilated into the phone. "I'm at the…airport… Dad…crashed…Mom won't…get up…"

"Wait right there," Andrew said, his voice firm. "Grace. Don't move. Stay exactly where you are. I'll find you."

"Help me," she said again, kneeling at her mom's body. Mom's mouth was open, the flesh of her face sagging and making her into an old woman.

"It's going to take me a while to get there. Grace, do you understand? Wait for me. I'm going to hang up now."

"No!"

"I have to. I can't come get you and talk on the phone at the same time. You have to stay exactly where you are."

Grace wanted to go home. She wanted her mom to wake up right now and fix everything. She wanted Andrew to rescue them. "When are you coming?"

She didn't hear Andrew's answer, for just then another jet came screaming across the tarmac in a fiery streak, breaking into flaming pieces as the friction and heat overcame the airframe's integrity. A section of wing, ejected from the fireball, tore through the airport's massive window. Grace threw her arms over her head and ducked against her mother's side as arrows of glass and twisted, flaming hunks of aluminum the size of cars rained down around her.

# CHAPTER 3

**June 10**
**Washington, D.C.**

Shawnika kept her eyes fixed ahead, trying not to think about dead people as she jogged around and between them. She prayed she would round the next corner and see cops and fire trucks on the way, and that grown-ups would be there to put things back in order. But as she approached the big intersection at New York Avenue and saw the massive jumble of trashed cars and trucks, she knew this thing was big. She knew it was everywhere.

Vernon Elementary lay like a shipwreck, lifeless, and Shawnika's skin tingled.

"Oh no," she said between heavy breaths. Poison gas. Poison gas killed everyone.

Then, as she drew close, she saw the faces of the children peering over the windowsills. They were too scared to leave.

Shawnika tugged the door handle. Locked. She pressed the buzzer for the security guard, but no one came. She shouted up to the kids watching from the second floor. "Somebody come open the door!"

She stood in the sunlight, catching her breath, waiting. After two minutes, she began to look for something to break the window—screw it, her mom would understand—when the door swung out. She recognized the rotund boy from a time he had come over to play with Tre. Shawnika brushed past him and into the hall, temporarily blinded after being in the bright sun. She tripped over the dead security guard.

Once back to her feet, she headed toward the stairway to the second-floor classrooms. "Tre Williams!" she bellowed. With her long, hurdler's legs she leapt, touching every third step.

At the top, she entered the fourth graders' wing. "Tre Williams!"

Each room played the same scene: dead teacher, crying and catatonic children. In the last room on the left, she found her brother standing alone by the dry erase board, his eyes wide and numb. "Tre!" Even as she ran to him and swept him into her arms, he didn't react. She put her hands on the sides of his face and rubbed under his eyes with her thumbs. "Tre," she said, this time in a lullaby voice.

He pulled her hands away and looked at them. "Why are your knuckles all cut up?"

"What?" She looked. "Oh, I got in a fight."

"They won't let you play sports anymore."

She took him by the hand. He was only a year and half younger but seemed like such a baby. Mama babied him. "Tre, I gotta take you out of here. Something bad happened, and we're going to go to the diner to get Mom."

"Is Mom okay?"

"Yeah," she said and then hesitated. The question twisted in her gut. "Yeah. Mama's gonna help us."

"I'm scared," Tre said.

\*\*\*

Block by block they walked, the same gruesome tableau unfolding before them: Crashed cars and trucks, lost children, and bodies. Bodies on the sidewalk and in the street. On porch stoops. In the doorways of nail shops. Blood dripping from faces and heads. At an abandoned house set to be torn down lay the corpses of construction workers. One must have fallen from the roof because his neck was twisted. Shawnika thought of her dad. *He's tough*, she told herself. He used to be a heavyweight boxer. He could take anything.

Tre did not speak or acknowledge the carnage. He stared ahead and held his sister's hand in obedience. Finally he said, "I'm thirsty."

"Mom'll get you something at the diner."

"My throat hurts."

Tre was famous for coming down with sore throats whenever they passed a shop that had Coke and ice cream. Sure enough, a newspaper shop, the narrow kind with the cooler in the back and the naughty magazines, stood to their left. "Okay," she said.

The bell above the door chimed as she tugged the handle. "Hold this open," she instructed her brother. No way was she letting that thing close behind her.

She stepped up onto the checkered floor and shivered as cool air enveloped her. A dead man lay sprawled in front of the counter. Shawnika imagined a cashier dead on the other side. The air conditioning unit kicked on, startling her.

"Let's just keep going," she said over her shoulder.

Tre, standing in the sunlight, made a visor with his free hand. "Come on. I'm thirsty. You can use my lunch money."

Shawnika sighed. "Don't worry about it. Just wait out there, and don't look at anything." Then she closed her eyes and shuffled past the body on the floor. She opened the cooler and looked for the all-natural juice. She took a grape and a mango, dug into her pocket, and left her lunch money on the counter. Two dollars, but the drinks cost $4.50. "I'll come back and pay the rest later," she said, in case there was a security camera.

The pair walked silently, sipping their drinks, for five blocks. An acrid smell grew ever more intense with each step, and bad thoughts rolling around Shawnika's head made her feel queasy. They turned onto Palmer NE. The butterflies in her gut were wiped out by a jolt of horror.

A tornado of black smoke billowed from the diner.

She launched into a run, leaping over a crashed motorcycle in the intersection, her heartbeat pulsing in her ears. Her speed would have carried her up the stairs and into the building like strong wind, but then she saw the fallen figure below the window in a pale pink dress and apron, white sneakers at the end of plump, brown calves. The left hand gripped a cell phone.

Shawnika braked, cut right, and tumbled to her knees before the fallen woman, abrading her skin without feeling it. She gripped the dead woman's face and stared into it.

"Mama!" she screamed. She wrapped her arms around her mother's neck and buried her face against her shoulder, wailing. Then a window cracked above her, sending down a shower of glass shards and a wave of blistering heat. She felt a tug on her arm. Tre.

The smoke began to burn her throat. She stood and pulled on her mother's arms as Tre tried to drag her away. "No," she said, sobbing and trying so hard to move the body, but the rough texture of the sidewalk held her mama in place. A second window blew out, filling her hair with glass, and she had to relent.

The two siblings fled to the street, turned, and held each other, crying and helpless as they watched the flames swallow Bernice Williams's body.

## Baltimore

"Ew. He stinks already."

Cara and Josie stood side by side, staring at the syrupy red pool around Hector's head.

"This is so fucked up," Cara said.

The frill of Josie's nightgown had dragged through the gore when she tried to open the bathroom door to help her mom ten minutes earlier. Even if it hadn't been locked, Hector's body lay in the way.

"What about Mom? She's stuck in the bathroom."

Cara leaned up to Josie's face, smiling for once, but it was fake and sad. Josie could see Cara's bra through her white pullover tee. "Josie, honey. You don't want to look in there. Trust me. This is a super fucked-up situation. We need to leave."

Josie didn't understand. Mom was still in the bathroom. They were home. "Why?"

Cara pointed down. "Because the floor is tilting. Did you notice there's a truck smashed through half the building? It's not safe."

As if cued, the frame of the apartment building groaned, and the room listed like a sinking ship. Josie shifted her weight to regain her balance.

"Jesus, Josie, we have to get out right now. Come on." Cara took hold of her wrist and pulled her toward the front door.

"I'm in a nightgown!"

"We'll steal something. I do it all the time. Come on."

Josie's socks slid as Cara tugged, and then a crack ran up the wall. And then Josie was out the door first.

Josie felt like she was in a cartoon trying to navigate the tilting steps. She began to climb around a big bag of laundry someone had left against the railing, but when she leaned her hand on it, she realized it wasn't laundry. It was the old German lady next door, dead now just like Hector.

She turned and scrambled back up the stairs, shoving Cara aside.

"Josie!"

"Forgot my train!"

## Charleston, West Virginia

Kneeling amid the gnarled wing parts and glass broken into jagged sheets, Grace prayed. She had moved away from her mom's body, mangled as it was now by the thick shard jutting from her shoulder and the flames crawling up her back. The smoke grew thicker as thousands of small fires one by one joined into a conflagration. Soon the airport would be engulfed.

Aware of a presence, Grace opened her eyes. Five toddlers surrounded her; at age nine, she was the closest thing to a living adult they could find. Grace wrapped her arms around two of the whimpering children. "Close your eyes," she said. The smoke began to burn her throat. She heard a popping noise and looked up. The flame was creeping across the ceiling and would soon be over them.

Grace bowed her head and whispered. "Our father, who art in heaven; hallowed be thy name. Thy kingdom come, thy will be done, on Earth as it is in—"

A hand gripped her arm. "It's me. Get up."

Grace waved the smoke away and coughed. Andrew's eyes met hers. "Where's Mom?"

She pointed to the wall of jet-fuel flame. Mom was underneath somewhere.

"Shit." Andrew took Grace's hand and dragged her toward the escalator. She looked back at the children, who scurried to follow her.

Andrew led her past the baggage claim littered with human bodies, through a set of sliding doors, and past the arrivals hall where still more lay dead. Grace took a deep breath of the clean air, but the great plumes of smoke caught up to her before she could take another. Sounds of glass popping and shattering chased them, and they broke into a sprint. One of the children, the smallest, wiped out, spilling onto the linoleum floor.

"Wait!"

Grace broke away from Andrew and scooped up the little girl. "Come on," she said, urging the others. She held the toddler to her chest and ran, determined to save at least this one. Andrew grabbed the two smallest, one under each arm. The two others would have to make it by themselves. The surging orange glow behind them and the heat on their backs propelled them forward as fast as they could go.

Andrew leapt through the sliding doors and onto the sidewalk. "Keep going!"

Grace charged across the car and bus lane, darting between crashed vehicles. They crossed the second set of lanes, ran along the fence, and then poured onto the parking lot. A blast sent them tumbling forward to the asphalt as if they had been kicked by a giant's foot. Grace rolled over in time to see a mushroom cloud of flame roil up from the terminal.

The fireball dissipated, its remnants chased by a dense column of black smoke, stark against the vivid blue of the late morning sky. Tears cleansed the sting from Grace's eyes. She felt hands gripping her firmly under her armpits, and she began to slide across the asphalt, away from the fire, the heels of her shoes scraping and bouncing over imperfections in the road surface. Facing the sun, she tilted her head back. Andrew appeared to be upside down, dragging her. Then her eyelids fluttered, and she went blank.

When she awoke, coughing, she was lying on a grass-covered island at the end of the parking lot near the exit. Andrew poured water from a Poland Spring bottle onto a rag and dabbed her face to remove the soot. "I'm sorry it took me so long to get here," he said.

Grace sat up, and Andrew held the bottle to her lips.

"I stole this from one of the cars," he said.

"What happened?"

"I don't know. Everybody's dead. There's crashed cars all over the highway. Like, everywhere."

Grace began to cry again. "Mom and Daddy."

"I know."

She noticed the five children they had rescued sitting on the grass as well, covered with dust and soot and in shock. The one Grace had carried had blood crusted under her nose and a cut lip. The little girl looked upon Grace as if she were her mother.

"What are we gonna do?"

"We have to go home, I guess. We gotta figure it out." Andrew hoisted himself to his feet. "You're gonna have to hold on."

"Hold onto what?"

Andrew pointed to a motorcycle leaning against the parking garage. "I took that from work. It's Mr. Klein's, the assistant manager. You're going to have to hang on to me on the way home."

"He let you borrow his motorcycle?"

"Grace. He's dead. They're all dead."

Grace rolled over and heaved herself up. "What about Mom's car? You can drive it! I've seen you."

Andrew stared into her eyes, hard and serious. It scared her. "The keys are in *there*," he said, pointing toward the destroyed terminal.

"Those kids we saved." The pitch of her voice rose. "What about them? We have to help them."

Andrew continued to stare, but sorry now, like when Mom told them Dad was moving out last year. "How? We're on a motorcycle."

"We'll take a car. I've seen you drive."

He laid a firm grip on her shoulder, but his answer came as a whisper. "The keys. We don't have the keys. All the keys are burning up inside that building."

She broke from his grip and held the little girl to her breast. "We have to," she cried.

"We can't. We have to leave them here." The pain in his voice made him sound like a grown-up.

Grace spun, looking for an adult, someone in a uniform. Somebody who didn't die. "We have to tell somebody."

"Grace!" Andrew pried the child from her arms and set her on the grass. "There is nobody! We can't help them. Come on."

She reached for the child, who began to cry, but Andrew took hold of Grace's arm and dragged her away. Grace let her body go limp. Andrew tossed her onto his shoulder and carried her toward the motorcycle. She screamed and clawed the air, watching through fresh tears as the five lost children faded into oblivion.

# CHAPTER 4

**July 1**
**Baltimore, Maryland**

Cara recoiled from the stench of rotting food and bodies. "No fucking way I'm going in there." Window glass crunched under her feet as she backed away.

Josie moved around her and stepped over the short ledge, avoiding the jagged bits jutting from the window frame. The power had gone off in the supermarket. She reached into her shoulder bag and took out a flashlight. She swept the beam across the floor. The light revealed three crumpled figures. "Stiffs."

"No shit," Cara said, shuffling in place and shooting nervous glances up and down the street.

Three weeks earlier, the sisters had stared in horror at Hector's dead body sprawled across the hallway in their crumbling apartment. They'd seen thousands since then, and lately the corpses weren't looking or smelling pretty in the summer heat.

Not to mention the flies. Flies everywhere.

Josie tugged at Cara's blouse, which the elder sister had stolen from a clothing shop an hour earlier. "If we don't take it, someone else will."

"Take what? Everything rotted." A few blocks away, a shot rang out, closer and louder than the last one. Cara screamed and jumped through the window frame. "What the fuck are we going to do?"

"Look for food," Josie said, skulking along the floor in a crouched position to stay below the level of the cash registers and out of sight. She'd learned it watching rats. She headed for the bread aisle, Number 16, far from the pungency of liquefied vegetables and decaying people.

Cara followed, gathering her limbs close to avoid bumping anything disgusting. Josie turned on the flashlight, revealing a debris field of items useless in a world with failing electricity: Laundry detergent. Cupcake wrappers. Cash.

Cara shook her head. "Everybody already took whatever was worth—ooh, cigarettes!" Josie's flashlight beam glinted off the cellophane. Two packs had fallen to the floor next to a hand basket under the register.

Cara scooped up the boxes, inspected them as best she could in the stark light, and stuck them in her bra. For the past two weeks, she'd been baring her chest to any boy who would give her a smoke. Josie figured this find would save her sister that humiliation for a while.

"Find me a lighter," Cara said. "And look for tampons."

Josie ducked down aisle 13 while Cara waited. She took inventory and returned to the front. "Just dry cat food," she said. She didn't tell Cara about the skinny, dead clerk and the obese lady decomposing next to a shopping cart.

Searching the rest of the store, Josie managed to locate spaghetti noodles and a pack of maxi pads for Cara. And, as if by divine intervention, a box of Brown Sugar Cinnamon Pop Tarts.

The girls watched the street from behind a cash register, trying to breathe less fetid air while still staying out of sight. They munched Pop Tarts and chased them with a can of seltzer they found in the minicooler at the endcap for Register 5. Cars driven by teenagers buzzed up and down the street, some trying to avoid the crashed vehicles, others not so much.

"This is so fucked up," Cara said. "We've got to find a gang or something."

"Why?" Gangs made Josie think of Hector.

"Because we need protection. We have no food. We have no way to get around. Are you dumb? I don't even have a cigarette lighter."

"I don't want to be in a gang," Josie said. "I'm pretty good at hiding, and there's other places to find food besides a supermarket. We don't need a gang. Boys are stupid."

Cara gave an impatient glare. "Dude. You carry around a toy train everywhere. That's majorly abnormal."

Josie reached into her canvas bag and felt around for the model. It was a diesel engine that belonged to her dad when they lived in a house in College Park. Before everything went wrong and they had to move to the apartment in the shitty section of Baltimore, as Mom described it. "Yeah? Which one of us thought of the can opener?"

While Cara had been busy looting an outfit for Josie the day after it happened, the younger Revelle sister, still barefoot and draped in a nightgown, swiped a can opener from a kitchen-gadget store.

Before Cara could respond, a Nissan Maxima bounded onto the sidewalk and stopped inches from the window ledge, tires further pulverizing the bits of window glass. Josie yanked Cara by the arm, dragging her over the customer service counter and into the darkness.

A boy in the front passenger seat smacked the window frame when he opened the door and squeezed out. The driver and another boy popped out on the left.

"Nice park job, asswipe," the front passenger said, climbing over the ledge into the store.

Ignoring him, the driver took a deep whiff. "Holy shit, it stinks in here. My eyes are watering."

Crouched behind that counter, Cara's ears perked. "I know that voice."

The passenger spoke again. "This place is fucked. Let's go."

Cara whispered, smearing lipstick and pop-tart crumbs on Josie's ear. "It's that dude Ronan from high school. He has *the best* parties."

She stood. "Wait!"

Josie, still crouching, wanted to bite her sister's leg. *Those boys were about to leave.*

"Who's that?" Ronan said, letting his rifle slide from his shoulder into his hands.

Cara climbed over the counter and into the light. She affected a pouty face. "Can we come with you?"

Ronan took a step closer. "Where do I know you from?"

Cara was good at manipulating boys. Even ones two years older. "You don't remember me? I'm Cara Revelle. I was at your house a couple times."

Josie, still hiding behind the counter, stayed still as a statue, as if the game were still on.

"Oh, yeah. Cara! I remember." Ronan slung his rifle and smiled. He patted the driver on the arm. "I know this chick. She's cool."

Cara stuck her hands in her pockets and shifted her hips. "So can we come?"

Ronan peered over her shoulder. "Who's 'we?'"

"My sister," Cara said. "She's back here."

Josie growled.

One of the other boys said, "How old is she?"

"Ten."

The boys conferred via eye contact, the driver looking none too pleased. Ronan won out. "Yeah, I guess it's okay."

***

Josie sat wedged between Cara and Richie, a tall, pimply kid with curly hair and a neck that reminded her of an inverted Tyrannosaurus ankle. She stared straight ahead as the passenger fumbled for radio stations and got static. Ronan, who insisted on driving this time, wove carelessly between wrecked cars.

"Anybody got a light?" Cara said, withdrawing a cigarette and gripping it with her lips. The front-seat passenger switched off the car stereo and reached back with a Bic. Cara cupped his hand and pressed her cigarette to the flame.

"So what happened to you guys?" Ronan asked.

Josie shook her head. *Really? The same thing that happened to everybody.*

"My mom died in the shower," Cara said. "Then our apartment building collapsed. We've just been running around, looking for food and stuff." She rolled down the window and flicked her ash, embracing the freedom of smoking with impunity. "You?"

"My mom died at the hospital," Ronan said. "She was a nurse. It's, like, ironic, because she had all that medicine around her, but it didn't matter."

"Yeah," Cara said, blowing a cloud of smoke that spread around the cabin and then vanished.

The pimply kid said, "My uncle—"

"No one gives a shit about your uncle, Richie."

Richie slapped Ronan's headrest. "Hey, fuck you, asshole."

Ronan stopped the car and twisted around. "You can walk if you want."

Richie didn't respond, and they resumed traveling.

Cara tossed her butt out the open window. "My dad's in prison. We were thinking of going out there and seeing if he's okay."

"Forget it," Ronan said. "I drove all the way down to DC. It's the same shit, just like this. You might as well stay with us."

*Please no*, Josie thought.

Cara was quiet for a minute, and Ronan said, "We got hot showers."

"Seriously?" This was the first day Cara hadn't bitched about not having a shower in three weeks. Josie was afraid she'd start up.

"Yup," Ronan said. "Here we are."

He pulled into the lot of a gym and parked crookedly in the first spot, bumping the curb. The five of them alighted the vehicle. Two boys about Cara's age guarded the entrance, one holding a handgun and the other the kind of rifle kids use to shoot squirrels. The gang members traded hand slaps and high-fives.

Josie scanned the façade of the two-story building and noticed the windows were covered from the inside with black paper. "I don't want to go in there."

Cara elbowed her. "Just be cool."

Ronan opened the Plexiglas door and waved them in. Cara sashayed forward, and Josie followed as if pulled unwillingly by an invisible rope. The boys from the car swept in behind them.

The door clicked shut, stifling the noise outside. Josie trained her ears on the footsteps behind her, wondering what Richie and Ronan were up to.

Two girls, thirteen or fourteen, were lounging in the lobby along with an older boy about Ronan's age. The girls glanced at each other, tossed down their magazines, and stood. Josie thought they acted nervous.

"Who are *they*," the new boy said.

"Chill," Ronan said. "That's Cara. She'd a friend of mine. And that's—"

"Josie," Cara said. "My sister."

The boy stepped closer to Ronan. "I'm not..."

Ronan put a hand on his shoulder. "I know. Of course not."

*He's not what?* Josie turned back toward Richie and the other kid from the car, who seemed to be watching Ronan for cues.

"Do you guys, like, sleep here?" Cara said.

Ronan set his rifle on the reception counter. "Yeah. My house got looted. Can you believe that shit? So me and my guys here decided to start a club. We got hot showers, a weight room, and all that. We're going to upgrade the weapons at some point."

"Can we stay? You can have all my cigarettes," Cara said. Josie yanked at the back of her shirt, and Cara swatted her hand away.

"Well, you kind of have to take an oath and stuff." Ronan grabbed a folded towel from the counter and tossed it to Cara. "And you definitely need a shower. You smell like a wet dog."

Cara laughed. "Screw you. You know what it's like out there."

Ronan flashed a phony smile and batted the other boy across the chest. "Hey, she's pretty feisty." Then he pointed to the sign that said *Women's Locker Room* over the entrance to a hallway with its doors propped open. "That way, your royal highness."

Cara whispered in Josie's ear. "Don't try to run away or do anything to get us thrown out. Understand?"

Josie didn't answer. She stared straight ahead as Cara strutted across the room and said, "No peeking," to Ronan as she passed. He gestured a scout's pledge and winked. Cara disappeared down the hallway.

Josie, sensing motion behind her, whirled around and glared at Richie and the other kid from the car, who joined Ronan and the new boy. The four of them began whispering.

"Why don't you have a seat," one of the girls said to Josie. She had a heavy Spanish accent. Josie eased into one of the lounge chairs, watching the boys and trying to figure out what they were so hush-hush about.

"You want a magazine?" the other girl asked. She was blond, like Josie and Cara, but her roots were dark.

"No thanks."

Ronan nodded to the Hispanic girl and picked up his rifle. At once, the boys turned and walked down the hall in the same direction Cara had gone. Josie jumped to her feet, but the bleached blonde stood to block the way. "Don't worry, honey. They're just checking the back of the building. They have to make sure no one gets in. You just have a seat."

Josie sat, peering down the hall. She wanted Cara to come out of the shower, and she wanted the two of them to get the hell out of this club. She waited for what seemed like an hour, but the clock over the reception desk only moved two minutes.

Those boys still hadn't returned. Josie stood and took a step toward the hallway.

The blonde stepped in her path again. "You want a Coke?" she said. "The Coke machine still works."

Josie looked past her. "I want my sister."

The blonde put her hands on Josie's shoulders and tried to steer her back toward the chair. "Just let her enjoy the shower for a minute. You can take one later." The girl turned toward the Hispanic girl and shrugged, as if unsure of her own words.

Then a muted scream emanated from somewhere down that hall, echoing off the hard surfaces. Cara's voice.

Josie raked her fingernails across the blonde's hand. The girl shrieked and let go, and Josie rocketed down the hall, her canvas bag of noodles and can openers and maxi pads rebounding off her hip with each step. She made a left into the locker room, around a painted barricade, and slid to a stop.

Cara lay on the floor, naked. The two boys from the car were holding her legs apart, and the other was leaning over her head, pinning her shoulders. Ronan was on top of her with his pants down. Cara's lip was bloody. "I told you not to scream," he said. "This will be done soon and then you're in the club, so shut the fuck up and enjoy it."

Josie leapt forward, driving her model train into the back of Ronan's head so hard the toy broke apart in her hand. He fell backward on his bare ass, howling and trying to stop the sudden geyser of blood spurting from his scalp. Josie tugged at Richie, the pimply one, who was holding Cara's leg, but another of the boys grabbed her and pulled her away.

Ronan stood and pulled his pants up. "You little fucking bitch," he said, wiping his bloody hand on the wall. "I knew I didn't like you for a reason."

Josie kicked the boy behind her in the shin, but he held on, and Richie took hold of her other arm.

Ronan, glaring at Josie, wound up and rammed his foot into Cara's kidney. Her body curled as she emitted a guttural groan. "Is that what you want, little lady? You want me to beat your sister to death?" Ronan landed another shot in Cara's lower back.

Josie stopped struggling and lost the strength to stand, going limp while her sister writhed on the floor.

"Hold her up," Ronan said, picking up his rifle and aiming the barrel at Josie's head.

The last thing Josie heard was one of the boys say, "Ronan, don't," followed by a popping noise.

# CHAPTER 5

**July 5**
**Alexandria, Virginia**

Her jungle-green eyes, unknowable and heavy with burden, cast a downward glance. A delicate forearm appeared from under the robe's sleeve, angling at the petite bones of her wrist. Her graceful finger pointing with inevitability. *You*, the finger said, *are chosen*. The angel, spilling golden curls and spreading white feathered wings, delivered God's message with solemn duty.

Zane's dart hit her square in the right eye. Not a bad throw from a seated position.

Some French guy painted this angel as a woman, though in the Bible the angel was a dude called Gabriel. Apparently the painter was mega famous back in the 1800s, but no one gave a shit anymore. In fact, this was only part of a painting. The left side used to be the Virgin Mary, but it got cut in half in 1920, on account of it not being canonical, and reframed. Zane's dad bought it twelve years ago for two hundred and fifty thousand dollars. A month ago, it was worth almost a million. Today, it wasn't even a good dart board.

Zane wound up for another throw when a rare twinge of guilt hit. He liked this painting and felt kind of shitty for knocking out the angel's eye.

He chucked the dart wide, and it lodged in the mahogany paneling. Then he kicked away from the desk, sending the leather chair into a spin, and he whipped the last dart into the blur passing before his eyes. He heard a thwack and jammed his foot down to brake the spin. His brain caught up a few seconds later. Equilibrium restored, he scanned the room for the strike point.

Lampshade.

Zane hopped out of the chair, walked to the window, and gazed toward the street. That iron fence was only good enough to keep people out until they realized gates didn't matter anymore and that no one would come when the alarm sounded. One of these days, the power would go out, and all the electronic security that ever existed couldn't stop someone with a hacksaw. The compound had generators, of course, but at that point Zane might as well put up a giant flashing arrow and a sign that read ATTACK HERE.

As if cued, a solitary kid, marching down the sidewalk with a shotgun, appeared from behind the stone pillar that anchored the fence. He wore a black T-shirt and jeans, and his face bore a warning frown and jutted lower jaw. Zane took a step back into the shade and did not let the punk out of his sight. "Fucking Neanderthal."

Zane swore the human race was devolving before his eyes. Idiots with dull expressions picking each other off with whatever guns they had lying around or could be ransacked. Disorganized idiots. Half their parents probably worked for Barzán Industries and took his dad's money to do nothing but sit around and waste space. Once upon a time, Zane couldn't wait for his father to drop dead. Zane would take over the company, fire all their stupid asses, and hire people who knew how to take orders.

Events had not quite played out as he'd expected.

"Be careful what you wish for," he said, aware he had been speaking aloud to himself with increasing frequency of late. Another reason to get out of this house, cushy though it was. Crazy people talk to themselves.

A gunshot sounded outside somewhere, audible even through the tempered windows of Dad's study. Zane shook his head. His dad had a warehouse with barrels of chlorine. Properly delivered, one of those drums could wipe out the population of four city blocks without damaging the structures. A chemical bomb made from other available supplies would doom the biggest nest of idiots in town in one shot. But Zane couldn't do it by himself. He needed labor. He needed to abandon the house and venture forth in search of idiots willing to do his bidding for no pay.

Piece of cake.

Without speaking aloud, Zane declared himself president and CEO of Zane Industries. His mission statement: *Destroy any motherfucker who tries to stop me.*

\*\*\*

Zane's right hand gripped the shifter knob of the Aston Martin, and his left caressed the top of the leather-wrapped steering wheel. His right foot eased off the gas pedal as his left pressed the clutch, and…the shift knob didn't move. He shook it and pushed it sideways and then forward. It still didn't move.

"Who designs this shit?"

Zane slid out and shut the door. *Yeah, the leather smells good,* he thought, *and it looks pretty inside, but what use is a sport coupe on a road littered with cars and bodies and no one to impress?* He knew from the dead phone lines and channel after channel of satellite TV with no signal that this thing was going on everywhere, not just in Virginia and DC.

Zane scanned the other choices in the garage.

Next to the DB8 was Dad's Dodge Ram, for when he visited a work site and wanted to look like one of the guys. Then the empty spot where old Charlie would have parked the Lincoln if he hadn't been fucking off with the two hundred bucks Zane gave him that morning when everyone in the world who shaved dropped dead. Zane figured the stores had long since been raided, with only razors and refill blades left behind. *I should go scoop them up*, he thought. *In a couple of years, when all the Neanderthals grow up, those refill cartridges will be worth a lot of whatever ends up being used for money.*

Zane decided the Dodge pickup would come in handy later if he needed to haul around a chemical bomb, but for now, that Escalade at the end of the garage looked pretty sweet. Stylish yet handy. Dad bought it with only nineteen thousand miles on it from some mobster on his way to prison. Why not just go to a Cadillac dealership, people wondered. Because *this* Cadillac had been custom reinforced to be bullet resistant. Not that Dad expected an assassination or anything, but you never know when some pissed off ex-employee is going to snap and pull out a .38.

Zane wondered, *Do people who shoot their bosses after getting fired for being bad employees understand the concept of irony?*

Since he didn't know how to drive, Zane spent twenty minutes practicing in the back yard. It seemed pretty easy, except for reverse because the wheel was twice as sensitive. He found out when he ran over the bushes. Unlike the Aston Martin, which boasted the scent of expensive leather, the Escalade reeked of cigar smoke. Dad must have been chain-smoking the damn things in here. But out in the yard, as he drove through the flower bed with a grin, Zane's entrepreneurial mind went to work. He drove around to the front of the house, parked, and went inside to grab a few useful items. And rescue that angel painting.

***

Two boys, each with a rifle across his lap, sat on a bench unwrapping and eating cakes from a white box. One tossed the plastic wrapper and watched it blow into the street, which had started to accumulate dirt and garbage. Otherwise, the tree-lined Georgetown avenue didn't look much different from the way it did before June 10.

A shiny black Cadillac Escalade, sunlight surfing its sexy curves and angles, pulled up and stopped clumsily before the boys. The driver's tinted window lowered to reveal a kid in sunglasses smoking a cigar. The boys, wary, rose to their feet.

"Gentlemen," Zane said, his eyes watering from the cigar smoke. He had no intention of inhaling, just of putting on a show. *First impressions count.* "Hell of a day, isn't it?"

The two boys looked at each other and back at Zane. "What do you want?"

Zane reached over to the passenger seat and grabbed the six-pack of Pepsi by the plastic ring. He reached it through the open window. "Thought you boys might like a drink. Sorry it's not cold."

They stared at him.

Zane gazed at the road ahead with an impatient face. "Five... four...three..."

One of the boys stepped forward and took the six-pack.

Zane reached over to the passenger seat again and produced a carton of Marlboros. "Here. You can smoke 'em or trade 'em."

The other kid took the carton and said, "What else you got in there?" He gestured toward the side of the Cadillac with his rifle. Zane assumed it to be a subtle threat.

"Odds and ends," he said. "Nothing compared to what I could get, though." Warehouses full of stuff. Warehouses that belonged to his father, with big metal doors and nondescript facades that Neanderthals like these two would never think of breaking into. No, these clowns would try raiding the same old supermarkets and convenience stores and Targets, wondering why they are starving to death. "So go ahead and take a shot at me with your pop gun. I'll roll up the window and drive away, and you'll never see me again."

The boys looked at each other again and then back at Zane.

"You guys have a hideout around here?" he asked.

"Who wants to know?"

"Not gifted in conversation, I see. Okay, you obviously have a hideout around here because you are on foot, and you're a couple of sitting ducks, especially now that you have Pepsi and smokes. You're not going to be sitting out here in the baking sun unless you can run back to your place in a hurry." Zane turned the AC on full blast and rolled his face in front of the vent. "Ooh. That's nice."

"I'm Nagesh," said the kid holding the Pepsi.

"Pleasure to make your acquaintance, Nagesh. I'm Zane." That was the way his dad used to greet new employees, as if he gave a shit. "And you?"

"Anthony."

"Well, Nagesh and Anthony. I will be back here the same time tomorrow with more items. If you guys are holding guns or have your pals hiding in the trees ready to ambush, I'm going to blow right past you, and you can suck my exhaust. If, on the other hand, you have half a brain and want to help me build an army to take over the city, be standing there, unarmed. Capiche?"

Zane raised the window and peeled out before they had a chance to answer. *This world-domination thing is going to be fun,* he thought.

# CHAPTER 6

**August 15**
**Washington, D.C.**

Shawnika's eyes burned from the urine vapor. The little ones were afraid to use the toilets because the older kids would rob their stuff and taunt them, so they peed in the corner of the classroom. Shawnika grew tired of scolding them.

"I hate it here," Tre said. He lay next to his sister on the gym mat she'd claimed for a bed. "I want to go home."

"We can't." Living alone in a ground-floor apartment got too dangerous with gangs breaking in all the time to take whatever food Shawnika and Tre had scavenged. Here, at the elementary school, they found safety in the herd. "Anyway, at least we got a mat to sleep on."

Most of the gym mats had been taken by boys, except for the one Tamara Toomey got, and this one. Even with the death of mankind looming, word still got around about Shawnika's fistfight. *There's the girl that kicked Tamara Toomey's ass*, kids would say as they pointed. One of these nights, someone tougher would steal her mat, but Shawnika didn't mind people thinking she was dangerous until then.

"It stinks," Tre said.

"What did I tell you about peeing on the floor?"

"There's mean kids in the bathrooms."

"I know," Shawnika said, pulling her little brother closer and laying her arm over him. *Anybody who fucks with him is going to pay, that's for sure.* "Go to sleep."

She owed it to her mom and her dad to keep Tre safe and to give him the best life she could for as long as she could. Mom had always worried about Tre ending up in a gang. *Love is the antidote,* she would say. With no adults around, Shawnika faced a steep challenge. Was her love enough?

"I can't sleep. It's hot."

"Tre, I know. It's August. It's hot everywhere." They'd made their home in Room 206, which used to be Mr. Bebbington's reading class. Shawnika didn't know who had moved his body or where they'd put it, but it wasn't in the room when she claimed her corner. Faces came and went, but at least twenty kids slept in here on any given night. Being on the second floor, the room was extra hot and stuffy, and it reeked of piss.

"It's too hot with your arm on me."

Shawnika rolled over, her skin sticking to the mat. She started naming the presidents in her head, in order, because that usually helped her fall asleep. If that didn't work, she'd move on to states and capitols, and then, if still awake, all the bones in the human b—

She sprang to a sitting position. "What was that?"

Tre leaned on an elbow. "What?"

"I thought I heard glass break."

A scream reverberated down the hall, and the other kids stirred. Shawnika, the oldest, rose and motioned for them to be quiet and stay still. She crept to the door and peered into the hall. Thumping sounded from another classroom, followed by another scream.

A figure moved into the hallway from Room 202. Shawnika ducked back in the darkness and closed the door. Pressing her face against the glass, she tried to peek through the narrow, rectangular window but couldn't see around the corner. Then she jumped as the figure, a boy, passed the door dragging a gym mat. As he did so, he caught Shawnika's eyes through the window and mouthed, "You're next."

Shawnika's hand trembled as she gripped the doorknob, but the boy kept going. Then another scream rang out, the same voice as before. "Help," the screamer begged. Shawnika looked back at Tre and then toward the door. She opened it and peered around the corner.

Tamara Toomey ran at her. She could tell it was Tamara only because of her size and the way she moved. Her face, arms, and chest were hemorrhaging red. Shawnika caught her and fought to keep Tamara from mowing her down.

"Tammy, stop." Shawnika held her by the shoulders, trying not to get blood on herself. Under the florescent light, she saw the extent of the injuries. Tamara's face had been hacked apart, and her arms and hands were crisscrossed with deep slashes. Shawnika fought the urge to throw up. "Sit on the floor. Come on."

Tamara looked down at her arms and screamed again. "He took my mat. He took my mat."

"What happened?"

Tamara wailed and held her arms out, blood drizzling from her fingertips like hot syrup. "Oh my god. Help me!"

Shawnika's heart pounded through her chest. She looked at the floor and saw the spatters of red merge and become pools. She felt panic rising, like when she saw her mom's body. "I don't know what to do."

She knew about direct pressure and tourniquets and all that, but how do you apply direct pressure to flesh hanging in ribbons, and how do you make tourniquets when you don't have any supplies because the whole place had been raided twenty times over?

"Let's go to the nurse's office," Shawnika said, which quieted Tamara, and she led her by the wrist down the main stairs. She glanced back toward 206 and felt acute anxiety for leaving her brother alone when some lunatic was running around cutting people up over floor mats.

She imagined Tre's voice. *I don't want to be here anymore.*

"Neither do I," she said, her voice bouncing back at her from the painted cinderblock walls.

In the nurse's office, trashed as it was, she could do nothing but lay Tamara on the examining table and hold her hand. No bandages. No pills. Not even a blanket to keep her warm. It didn't matter. In a few moments, the bigger girl's moaning and crying trailed off, and her grip loosened.

Shawnika left the lights off because she didn't want to see Tamara's cut-up face and because she didn't want the mat thief to know she was in there. She lifted up Tamara's bloody shirt and laid her head on her chest. Thump-thump…thump-thump… Shawnika counted three seconds between beats. She figured that was bad news. She put the bloody shirt back in place.

"I'm cold."

Shawnika jumped back from the table. Then Tamara said it again. "I'm cold." Her voice sounded far away.

Shawnika did another sweep of the room but found nothing to cover the poor girl. She whispered in her ear, "I'll go look for a blanket," but Tamara didn't respond.

In the silent, empty corridor, lit only by two florescent overheads, jagged shadows jutted like shards of glass. Shawnika crept across the cool linoleum in her stocking feet, peering into each room, half expecting to find some junkie who had broken in to steal syringes and decided to shoot up right there. She'd never seen junkies until her family moved to this neighborhood. After her dad lost his full-time work.

Dad.

She eyed the tiled ceiling as if she could see through to the next floor and make sure Tre was all right. She realized should have taken him off the mat in case the lunatic came back for more.

Shawnika picked up her pace, reaching the end of the hall and the doors to the cafeteria. Despite the Keep Out warning spray-painted on them, she pulled the handle, cringing at the squeal the hinges produced, and stepped into the dank, musty air of the pitch black, windowless cavern. The heat and the rancid smell gagged her. *Those kids must have let all the food go to rot. Can't anyone use their brains?*

*Screw it*, she thought. *I gotta find a blanket for Tamara*, because she had to do something for the poor girl, even if she hated her. Shawnika ran her fingers up and down the wall until she felt the plastic nubs all pointed down. She pushed them up. Some of the lights flickered on for a half second, then off, but long enough for her to see the lumps scattered across the floor. The afterimage floated before her in the dark. *Was that...*

Then the lights stayed on.

*...the dead teachers?*

Someone had dragged their corpses in here.

Shawnika turned to run but stopped herself. Another after-image, this time in her memory. A blanket? She pivoted back to see that the body closest to her covered with a makeshift tarp made from a school banner. She crouched and leaned forward, keeping her ankles far enough away so they couldn't be clutched by some zombie teacher hand, and whisked it free. Whirling before she could see who lay beneath, she shoved the doors open and charged into the shadowy hall, racing past all the gaping rectangles of darkness that led to who knows what, back to the nurse's office.

"Tamara?" she whispered. Tamara did not respond. She laid her hand over Tamara's chest to feel for the rise and fall of breathing, but her own hand shook too much to make a diagnosis. Tamara's congealing blood made her palm stick to the T-shirt for a moment. Shawnika laid the fetid tarp over the supine girl, wiped the blood from her hand, and fled back upstairs, jumping three steps at a time. That mat slasher was going to get a face full of fist if he tried to mess with her.

In Room 206 again, her eyes needed a moment to adjust. At last, she spotted Tre sleeping on the floor. He had rolled off the mat. "Little bastard," she said, kissing him on the cheek. She dragged the gym mat into the hall and leaned it against a row of lockers. Let the lunatic take it. She didn't want to end up under a tarp in that cafeteria over a stupid mat.

Once back at Tre's side, she laid down on the hard linoleum, the smell of death fading from her nostrils and the scent of little-kid piss taking its place. She snuggled against her little brother and whispered, "We're leaving in the morning."

# CHAPTER 7

**October 31**
**Baltimore, Maryland**

*T*he sky. No clouds. No breeze. Not hot, not cold. Three turkey vultures loop, pinned to the flat blue.

*Something is interfering with her vision, disorienting her. From someplace far off, her brain commands her to reach up and brush the blockage away.*

*Her fingers make contact, but they are a sledgehammer, sending a devastating jolt of pain into her skull, an agony she never thought possible. It seems like forever, but it subsides. This time, her hand creeps up delicately to find the thing blocking her view. Tentative fingertips probe. She feels rough, crusted material where her forehead and cheek should be. Her fingertips find the edge and pull. The agony seers her again, and a scream punishes her ears.*

*The scream is hers.*

*She tilts her head to the left, and more pain explodes, this time from deep inside. Dirt and garbage surround her. Old beer bottles and fast food wrappers stuck in the dirt. Someone is lying next to her. A naked girl with blonde hair.*

*She places a hand on the naked girl's shoulder, but the girl is stiff and cool. A faraway voice says, "What happened?" but it came out of her own mouth.*

*Rolling onto her knees, a new wave of pain wracking her skull, she crawls to the blonde. Rivulets of dried brown blood are streaked from the girl's mouth and nose and run down the side of her face. Her throat is stained with purple bruises that look like handprints. Around her eyes are spider webs of burst blood vessels. Great purple blotches radiate from her rump and the back of her legs where the blood pooled. The girl is dead. The girl is Cara, her sister.*

Josie jerked upright, her heart pounding, and pulled her knees to her chest, trembling. Then she swung back and punched the side—formerly the ceiling—of the overturned trailer, generating a dull metallic thud. That same damn dream. It was like getting shot in the face over and over.

"Good morning!"

Josie peered at Rogelio from under scraggly bangs. Every morning, after she awoke in heart-pounding terror from discovering Cara's body in the garbage dump yet again, Rogelio greeted her with a smile. He never said anything about the dream. Why would he? They all had bad dreams.

"Happy Halloween. Have you decided on costume yet?"

Josie blew out the last breath of nightmare air. "A princess. Or an angel." Something pretty. Something with two eyes and access to a hot shower. "Fuck."

Rogelio gave a disapproving glare. "How old are you again?"

"Ten."

"Is that any way for a ten-year-old to talk?" Rogelio was fourteen.

"You curse."

"I'm a boy."

"So?"

Rogelio waved the topic away. "So. Are you ready?"

Her heart began pounding anew. "Right now?"

"Josephine, we're kind of getting to the now-or-never point."
Rogelio turned on the battery-powered lantern, which cast a dim
glow halfway through the trailer. The overcast morning threatened to ruin the holiday and make them use precious battery
power, a finite commodity.

"Can we do it tomorrow?" she said. She had said that yesterday
and the day before, too.

"No. We have to do it today. I'm running out of time." He
reached into his nylon backpack and withdrew an object.
"Besides," he said, waving a king-size Snickers bar, "You get this if
we do it today. If you wait until tomorrow, I'm eating it."

Josie leaned closer. "Where did you get that!"

He stuffed it into a zippered pocket. "I found it in some lady's
purse on my last supply run. I was saving it for a special occasion."

By *last* he meant *final*. Rogelio had cancer, and his treatments
had stopped abruptly on June 10 at 9:27 in the morning. He no
longer knew for sure what was happening inside his body, he told
Josie, but he could feel it in his bones and his lungs. He couldn't
leave the trailer anymore, or eat much, and Josie had been going
out to dump his pee bottle when it got full.

Josie wiped a tear from her cheek. "Okay. Let me eat breakfast
first."

She grabbed a handful of Slim Jims and made her way to the
back of the trailer across a slightly off-level floor, pushing aside
the blanket they'd hung for a door, and stepped into the brisk
autumn air. Shivering, she peeled back the plastic and took a bite.

They only had unspicy ones left, which she didn't like, but food was food.

Josie felt bad eating in front of Rogelio, so lately she had been taking breakfast outside. She walked along the trailer, trying to escape the wind. This truck they used for a home had crashed into a ravine. It was a good spot for staying out of sight but a terrible spot, she discovered with the changing season, for keeping warm. Soon it would be freezing outside, and she would have to find a real building to live in. And maybe something to eat besides Slim Jims and pretzels.

As she rounded the smashed cab, which she'd covered with branches to help keep their hideout a hideout, the first drops of cold drizzle landed on her. "Shit." Rain made her head hurt.

She finished the second Slim Jim as she stood under the propped-up back door of the trailer, in front of the hanging blanket, reminding herself of the way Cara used to shiver under an awning somewhere, smoking cigarettes and watching the rain. Cara usually had friends with her, though. Josie had but one friend, and he was about to die of cancer.

In July, Josie had staggered into Saint Agnes Hospital looking for help for her gunshot wound, as if they were still open for business. There she met Rogelio wandering the halls. He gave her painkillers, disinfected her, put a bandage on her face, and found her an empty bed. He sat in a chair beside her as she slept, holding a scalpel to protect her from druggies looking for needles and meds.

He also held the mirror when she saw the injury for the first time. Her eye gone, the right side of her face was swollen and covered with scabs and misshapen from a shattered orbital bone. She cried on his shoulder, though she was alive and he was doomed.

***

Rogelio's coughing stirred Josie from her daydream. She went back inside the trailer, out of the wind.

"You ready now?" he said, cheerful as ever. "You want to look your best when you go trick-or-treating tonight."

Josie sighed and sat next to him on his quilt, pretending she wasn't shaking with dread. "Maybe I'll wear a mask instead."

He turned on a pocket flashlight and handed it to her. "Here," he said, adjusting her hand so the beam aimed into her face. "Like that."

She tried to hold it straight, but her hand trembled. She heard him open a bottle and pour, and the acute odor of rubbing alcohol filled the space around them.

"Josephine. This is going to hurt like all fucking hell. But I promise you…I promise you, because I know…you will remember that you had pain, but you won't remember the pain. Okay?"

"See, *you* curse," she said, trying to laugh through the welling tears. She remembered the pain every day.

"Hold still."

"Please don't do this."

"You know how many times a doctor or a nurse told me to hold still? I always listened because it was for my own good." He lifted the tweezers to Josie's face and, softly, began to probe for the back end of the slug embedded in the soft tissue of her right eye socket. Josie gripped the flashlight harder and harder until the plastic began to creak, and she bit down on a bundle of still-wrapped Slim Jims.

"Found it."

The meat sticks fell from her mouth. "Wait!"

"No," he said, jerking his arm back.

56

Josie let out a scream and fell over, slapping the sheet metal floor again and again in time with the jolts of pain pulsing through her body. But she didn't black out. Not like when they'd shot her. This time she took it.

"Fuck. That hurt a lot worse coming out than it did going in," she said, trying not to hyperventilate.

Rogelio shoved a rag into her hand. "Here. It's bleeding."

She pressed the rag against her eye socket, not smelling the fresh dousing of rubbing alcohol until it was already against her and burning. "Ow! You bastard!"

Rogelio pressed his hand against hers to hold the rag in place. "Sorry, but you have to disinfect it."

In his cancer-shrunken state, she could have easily pushed him away, but she bore down and waited for the burning to subside. When it did, she lowered the bloody rag and turned to her ersatz surgeon. "How do I look?"

"Like an angel," he said.

# CHAPTER 8

**November 30**
**Charleston, West Virginia**

Andrew Cavanaugh crouched, hooked the drape aside with his finger, and peered outside toward the barn. His right hand gripped the barrel of his hunting rifle. "They left Becca standing guard. Can you believe that? A little kid."

Grace stuck her head out from under the bed, where Andrew had ordered her to hide. "What are they doing?"

"I guess they're in the barn looking for our animals," he said, standing and pressing the rifle's barrel to the glass. He closed one eye and lined up the sight. "I could take her out from right here. Idiots."

"Andrew! It's Becca Fisher. She's our friend."

"They're trying to take our food. They have a goddamned working farm, and they are trying to steal *our* food."

A couple months ago, Andrew and the Fisher boys had been out in that same field behind the house, shooting up at the Canadian geese. They'd gone deer hunting too. Then a storm had knocked out the power, and it never came back on.

All the food rotted.

Andrew pivoted away from the window and put his back to the wall. "They're coming out." He laid down his weapon and crawled under the window to open it without being seen.

Icy air flooded the room. Grace could hear the Fisher boys' footsteps crunch across the hard-packed, crusty snow. Andrew waved her out from under the bed.

Grace shimmied out, wearing the flak jacket her father had brought back from Desert Storm, which had happened way before she was born. She reached back under the bed and felt around for her shotgun.

"Hey Andy!"

The voice belonged to Kyle Fisher, calling up to them from the back yard.

Andrew whispered to Grace. "You talk to them, but don't let them see you. I'm going up to the attic."

Grace grabbed his wrist. "What are you gonna do?"

"Just keep them talking."

Kyle Fisher shouted again.

Grace pulled her brother closer. "What am I supposed to say?"

Andrew pried himself loose. "How should I know? Just don't let them see you. They probably have guns."

Grace's heart pounded. Why would they have guns? They'd been friends with the Fishers her whole life. Even after the grownups died, the Cavanaughs and Fishers still checked on each other and hunted together and shared food. "Are they going to kill us?"

"Shhhh. Stay along the wall, and don't get shot." With that, Andrew left. In the hallway, he pulled down the attic ladder and climbed up.

Grace sat next to the window and clutched the shotgun to her chest.

"I'm not fucking around out here," Kyle said. "Tell us where you put your chickens."

All this for a bunch of stupid chickens? Grace inched the curtain aside and peeked toward the yard below. The snow tinted everything blue, even their shadows.

John, Kyle's twin, fired a shotgun shell into the air. Grace let out a shriek and spun away from the window. John said, "The next one isn't a warning shot. Now give over the chickens if you still got 'em."

Grace heard Andrew rustling around in the attic and remembered she was supposed to be talking to them. She got as close as she dared the window frame and said, "I thought you were our friends."

Kyle spoke again. "Sorry, but things are different now. There's no food. We don't want to hurt you guys, but you gotta give over those animals."

"Just give us the animals," Becca said in that high-pitched rasp they all used to make fun of. Did she understand this wasn't a game?

"What happened to all your crops?" Grace asked.

"The crops is frozen," John said.

Grace peeked. The three of them stood side by side about twenty feet from the back of the house. "Well, why didn't you dig them up before they froze?" Grace said. "Your dad didn't teach you anything?"

"You shut up about my dad," John said.

Kyle rapped his brother across the chest. Then he said to Grace, "There's no gas for the combine, and you know it. Now stop talking, and tell us where the animals are. We don't want to shoot nobody, but we will."

Becca said, her voice shrill and cutting, "Give us the animals, or we'll burn your house down."

The animals were in the storm cellar. Andrew put them there after the Fisher's pigs got attacked by a pack of wild dogs. *If they burn the house down*, she thought, *nobody gets the animals.*

"Becca," Grace said. "Is that way for a seven-year-old to talk? What would your mom say?"

How long did Andrew expect her to keep them talking? Maybe they should just give up the chickens. They were friends after all. She poked her head out into the cold, prepared to make a deal.

"Don't you ever mention my mother again," John said, whirling and training his shotgun on her. Grace screamed and flung herself to the floor as a boom rang out and the window blew apart. Kyle began hollering at his brother, calling him names. Even as she huddled in terror, she knew Kyle wanted to negotiate. If she could just talk to him…

Her thoughts were dispersed by the sound of two stark pops followed by something heavy thumping onto the encrusted snow. Silence followed, then a screech. Becca.

Grace crawled to the window, careful to avoid the broken glass, and craned her neck. Becca was fleeing across the hard-packed snow, up the incline toward the Fisher farm, her screams vanishing into the frigid morning. Grace shuffled a few inches closer and peered down at the two sprawled figures. Kyle's arm rested on John's face. Their shotguns sat across their midsections. They weren't moving.

Grace stared and, aided by light of the rising sun, began to make out red speckles in the snow around the two boys. Becca's shrieks faded away, and the still morning deafened her with silence. Maybe she heard Andrew come down the attic ladder, maybe she didn't. She realized he had entered the room when a floorboard groaned under his foot.

He still held the rifle, but his face had gone blank. He walked past her to the hole where the window used to be and gazed down at the bodies. He stared for a good long while.

Neither of them spoke.

***

Andrew pulled the rope tight, forcing John Fisher's nylon jacket to bunch up on either side. The body jiggled when Andrew gave one last tug to make sure the nylon was secure. Grace felt sick, imagining the friction of the rope cutting into John's flesh. She wanted Andrew to be gentle, though it hardly mattered.

Snow crunched under her feet as she shifted back and forth, watching her brother work. Steam shot from her mouth with each breath she exhaled. The stinging of her cheeks and nose had given way to numbness.

John and Kyle Fisher were dead. Andrew had killed them. It was like one of those horrible nightmares when you hurt someone you care about and still feel sick over it when you wake up.

"Now you gotta be careful not to let him pick up too much speed," Andrew said. "We don't want them sailing off into the sticker bushes or knocking your feet out."

He had tied the boys to sleds he'd rummaged from the barn.

"Do we have to do this?"

"You want to leave them right here in the yard so you have to look at them every day?" Andrew marched to the front of the sled to which John was fastened and picked up the yellow nylon rope. John was the far chunkier of the twins. Grace would pull Kyle.

"Can't we bury them?" she said, draping the other nylon cord over her shoulder. She tugged down on her purple knit cap with her matching mittens, trying to protect herself from frostbite. Then she took hold of the bowline loop Andrew had tied at the end of the rope.

Andrew pulled. "The ground is frozen. Anyway, I don't want to go outside and see their graves all the time." The rope stretched and fully extended a moment before the sled budged. It jerked forward and stopped, but soon Andrew found the flow. "Come on."

Grace tugged and marched but got nowhere, her feet bearing down the same patch of snow. Andrew jogged to the back of her sled and shoved with his boot. It started sliding forward.

"We gotta get rid of them. We don't want scavengers in the yard, tearing them up," Andrew said, now marching beside his sister. "Watch out, the ground dips here."

Grace couldn't help but look ahead to the left, toward the big oak they called the Baby Tree because it looked like a giant fetus in the summer, its trunk serving as the umbilical cord. From the ground at its base rose a wooden cross.

She noticed that Andrew was staring at it too. This was not the first time they had hauled a body out here. The other time was June 11, they day after *it* happened, and they had to use a blue plastic tarp to slide that body over the grass. Grace cried so hard that day she couldn't see, and Andrew had to tell her to shut up a bunch of times.

They let go of the ropes and stepped somberly to the wooden cross. Carved on the horizontal bar was GREG CAVANAUGH JR. AGE 19. Their older brother. They had found him on the family room couch when they got back from the airport. Three of five

Cavanaughs dead on the same day. Andrew had spent two days making the grave marker.

Grace shuffled across the snow and wrapped an arm around Andrew, whose gaze seemed to reach past the grave, past this moment.

"We can't stay here much longer," he said.

"Just for another minute," she said.

"I mean at the house. We can't stay. We're sitting ducks."

A tear came to Grace's eye. "I don't want to leave. It's our home. Let's just wait until the police come."

He pulled her in for a hug. "Grace, the police aren't coming. They're all dead. No one is coming."

She pulled away from him, picked up the rope, and started dragging Kyle Fisher's corpse. "What do you mean about sitting ducks?"

Andrew resumed his burden. "Anybody with a gun can walk up and start shooting. We need a safer place where there's more people. Strength in numbers."

Before Grace could respond, a din arose from beyond a distant cluster of trees, on the other side of the ridge. A pack of dogs howling.

"Let's hurry up," Andrew said.

# CHAPTER 9

**November 30**
**Alexandria, Virginia**

"To be, or not to be? That is the question."

Zane cradled the skull—made of resin—as he paced across the stage. "Whether 'tis nobler to suffer the slings and arrows of outrageous fortune or to take arms against a sea of troubles…"

The theater's red velvet curtains, tattered and thick with dust, swallowed most of the light from the torches. Four on the stage, another twelve in the aisles, but it was still not bright enough. Any more fire and they'd start choking on the smoke. The biting cold did not permit them to open the doors and let in fresh air. Yet, despite the ragged condition of the old hall, with cracks spider-webbing across its stucco ceiling and creaking, careworn seats, Zane enjoyed the ambiance.

The flame cast an orange glow across the faces of the children seated before him. He continued his monologue as he watched them watching him. He could do the whole thing on autopilot. "When we have shuffled off this mortal coil, must give us pause. There's the respect that makes calamity of so long life."

All those fresh young faces belonging to eight-, nine-, and ten-year-old boys and girls gazing up at him with reverence. The older kids treated them like gnats, always shoving them and shouting, "Get the fuck out of the way!" Not Zane. Zane ministered to them. He remembered how, back before his mom had died of cancer and still dragged his ass to church every Sunday, people looked up to Reverend Moore like he was a messenger from heaven. Zane used to sit in the pew thinking, *If this guy told us to go out and kill somebody, we would.*

Meanwhile, Nagesh and Anthony, both fourteen like Zane, sat in a row to the right of the aisle, huddled in a chat and ignoring him. He pivoted and stormed the edge of the stage. "I'm performing up here. Do you mind not talking so loud?"

Nagesh said, "Why are you carrying a skull? It's the wrong scene, Hamlet."

Zane hurled the prop at their feet, hoping it would shatter. It didn't. It bounced up and hit an armrest before falling back and spinning twice. The two boys glared at Zane. "What's your problem?" Nagesh said.

"Yorick is my best fucking friend," Zane said. "Maybe I feel like carrying him around all the time."

"Whatever, dude." Nagesh said. "These are your plans we're discussing. You might want to get involved." He and Anthony shook their heads and resumed their conversation.

Zane frowned. Nagesh and Anthony were getting too full of themselves lately. He gestured for the children to sit still and then trotted down the stairs stage right. His two junior partners, as he viewed them, showed less bravado as he drew nearer.

He sat. "Nagesh, if you have a problem, you know you can come to me any time. But let's can the attitude. Zane giveth, and

Zane taketh away, and your life is much better when Zane giveth. No?"

Anthony, bigger and dumber and, for now, easier to control, said, "We just want you to help us more. This is some serious shit you want us to do."

What more did these clowns want? Zane wrote, in exacting detail, how to build the bomb, and he supplied them with all the material, including the explosives (thanks, Dad), the Dodge Ram (thanks, Dad), and the makeshift detonator. He told them where: Metro Center subway station in downtown DC. The biggest gang in the city was using that as a base, a decision so stupid it made Zane giddy.

"It's not really all that difficult. Stage it and wait for the next storm. They'll all be down there, and you just send it down the tracks. Boom. Done."

Nagesh shook his head but spoke in politer tones with Zane now staring a hole in him. "Nobody likes those tunnels, man. I've heard stories about some crazy shit down there."

Zane placed a hand on Nagesh's shoulder like Dad used to do to him. "Look, a cruise missile with a warhead would be nice, but you may have noticed the world is a bit fucked up technology-wise. If you guys don't want to do it yourselves, recruit some idiot. Promise him and his buddies that I'll give them all kinds of booze and cars or whatever. Take some gifts with you to sell it."

Anthony stirred. "Dude, we're your partners. That's not fair if you give them all the shit you promised us."

Sometimes people's stupidity hurt Zane's brain, as if they were giving off moron shock waves. "Anthony. We're not really going to give it to them. We say we we're going to give it to them after they set off the bomb. Tell them the detonator is on a timer that takes twenty minutes, when it really takes a half a second. They are on a suicide mission and don't know it. You sit back and laugh. It's a good time."

The junior associates eyed each other and nodded. "That works," Anthony said. "You have to do the talking, though. You're way better at that part."

"Deal. Now go find me some idiots. And make sure they are indeed idiots."

Zane returned to center stage. The children, twelve of them, stared at the two transgressors with a mixture of alarm and offense for interrupting their leader's performance. Zane thought of Reverend Moore again, of loyalty and surrender. Of gods. He smiled as a notion sparked in his mind.

"Hey, kids."

They all turned to him.

"Who wants to come up here and be part of the show?"

All twelve jumped to their feet and cheered.

# CHAPTER 10

## November 30
## Charleston, West Virginia

Andrew finished untying the nylon cord that held John Fisher to the sled. Kyle had already been cut loose. The two bodies rested side-by-side on the stone ledge that jutted over the water's surface ten feet below. Just a few months ago, the three of them had come down here to swim.

The river ran through the center of the valley, a mile below the open expanse of the Fisher's farm. The damp air chilled Grace, turning the sweat of her exertion cold and her skin clammy.

Andrew removed his hat and nodded to his sister, and she followed his lead.

"Dear Lord," Andrew said. "We give unto you the bodies of your faithful servants, Kyle and John Fisher, whom I had to shoot in self-defense today, and for which I am very sorry. I know it wasn't very Christian of me, Lord, but it was us or them. When you take their souls, just remember that they were mostly good people who…Hey, get off!"

Grace opened her eyes. A turkey vulture crouched on John's chest, pecking at the bullet hole. Andrew kicked at it, and the big black bird squawked and flew off into the trees. John resumed his pious stance.

"So anyway, dear Lord, please accept them into your kingdom and realize that they were just desperate, and please forgive me when it's my turn, in case no one is around to pray for me. Amen."

"Amen," Grace said. She wondered if God was mad at her too, even though she hadn't done anything wrong that she knew of.

Andrew placed his arms against John Fisher's supine form. "God have mercy," he said, and pressed his weight into the task. A creaky noise emanated from the rocky outcropping, and Grace scurried back a few feet in case it decided to give way and dump all of them into the frigid river. With one final nudge from Andrew, John slipped from the icy crag and splashed into the water. The corpse popped to the surface, bobbed, and joined the current.

Andrew stared at Grace. She shrugged, and he gestured toward Kyle.

"Me?"

"Yeah. He's yours."

"Ew. Andrew. I'm not pushing a dead body into the river."

Andrew took her by the arm and tugged. "Come on. Use those thick Cavanaugh thighs you got from Grandpa."

Grace grumbled and yanked free. "Fine!"

She stomped to the ledge, kneeled, and pushed. Kyle flipped over and hit the water with a hard slap. Then she stood and booted both sleds in after him. "Happy now?"

\*\*\*

Andrew marched up the slow incline, stone-faced. Grace followed, quite relieved at not having to haul sleds with dead people on them. She didn't know why her brother was so upset. Before he was saying they should go live somewhere else. Like they were going to carry sleds around! She had no intention of leaving, though, so she didn't bring it up.

"That was disrespectful," he finally said.

"What's the big deal about the sleds? We never use them."

Andrew began to huff as the ground became steeper. They had been hiking steadily uphill for a while. "I mean to Kyle."

"I didn't shoot him. You did."

Andrew stopped and turned. "I had to. That's how it works now. It doesn't mean we have to act like subhumans."

Grace noticed a dark red patch as he gesticulated. "You got blood on your glove."

He turned his right hand over and poked the stain with his left index finger. He removed the glove and found blood seeping from a deep cut on his finger. The blood quickly began to thicken in the cold. "Must be from when I cut John free. I didn't even feel it."

The two of them resumed walking. The top of their house came into view over the ridge, still two hundred yards away.

"We should have offered to share the food. You didn't have to shoot them."

He waved her off. "Don't be an idiot. No one is coming to rescue us. There's no more rules. We gotta fend for ourselves and go find somewhere warmer to live."

"Andrew," she said with a sigh.

"We're going to starve here. It's not even technically winter yet."

Grace put her forearm over her face to block the noisy, biting wind gust that greeted them at the top of the hill. "What are we going to do, ride our bikes?"

"You know how we're going to get out of here."

"No, I don't, and shut up. We shouldn't argue in front of Greg." She nodded toward their brother's grave.

"You know—"

Andrew stopped and pivoted to his right with a jolt, his attention caught by several dark shapes emerging from the shadows of the pine trees. Bearing down on them with speed. The first dog, a German shepherd, chomped down on his bloody hand a half second before a Rottweiler leaped onto his chest and knocked him to the hard snow.

Grace screamed.

The rest of the pack charged in, biting at Andrew's arms. He fought to stand but was overwhelmed. He fell backward and rolled, covering his head as the starving beasts gnawed at his fingers and scalp. "Run," he grunted. "Grace, run!"

Grace took a step closer to the swarm of gnarled, mangy, and gaunt animals. She grabbed one by the rump and yanked it away. It twisted back, snarling, and snapped its jaws. The dog's fangs missed her face by an inch.

She let go and ran, the crunch of the snow under her feet the only thing she could hear. The house didn't seem to be getting closer. She looked back, still running, to see Andrew rolling on the ground as the dogs tore at him. Why didn't he get up and run?

She turned forward too late to see the porch steps and plowed into them, whacking her knees and forearms. Her head cracked off the railing, sending a pulse of pain through her temple. The momentum pushed her back to her feet, and she continued into the house. Into the darkness. She ran into the living room and ripped the shotgun down from the rack.

When she came back outside, her flank aching from the panicked sprint, Andrew was no longer struggling. The dogs were circling and barking and nipping at each other.

Grace propped the shotgun against her shoulder, whipped her mitten away, and fired into the pack. The recoil tossed her onto her backside. She rolled over and saw the dogs fleeing, one trailing behind the others with its hindquarters covered in blood, whimpering. It took three more steps and dropped.

Grace's body ached. "Andrew," she huffed, crawling to her brother.

His arms and legs were chewed to the bone, and his scalp had been ripped away. Blood streaked the snow for fifteen feet, some of it spattering the cross that marked Greg's burial spot. Grace put her hand on her brother's chest. "Andrew!"

His eyelids fluttered. "You can do it," he said.

Grace pulled at his jacket. "Come on, we have to get you inside."

"You have to," he whispered. "You can."

She wiped her tears. "I can what?"

Andrew's eyes closed.

"I can what?"

His chest rose with a sudden gasp. He opened his eyes again.

Grace patted his chest, her teardrops freezing on her face. "I can what? What can I do?"

He mouthed the word, "Fly." Then his head dropped to the side. After that, the world fell still, save for the blood draining from the tear in Andrew's throat.

Grace tucked her face into her hands and fell into screaming sobs as hungry, frightened dogs looked on from the edge of the woods.

# CHAPTER 11

**December 25**
**Baltimore, Maryland**

She went looking for a prison and found a church.

That's what it looked like at first: The big, gray stone walls, the tower, and the pointy roof all looking so gloomy and medieval. The tall fence topped by coils of barbed wire said *prison*, though. A stark, gray sky threatening snow completed the grim vignette.

By Josie's estimation, today was Christmas Day. She cared little for the holiday, for it reminded her mostly of disposable gifts from the dollar store and yet another of her mom's boyfriends trying to buy Josie's approval with a twenty-dollar bill or a Barbie.

Last year, Cara had given Josie a box of old *Incredible Hulk* comics she had flirted away from some nerd. Easily the best Christmas gift of all time. The poor kid probably turned over his entire collection for the promise of a kiss. Cara Revelle positively owned boys.

Josie stepped sideways and slid through an opening cut into the prison fence. No doubt some gang had tried to use the place for a fortress, but a hideout this big and cold and damp is too much trouble. And the dumbest thing you could do these days was have something everyone else wants.

Crouching in the shadows, Josie inched along the rusticated façade in search of an entrance. On the far end, she found a metal door hanging half open. Someone had dragged the bodies of two guards and a prisoner to the side. Josie tugged on the decayed inmate's uniform looking for a name tag. No luck.

With expert silence, she slipped into the building and made for the darkest spot, an easy enough tasks since only high slits for windows let in light. She removed her ski mask and gloves, finding it nearly as cold in here as outside.

If the prisoners didn't have name tags, finding her dad would be impossible. She didn't even know if he was in here or some other lock-up. Or if he was a prisoner at all. Maybe he really did work on the railroad.

Josie produced a flashlight and began to search the halls for an office. She had noticed from raiding office buildings for food that companies had all kinds of files. Maybe her dad's name was on a list around here somewh—

Footsteps.

She stowed the flashlight and ducked behind bolted-down row of chairs.

"Hello?" a voiced called from beyond a propped-open door connected to a corridor that led deeper into the building.

Josie moved into a crouch, ready to flee.

"Hello? Are you here for the Christmas party?"

She peeked over a chair back. A boy poked his head through the doorway. "Is someone in here?" he said.

He turned on a flashlight and swept the room, stopping the circle of light on the cluster of chairs in front of her. "Uh, I can see your hair."

*Damn it!*

"It's all right," he said. "I'm not going to hurt you. We're having a Christmas party. You can come out. I swear we're not a gang or anything."

Josie flashed her beam back at him. He wore a green sweater with a red Rudolf the Red-Nosed Reindeer on the front. Definitely not a gangster.

She stood. "I wasn't invited."

"I'm inviting you right now."

***

The boy, who called himself Jason Kim, led Josie through a series of connecting corridors. She flashed her beam left and right for markers in case she had to turn and run. They emerged into a cafeteria with candles on some of the tables, camping lanterns on others, and a twelve-inch tall, battery-powered, fiber optic, spinning Christmas tree on the one in the middle. A group of about thirty kids sat scattered around the room.

"This is Josie," Jason said, receiving a few half-hearted waves in response. He pressed a switch on the tree, and a chime-bell version of "O Christmas Tree" emerged from a tiny speaker hidden somewhere on the decoration. Half the kids groaned, and one said, "Please, not again."

Jason reached into a bag and came out with a sealed pouch of peanut butter crackers. Then he took a Coke from a cooler and handed the items to Josie. "Merry Christmas," he said. She thought he did a better job than most at not flinching when he noticed she had one eye. Josie devoured the crackers in seconds, and Jason handed her a second bag.

She glanced at the others, expecting someone to gripe at her taking seconds.

"Don't worry," Jason said. "They all got the cookies before. These are leftovers."

Josie shrugged and gulped the Coke so fast her sinuses burned.

Another boy sat at a nearby table with his knees pulled up to his chin. "Who told you about the party? Blinky?"

Josie wondered how someone named Blinky could still be alive seven months in. "I came looking for my dad."

The party guests within earshot exchanged curious glances.

Jason sat beside her. "Josie. I don't know how to tell you this, but..."

Josie stood and peered into the snack bag. She fished out two handfuls of peanut butter cracker packages and stuffed them into her pockets. She sat back down next to Jason and took another sip of Coke. "That's the ugliest sweater I've ever seen."

Jason laughed. "It's pretty warm."

"Well, I wouldn't wear it outside unless you want to get shot."

Jason put his fingertips together like a grown-up about to say something serious. "Your dad is dead, Josie. They all are."

Josie studied his face. He was all right. Some boys were cool, and she usually knew within a minute. Maybe she could hang out with Jason and he wouldn't die of cancer like Rogelio did.

She explained: "My apartment building collapsed with my mom in it, so I can't go there, and I don't remember where my sister died because...I don't. I think my dad might have been a prisoner here. I just thought I should visit him on Christmas. I didn't have other plans."

"You can hang with us. There's plenty of mattresses."

*That might not be too bad*, she thought, *not having to sneak around and forage for a day.* She didn't mind talking to Jason, either.

"You!"

Two kids moved aside as an older girl wandered into their circle of light. Long pink scars crisscrossed her face like a tic-tac-toe game gone mad, paralyzing one side of her mouth. She pointed at Josie.

"You're that little fucking bitch that did this to me. How come you didn't die?"

Josie climbed over the table to the far side. "I never saw you before."

Jason said, "Hey," and placed his arm in the girl's path, but she smacked it away.

"Liar. All you had to do was sit there and wait 'til it was done, then you and your sister would have been in the club. It was that simple. Nothing would have even happened to you."

The club. Ronan and his gang. Josie stared at the girl, looking past the scars and the jagged cut of her brown hair. She *had* seen her before. This was the girl who had tried to stop Josie from rescuing Cara. Back then, her hair was bleached blond and she had normal skin.

"I only scratched your arm. I didn't cut up your face."

The girl pointed to herself, her hand trembling. "They did this to me for letting you get away, you dumb fucking bitch. This is your fault."

Josie's mouth froze open, and no words came. How could this girl blame her for what Ronan did? Both of them were maimed by him that day.

"You get out. You get the fuck out," the girl said. Two boys tried to sit her down, but she broke free and took a swipe at Josie with her fingernails, screaming one more time for her to get out, her face wet with tears and spit flying from her lips.

Josie ran, her face hot with humiliation. She fled through the corridors and the waiting area and past that half-open metal door into the cold, gloomy afternoon. Reaching into her pockets, she realized she'd lost her ski mask and one of her gloves during her flight. After debating with herself for a minute about retrieving her hat, she turned back toward the building, only to see Jason pull the door shut. His eyes said *I'm sorry.*

"Why does everyone hate me all the time," she said, immediately regretting her self-pitying words. She changed her statement to "people suck" and began the long journey back to her nest inside the boiler room of a school, her pockets stuffed with peanut butter crackers. The second-best Christmas gift she'd ever gotten.

# CHAPTER 12

**January 28**
**Washington, D.C.**

The snow kept coming, and not the fluffy kind, but the tiny, hard pebbles that sound like sewing pins bombarding the window. It grew deep enough, finally, that she could no longer spot the dead bodies under it.

Shawnika got so used to seeing corpses that she hardly noticed them anymore, especially now that they were frozen and didn't stink. Most of them were so rotted they looked like props from a movie, not real people. Sometimes, though, opening up a room that had been closed since June 10 was a putrid reminder of what happens to flesh after people die.

But right now the snow was covering it all, and she felt transported to a peaceful place. She wanted more of that feeling in her life.

Behind her, sitting cross-legged at the entrance of their make-shift tent of blankets and towels, Tre stuck his spoon back into the jar of peanut butter. Shawnika saw, in the faint reflection cast by the window, her little brother eying her.

"No double-dipping, I said."

He slumped, caught again. Then he shoved the spoon in a third time. "Who cares?"

"You're getting kind of recalcitrant these days."

Tre shrugged. "It's just peanut butter."

"Do you know what recalcitrant means?" This new hideout was short on reading material, leaving Shawnika to try memorizing a dictionary she'd found in the basement.

"I don't even care."

"It means you like to argue with me and disagree with me just to be difficult. It means you are contrary."

"Stop using dictionary words."

Shawnika turned to him. "I already knew what contrary means. I train my brain because we need to be able to think. Thinking keeps us alive."

Thinking led them here. With all the gangs in the streets and people fighting and raiding hideouts, Shawnika went low profile: an apartment above a tax office. There was nothing to raid here. Anyplace with food, forget about it. Clothing stores got targeted a lot too. Liquor stores were no good. Their last hide was a sewing shop, and even that got ransacked weekly for fabric. A toy store was flat-out suicide. Kids got stabbed for a Spider-Man action figure. But everyone right walked past an H&R Block without even seeing it.

Tre came to the window and peered into the blizzard. "Who's that?"

Shawnika snapped back into the moment. "Who's what?"

Her brother pressed his index finger to the glass. "That kid outside."

She squinted. With night approaching and the world fading into a blue-gray haze, she needed a moment to focus. Then she homed in on something moving counter to the downward blasting snow. A child, shorter than Tre and up to his hips in snow, was bearing down against the beating storm. "What's he doing?"

"Hey! That's Melvin."

"Who?"

"From school. He was in my class. He came over that one time."

Shawnika cupped her hands to the glass. "How can you tell?"

"Cause he's fat. He was the fattest kid in the school."

"Maybe it's some other fat kid."

Tre wrapped his hand on the glass and shouted, "Melvin!"

Shawnika cracked him across the arm. "Are you stupid? Never do that again. You'll give us away."

Tre gazed up at her with big puppy eyes. "He's my friend."

She rolled her head back, looked toward the heavens, and grunted. "You really want me to go out there and get this kid?"

"He was the only kid who liked me when I started the new school."

Shawnika thought of their four jars of peanut butter and their two boxes of stale crackers from the Jewish center they'd ransacked, and then she thought about that kid outside not exactly being skinny. Then she thought about that kid freezing to death, and what kind of Christian lets that happen? And her brother was probably getting sick of his dumb old sister for company.

She sighed and said, "All right. But the second you guys start with the underarm farts, I'm going to the Bahamas, and you can both stay here and freeze to death. Got it?"

Shawnika shoved her arms into the sleeves of an oversized parka she'd found in a bedroom closet and carried a pair of size twelve men's work boots down the stairs, which terminated near the back of the building. In the dark, she slinked through the hallway, did a quick scan of the tax office to make sure it was empty, and crept to the Plexiglas front door. She slipped into the boots and pressed the handle, hardly budging the door with the snowy gale pounding on it from the other side. She lowered her shoulder and pushed through.

At once, snow began pouring into the boots, wetting her socks. She pulled the parka hood over her head and scanned the scene to orient herself. The block of shops and apartments across the street appeared as flat, gray rectangles, and the street to her left and right faded into mad swirls of flurries. As far as Shawnika could tell, this was the whole world.

She tripped over a stiff hump and face-planted into the snow pile. "Damn it," she mumbled, pushing herself back to her feet. Now her hands stung, and the sleeves of her parka were full of icy beads. *Where's that kid?*

To her left, a small round lump protruded from the snow like a squat snowman. She felt it looking at her. She hollered over the noisy wind. "Melvin!"

It kept staring, faceless. What the hell. Maybe Tre was even more of a knucklehead than she thought. Was she out here chasing an abandoned shopping cart or something? Shawnika bellowed again. "If your name is Melvin, come over here. I'm only going to invite you once."

The blob began to drift in her direction. It stopped a few feet away, gazing up, its face round, and its eyes sadder than a dog that just got kicked. The blob shivered.

"What are you doing out here in the cold?"

"I'm sorry," Melvin said.

Oh, great. Another charity case. "Well, let's get inside before we freeze to death, huh? My brother Tre is in there."

Shawnika warned Melvin not to trip over the frozen corpse in the snow, but he did anyway, and helping him up was quite a bigger challenge than scraping up Tre whenever he fell over something, which was often.

She led him through the shop and up the stairs, shaking her head at his thumping footsteps. In the apartment, Shawnika peeled his wet jacket and put him into a double XL Washington Redskins sweatshirt that made him look like he was wearing a tomato.

She gave him a handful of crackers and sat him next to Tre. The two boys exchanged shy greetings.

"What were you doing out in the snow?" she asked.

Crumbs fell as he spoke. "Some big kids set my hideout on fire cause they were cold I guess. I got scared."

Shawnika's anger swelled. What was everyone supposed to do when all the buildings are burned down and it snows again?

"Where was this?"

"Some place."

"What place?"

"I don't know. A house or something."

"Melvin. How did you stay alive? You don't exactly look like you been going hungry."

He shoved another cracker in his mouth. "Do you have any chocolate milk?"

"Seriously? You see a chocolate cow in here?"

"They have 'em. Chocolate milks with little straws attached that you don't need to 'frigerate."

Shawnika ran her hand over her hair, which was starting to look like her grandma's natural in those hippie photos from 1970. "What's your last name, kid?"

"Tubbs."

She stifled a laugh. "Of course it is. Melvin Tubbs, what am I going to do with you? I don't have enough food for me and Tre, much less a walking garbage disposal. You have anywhere I can take you when the snow melts?"

Melvin pondered. "The White House?"

"The White House."

"Sure. The president is there. He knows what to do."

"The president's dead."

"No he's not," Tre said.

She gave him the *don't be dumb* look. "All the grown-ups are dead. What's so special about the president?"

"He isn't dead," Melvin said. "The White House has secret bunkers that block radiation and stuff. They move the president into the bunker when there's a war or whatever. Everybody says it was radiation."

"Who's everybody?"

"Everybody. Every kid says radiation killed the teachers and police and everything."

Tre gazed at Melvin with admiration. His eyes said: *Finally, someone who knows something!*

At that, Shawnika decided she had to break up this bromance as soon as possible. "Then why are *we* alive?"

"'Cause we're invisible."

"Invincible, you mean?"

"Some smart kid was talking about Jean…Mutajin."

"Gene mutation?"

Melvin nodded. Shawnika was more into history than science, but maybe this Melvin kid wasn't one hundred percent silly. Maybe—

The explosion shook the floor hard enough to knock the candle off the little trunk they used for a table, snuffing out the flame's golden glow. The windows rattled but held. Shawnika turned around in time to see a yellow fireball mushroom into the sky.

She crawled to the window and peered through as the flames dissipated, a shimmer of orange remaining just beyond the buildings yonder. Did some fool just get more than he planned for trying to burn the wrong thing for heat?

"Keep it on your block, guys," she said to herself.

She stared for a while at the orange glow. It seemed to be devouring the blizzard and illuminating the cloud ceiling like a god of fire escaped from the underworld.

It was a lot more than a few blocks away. More like a few miles, and massive. Shawnika realized a lot of people just died.

"Keep it on your block."

# CHAPTER 13

**February 19**
**Alexandria, Virginia**

"Gangs are so banal."

Zane had said that to Nagesh and Anthony and the boys upstairs. They had just blown the shit out of the biggest gang in DC...killed those pig scum with a bomb he'd taught them how to make...and what do they do? Start talking about coming up with their own gang name and symbol and initiation rites. Zane had simply offered his opinion about that. He got the feeling they didn't understand.

After that, he told them he would not attend another meeting until they stopped behaving like Neanderthals. He did not worry about getting kicked out because they were all stupid and needed his brain. And all his dad's stuff.

Now he was in the basement of the theater, always a crisp fifty-five degrees and a perfect thinking temperature. The costumes were stored down here. *Costumes are half the fun of acting*, he thought.

Zane slid the Santa Claus suit to the right and began to check the tags on the elf costumes. They were intended for adult dwarf actors, but they'd serve his purpose. He pulled a small from the rack.

"Here you go," he said, handing the green-and-red outfit to the seven-year-old girl following him. He imagined this was the first time in forty years this shabby theater had failed to stage its annual Christmas spectacular, what with civilization destroyed and all.

"I can really wear this?"

"Of course you may, young lady." Zane patted her head the way the Grinch patted Cindy Loo Who in the cartoon. "Now you go to that changing room over there and put it on. It's yours to wear whenever you want."

As the smiling half-pint hurried off, Zane made a mental note to remember her name. He'd taken in so many young orphans lately that he couldn't keep track of them. The other so-called leaders upstairs complained regularly about feeding the "rug rats," but Zane promised them he was raising future slave labor. *Once we take over the city*, Zane would say, *we'll be like kings*. That always worked.

Zane abandoned the costume rack and entered the script library. Here were all the Shakespeares, the Tennessee Williams, and the Andrew Lloyd Webbers on heavy shelves. Plus scripts based on classic novellas like *A Christmas Carol* and *Dr. Jekyll and Mr. Hyde*, filed alphabetically by title in cabinets. Over the unused radiator were biographies of famous historical figures and playwrights.

Zane removed the volume on Vlad Tepes, the real-life Romanian prince better known to history as Dracula. He flipped to the middle of the book to the reproductions of medieval wood carvings. One showed Tepes's castle surrounded by thousands of men impaled on stakes. Old Vlad knew how to send a message.

"Mr. Zane?" The little girl's voice echoed down the corridor.

"In here, dear," Zane said. She came to the doorway and peeked in. He stood. "Come on in."

She stepped into the library and stood with her arms at her sides, waiting for his assessment.

Zane clapped. "Well, aren't you the prettiest elf I've ever seen." He crouched before her and spoke the phrase that had been working like an enchanting spell lately: "The Lord is pleased."

Like a rose blooming, a smile unfolded across her face. "Really?"

"Really," Zane said. "The Lord told me."

\*\*\*

Zane strode back into the meeting of the elders and took his seat at the oval table. Once a place for script read-throughs, it now served as their war room. Or, as far as the other elders were concerned, a place to debate inane shit like gang logos.

The eleven other boys shot nervous glances at Zane as he took his seat. Anthony continued orating.

"Fifty miles is a long trip for a covert mission, but if we leave before dawn, we can get down there, do some recon, and get back before nightfall."

Anthony loved military-sounding words like *recon* and *covert*.

"If the place is easy-access, we take whatever we want. If the place is locked down, we do some surveillance, find out when they change guards or whatever, and then come back with enough bodies to take it."

They must have decided to raid the National Guard armory while Zane was downstairs.

One of the other boys interrupted. "Dude, the place is going to be ransacked by now. Anyway, they have, like, tanks in there. We'll get killed."

"We don't know if it's ransacked until we check it out. They probably have shoulder-rocket launchers and stuff. No one would fuck with us if we had that shit."

Zane raised his hand as if seeking permission to speak. They all looked at him. He said: "Chocolate."

Wary and confused glances were exchanged.

Zane continued. "About six miles from here is a company that made gourmet chocolate. There's no reason to think the equipment doesn't still work. They have files with recipes. Probably supplies too, at least whatever the bugs didn't get into. We should get that working."

"Um, why?"

"Um, I'm sure you guys are great at paramilitary raids and at operating rocket launchers, but it's not really like X-Box. Not in real life. It would be a lot less dangerous to make chocolate. People love that stuff."

Anthony beckoned with his finger, and one of the younger kids—the slaves—came forward with an open-topped box. Anthony reached in and fished out a Milky Way. "We have chocolate right here, man. Are you talking just to be a pain in the ass?" Something had clicked in Anthony's brain after they'd blown up the Metro station four weeks earlier, and he'd begun talking tough.

Zane shook his head and gave his most dismissive look. "Ten months ago, civilization went belly up. No one has made a fucking candy bar since June. How many Milky Ways do you think will be in that box two years from now?"

Anthony dropped the candy bar in the box and motioned for the boy to get lost. "Dude, what the hell is wrong with you. We need weapons. Nobody gives a shit about candy bars."

Zane waved the child over. The child circled the table and held the box forth. Zane took the box, laid it on the table, and fished out the Milky Way. He peeled the wrapper halfway. "Thank you," he said to the young boy. "What's your name again?"

"Jorge."

Zane placed the Milky Way in the boy's hand. "This is for you, Jorge, for doing such a good job."

Anthony stood up. "Hey. That twerp doesn't get candy bars. That's for *us*."

Zane gave Jorge a reassuring nod and turned to Anthony. "See? People do care about candy bars. And cars and gas and electricity and clothes and whatever. This country has oil refineries and power plants and car assembly lines just sitting there waiting to be used. We don't have to build anything. We just have to figure out how the shit works and then get it working."

Anthony stared at him. At last he said, "There's thirteen of us and about fifty of your rug rats. You want to do all that with a bunch of kids?"

Zane shook his head in pretend agreement. "Good point." It was actually a stupid point, but Zane wanted Anthony to think they had a partnership. "So, instead of going on same half-baked raid of an armory that has nothing left or is being guarded like a fortress, why don't we go out there and recruit some labor? You can't be a king without subjects to rule."

Zane looked from face to face and sensed the room starting to slip from his control. Perhaps words were no longer powerful enough.

# CHAPTER 14

**March 21**
**Charleston, West Virginia**

Grace opened her eyes, dreams at once flushed away. Almost. She remembered something about breaking glass.

Then a crash sounded, followed by the immediate tinkling of shards on the floor. Then another. Boot steps.

Someone was in the house. For real.

She shot upright and threw off the wool blankets. Someone was upstairs smashing the windows and stomping around. Every night, before descending into the storm cellar, she did her best to hide evidence of her presence. No tea kettles. No dirty plates or silverware. No washed plates or silverware. She did that in preparation for what was now taking place: people ransacking her home.

The chickens! The last two chickens were in the basement. She'd started with twenty, and they'd fed her all winter. At first the din infuriated her, then she got lonely and they kept her company. And every five days, the cages became less crowded by one chicken, but she couldn't bear to kill these last two. Now she feared they would betray her loyalty and give away her presence.

In the storm cellar, with its steel frame and insulated walls, she couldn't hear much of what was going on upstairs, but she felt the vibration of doors being opened and closed. The boot steps grew louder, and she realized the burglars were coming down the basement steps. Now, muffled voices discussed plans and exchanged ideas on the other side of the metal storm door. If they saw the chickens, they'd know she was in the house. She covered the cages with a canvas tarp to shut them up at night, but a chicken cage is a pretty obvious sha—

A boot landed hard against the storm door. Grace reached to her right, in the dark, and felt for the pistol she kept on top of her dad's maintenance manuals and magazines beside her cot. Her hand closed around the grip. She picked it up.

Another kick.

She held the pistol out, aiming, as best she could, toward the door. Her own heartbeat drummed in her ears.

A muffled voice, belonging to a boy, said, "What are you doing, dude?"

A second voice, closer and clearer, just opposite the door: "I wanna see what's in here."

Grace tilted the pistol so the barrel's tip pressed against the soft tissue on the bottom of her jaw. She'd been doing that a lot lately. All it would take was one squeeze, but she chickened out every time.

Ha. Life and death revolved around the word *chicken*.

"It's a bunch of fucking dead bodies, man," the first voice said. Seconds of silence, then: "Can't you fucking smell it? My fucking eyes are watering down here."

The chicken poop! Grace had become so used to it that she didn't notice the odor, except on those days she felt brave enough to poke around outside and then come back in.

Boot steps up the stairs. Grace exhaled and realized she hadn't breathed for almost a minute. Then she noticed the gun barrel still pointed into her skull, so she tilted her head back gingerly and returned the weapon to her stack of magazines, its business end aimed toward the wall. She sat in the dark and waited for a half hour before unbolting the storm door and checking on her birds.

Chickens intact, Grace tiptoed up the steps, peeked left and right, and stepped into the kitchen. The cabinets stood open, and a chair lay on its side. A breeze blew through the passageway to the hall. The air felt fresh, like outside air. That shouldn't happen. She skulked around the corner and into the living room.

The windows were smashed, and the screen door hung on one hinge. The coffee table lay on its side. She approached the gaping frame that had housed the picture window, careful to avoid glass shards, and looked over the edge. On the grass below lay her mom's porcelain angel figurine from the mantelpiece, its head broken off. Like it had a heart attack midflight and plummeted to the Earth.

Those boys smashed up her house for no reason other than they could. Grace wished she had shot them. Then she thought of those dead Fisher kids and how Andrew had killed them outright. She thought of Becca Fisher with no one to take care of her.

The breeze picked up again, parading right into her living room like it owned the place. Grace closed her eyes. The breeze felt good. It felt warm.

She had no idea what day it was, but the cold and the snow seemed like it had been around forever. *In like a lion*, her mom used to say about March on account of the wind. Perhaps spring had come at last, bringing home invaders no doubt, but also something more.

Hope?

Grace put on her jacket and snow boots, which were way too small since she'd worn them last winter too, before everyone died. Once outside, she lifted the heavy wooden lid of the trash bin designed to keep out raccoons and withdrew a small basket of chicken eggs. She hid them out here in nature's refrigerator, but if warm weather was coming, she'd have to use them up before they spoiled.

She let the lid slam shut, picked up her basket, and marched up the incline toward the Fisher place.

When the ground leveled off, the Fisher's farmhouse came into view. Their house was big and bulky and had real shingles, unlike the white vinyl siding on Grace's home. As she drew closer, she began to feel exposed, like someone might take a potshot at her from an upstairs window. But, of course, Kyle and John were dead.

The events of that day replayed in her mind like a ten-second movie.

Pop. Pop. Sleds. Andrew. Wild dogs.

She twirled to check for mongrels on the prowl and, seeing none, continued on. She passed under the shade of a big, old pine tree, where the morning air felt so much cooler, and then crouched as she slunk toward the porch. She realized those invaders could have come here after trashing her place.

Grace climbed the porch stairs in a manner befitting her name, not making a sound. She put her ear to the door and listened. Nothing. She tugged the handle, and the door opened with a loud creek.

"Becca?"

She stepped into the gloom of the kitchen. She had played here so many times it used to feel like her second house. Now she entered as the girl who helped wipe out the family that owned it.

"Becca. It's Grace. Are you home? I brought you some eggs."

She set them on the table and checked the dining room and the enormous living room that stretched nearly the length of the house. Streaming sunbeams lit up a million gray dashes and dots of dust moving along a conveyor of air currents. Spider webs stretched from the floor lamp to the wall and from the sofa to the recliner.

In the dim hall, she peered into the bathroom and the two bedrooms. Finding them empty, she returned to the living room and positioned herself at the bottom of the stairs. "Becca?"

A little louder. "Becca!"

She had taken two steps into the shadows when she was clotheslined by thick strands of web connecting the banister to the wall. She scrunched her face and wiped them way, and then she continued up. She skipped Kyle's and John's bedrooms, checked the upstairs bathroom, and finally reached Becca's room at the end of the hall. She pushed the door a crack with one finger. "Becca?"

The space smelled dank and musty. Grace stepped in. In the middle stood a canopy bed, the blankets pulled up over a child's form. Grace recognized Becca's long brown hair. "Becca?"

The seven-year-old did not respond.

"It's me. Grace."

Grace tiptoed to the bed and hesitated. She took three deep breaths and then peeled the cover down.

Her next breath stopped short.

Rebecca Fisher's mummified body lay curled, as if for warmth. Her skin, now caramel colored, looked dry like a beetle shell. A withered arm gripped a moth-eaten teddy bear.

Grace kneeled, buried her head in her hands, and screamed into the mattress. Then she surrendered to sobs that shook her

entire body. Everything she ever knew...her family, her neigh-
bors, her friends, her home, her life...

Lost.

# CHAPTER 15

**April 10**
**Baltimore, Maryland**

Josie followed the sound of laughter for ten minutes, distrusting her own senses. After three months in the cafeteria of an office building eating stale taco shells and pretzels and cans of chopped pineapples with only the withering dead for company, she scarcely knew how to react to human voices.

She wore tan pants she'd taken off a dead woman, who Josie was grateful to discover had not shit herself upon death like so many others had, a tendency that made clothes scavenging a hit-or-miss endeavor. Josie's top half sported a stone-gray hoodie she'd pulled off some kid who had been shot. He hadn't shit himself either. No clothes with shit. That was her policy.

She sought garments that blended with the asphalt and sidewalks because surviving wasn't all sneaking around garbage dumps and hiding in overturned trucks. Sometimes you had to be out in the open. The best way to blend with Baltimore was to dress like dirty asphalt and sidewalks. She'd had to cut four inches from the legs of this particular pair of corduroys so she didn't trip over them.

With Baltimore's harbor docks up ahead and the sound of laughter growing louder, Josie ducked into a parking garage, using the shadows as cover. Darting between cars, she made a mental note to come back later and check if any were unlocked. Cars in constant shade were the best because the stuff inside wasn't baked or melted. Sometimes she found cool things like iPods, which she would listen to if the music was decent. And even if it sucked, she listened until the battery ran down. She drew the line at taking earbuds out of a dead person's head, though.

At the other end of the garage, she followed the exit signs until she found a down ramp. She slithered along the wall, couched by the exit, and poked her head into the street for a look around. She felt vulnerable doing this since she only had about sixty-five percent of a normal field of vision. Especially looking left, since her blind half had to stick out first.

There they were. Out on Pier 3, across the wide boulevard of East Pratt in the courtyard in front of the aquarium, a bunch of kids were hopping around and playing and laughing like any old day in the park.

Josie stared for a good while, running a sanity check. She knew about mirages from movies and TV commercials.

The sidewalk lay in shade, and the leaves were budding. She hopped and ducked behind a tree. Then the next and the next, until she reached the wide boulevard running perpendicular to the pier. She stepped to the corner traffic light and hid behind the pole. Here, the direct sunlight made her sweatshirt an oven. Hadn't she been shivering and huddled under blankets just a few weeks earlier?

She stared, but the mirage did not fade. Indeed, she saw the most shocking thing since Hector had dropped dead: kids having fun. A circle of four boys kicking a beanbag. Behind them, two kids, a boy and a girl, were throwing a Nerf football. To their left, two girls swung jump ropes while others hopped and skipped over and under the nylon. One girl stepped on the rope, knocking it out of another's hand. They laughed and started again.

"Wanna play?"

Josie had been so mesmerized she hadn't noticed one of the girls watching her.

"Yo. I'm talking to you." The girl's voice carried over East Pratt as if amplified by a bullhorn.

Josie grabbed of clump of hair and laid it across the right side of her face to hide her disfigurement. Then she pulled her hood up and marched across the boulevard, glancing both ways out of habit and because bigger kids were known to joyride on wide streets and play smashup derby with crashed cars.

She stopped at the sidewalk on the opposite side to reevaluate the situation and make a choice; did humans deserve one more chance not to disappoint her?

"Come on," the girl said again, waving her on. Before The Fall, Josie never hung out with the black girls in her school just because she didn't. For a minute, she wondered if these girls were going to beat her up and take her clothes because Hector had said that's the kind of thing black people do. Then again, she hated Hector and everything else he'd ever said. Anyway, some white kids were playing on the pier too. Nobody fought or screamed, a weird thing in itself these days.

"You wanna try it?' the girl asked again.

Josie didn't know how to answer. This time yesterday she was yanking the pants from a corpse and checking for shit stains. "Uh."

"Or you can just watch if you want."

Josie shuffled closer. Overheating in the hot sun, she pulled her hoodie off and tossed it to the ground. "I'll try it." In old times, Josie never got too friendly with anyone on her block, but rope jumping was okay because no one had to talk that much. The two girls began making arcs with the rope. Josie counted one, two, three, four and stepped into the spin. She made four hops before stepping on the rope.

"Sorry."

"It's okay. You need to warm up."

The arc formed again, and Josie fell into the rhythm. Four steps, eight steps, twelve. She stared grimly at her feet, trying not to mess up.

"You're pretty good," the girl said. Josie didn't answer.

A few minutes later, Josie swung while another girl jumped. She skipped her next turn because she liked swinging better, and that kept going until the girl who'd invited her to play hollered, "Crabs is ready!"

Near the edge of the pier, a group of kids had a fire going under a big stainless steel pot like the ones in Josie's cafeteria hideout. Steam rose from the uncovered opening. Josie found herself moving toward it with the other girls. The chef, a pasty white kid, began lifting crabs one at a time with salad tongs and placing them on a beach towel next to the pot.

"You ever eat crabs before?" the jump-rope girl with the loud voice asked Josie.

"No." She hadn't. Crabs were expensive.

"You live in Baltimore and you ain't never had Maryland crabs?"

"No."

"Me neither." The girl elbowed Josie and laughed. To the chef, she said, "You know how to cook crabs?"

"Not really."

Loud Girl made a face. "Are these gonna be edible?"

Unfazed by the interrogation, Chef laid two more crabs on the towel. "Probably not."

\*\*\*

Josie, having retrieved her sweatshirt, leaned against a tree trunk, ripping a crab apart and sucking the meat out. She didn't care if they were cooked right or not. It beat her usual dinner that came out of a can or a plastic rapper. Loud Girl and Chef sat with her, forming a triangle. Sunbeams, low and orange in the late afternoon, lit the sides of their faces.

"You don't talk much, do you?"

Josie shrugged. "I guess not."

"What's your name?"

"Josie."

"How old are you?"

"Ten. I'm going to be eleven soon."

"When?"

"June sixteenth."

Loud Girl waved at the air. "I lost track of days."

"It's April tenth."

"Yeah? You usually gotta find a kid with a digital watch to know what day it is."

A chill breeze swept in from the harbor and raised bumps on Josie's arm. She wiped her hands clean on the paving stones and slid into her sweatshirt. "It doesn't really matter."

Chef joined the conversation. "So what happened to your eye?" Loud Girl chucked a piece of crab shell at him and shook her head in disapproval. "What did I say?"

"Pay him no mind," she said to Josie. She rolled up her right pant leg, revealing a gnarl of twisted tissue and pink scars on her calf. "I got chewed up by a pit bull."

Chef threw the shell back at her. "That happened *before.*"

"I was supposed to get surgery. My doctor went dead right in front of me. Now I gotta walk around with a leg looking like a piece of roast beef for the rest of my life."

Chef rolled up the sleeve of his flannel. "Look at this. I tried to rescue some dumb cat, and he scratched the shit out of my arm."

Loud Girl slapped his hand away. "Get away from me with that. Cat scratches!"

Josie decided to lay it on them. "I got shot in the face by a guy who raped and killed my sister."

Loud Girl and Chef fell silent and stared at Josie. Twenty seconds passed, and Loud Girl said, "Oh, honey…"

Josie looked at the pile of shell parts scattered beside her on the pavement. "Any crabs left?"

Later, the three of them lay on the ground and watched as the daylight faded and the stars unveiled themselves. Josie heard a rustling and rolled over. A rat scurried across the pier and vanished into the shadow of the aquarium. She turned back to see the stars some more.

"What were you looking at?"

Damn. That girl's voice was loud. "Nothing," Josie said. Rats tended to freak people out. She didn't mind them. Rats knew all the good hiding spots.

Loud Girl said, "Did you watch your parents die?"

Josie had not had this much conversation since she'd lived with Rogelio. His cancer took him the day after he pulled the bullet from her head. "No. My dad was in prison or driving a train or something. My mom was in the shower."

"I walked in on my mom when she was in the shower once. Christ. Turned me gay on the spot."

Loud Girl slapped Chef across the chest. "Are you dumb? This is personal shit she's discussing."

Josie didn't care. Chef was the kind of guy who would be killed one of these days. He was too soft.

Loud Girl said, "I didn't see mine die, either. I was in the hospital with my leg all bandaged up. The doctors and nurses was talking to me and trying to cheer me up 'cause I was scared. My mom was in the lobby, and my dad was sleeping off a drunk. Kids who saw their parents die right in front of them got the most messed up by this whole thing."

That's what most kids called it. The end of the world was "This Whole Thing." Josie called it "The Fall" because she saw Hector fall and break his face open. Sometimes she got mad that Hector would forever be her mental image of This Whole Thing. Hector, her mom's stupid boyfriend with Nazi tattoos.

"I was at the national skateboard championship," Chef said. "I was in the middle of my routine when all of a sudden the judges and the people in the audience just went *down*."

"You were in school, clown, probably getting an F on something."

"It was the best routine I ever skated. I would have won!"

"At nine-thirty in the morning on a Friday?" Loud Girl shook her head. "You were in school kissing your boyfriend."

"Don't be a hater, home girl."

"You did come up Gay Street this morning, and that's a true story."

Chef slapped at her and missed. "No such place."

Loud Girl leaned on her elbows. "I'm serious. Go look at the road sign back there. It's called 'Gay Street.'"

"Then you must have come down Black Bitch Street, because you a—"

Josie jerked upright. "Shut up!"

"Excuse me?"

Josie held up her hand to silence them and peered across the courtyard, toward the black silhouette of the city. A bunch of kids had replaced the crab pot with a bonfire and were standing around the yellow flame and talking. She tried to pierce the darkness beyond, but the flames were too bright. "Something's coming." She swept herself into a crouch.

Loud Girl and Chef began to look around, alarmed. "You're scaring me, kid," Loud Girl said.

Chef stood up and looked toward the boulevard. "I don't see anything. You're just having a panic attack."

Josie lacked a normal field of vision, but she had the hearing of an owl. Something was heading their way. She began backing toward the shadows. "You should probably run."

Now the other kids began to hear the sounds of footfalls and drew closer to the fire. Loud Girl and Chef moved toward the flame too, on instinct, to huddle with the herd. Only Josie moved away and into the darkness. She turned toward the crosswalk that connected Pier 3 to Pier 4, ready to dart across, when she spotted two boys with shotguns marching from the other side. Gasps came from around the fire as another group of armed boys crossed East Pratt to the pier. The party was over, and the partiers were being surrounded.

Josie ducked behind a tree and peeked around.

"This is our turf," the gang leader said. "I don't remember giving anyone permission to have a party."

Josie knew that voice. It had gotten lower, but…

"You," the gangster said, pointing his shotgun at Chef. "What's that shit on the ground?"

Chef froze. The leader nodded to one of his thugs, who fired his shotgun at the sky. Their captives issued cries and dropped, covering their heads.

"I *said*, 'What's that shit on the ground?'"

Cowering, Chef stuttered, "Jump ropes."

"Jump ropes? Are you some kind of faggot? Jump ropes are for girls. Put 'em in the fire."

Chef crawled to the ropes, dragged them to the bonfire, and tossed them in. A plume of embers shot up and over the water, little orange specks that soared for a moment and then died.

"Good boy. Now, y'all have a choice. You can join our club. Or you can die right here. But you gotta take an oath."

The fine hairs on the back of Josie's neck stood up.

Ronan. The sadist. Haunting her wherever she went.

Ronan kicked Chef in the hip. "You ready to take an oath, partner?"

Chef hurried a jittery nod.

"Sorry. No faggots in our club." Ronan fired a round into Chef's ribs. A roar of screams exploded from the prisoners, who began to panic and scatter. More shots were fired and commands shouted. Josie took advantage of the chaos by backing along farther down the pier, following the same path as the rat. Over the din, someone shouted, "Hey! Get her!"

She turned and sprinted. The doors of the aquarium had been smashed. Josie leapt over the jagged spikes of glass like a hurdler and—

The smell.

The dense odor of rotting fish blasted her so hard she grimaced and cupped her mouth to stop a flood of vomit. The dead sea creatures must have been frozen all winter and just begun to thaw. She crawled on all fours through the dank muck, trying to scurry up a curved ramp but sliding backward as she clawed with futility at the slime.

Plan B: find an escalator. Crouching against the wall, she squinted and scanned the shadows. Against the lighter background she saw lumps. Big ones. Those were the dead people. Smaller lumps, fish. The tanks must have burst open when the water froze, pouring the dead animals down the ramp and into the lobby.

She noticed one of those lumps moving. *What the hell is that?* It inched closer. Fleeing might betray her location to Ronan and his gang, but…

The lump brushed against her thigh and let out a meow. Without thinking, Josie scooped up the cat, holding it to her bosom and stroking it. "You like the smell in here, don't you," she whispered. The animal's fur was matted and coarse.

A piece of glass fell away from the doorway. The cat skittered off, and Josie turned. About thirty feet away, the silhouette of a boy stood out against the deep blue of the night sky. The gangster mumbled curses at the odor. Josie slithered backward through the slime, imagining herself as an eel.

The gangster tried to stalk in silence but almost wiped out when he hit the slop coating the lobby floor. His eyes must have adjusted, for he was stepping over the dead bodies and sweeping the darkness with his weapon. "Look, just come out. If I find you, I'm going to shoot you dead. If you surrender, I'll take you back to the clubhouse and give you something to eat."

She knew this voice too. It belonged to Richie, Ronan's sidekick with the bad complexion and curly hair.

Josie, hiding behind a support pillar, shifted her weight and slipped. Reaching back to block her fall, her hand landed on something scaly and icy cold.

"I hear you over there," Richie said. "I'm going to kill you if I find you first, so you better surrender right now." He aimed his rifle forward as he approached the pillar, paused, and then hopped around the corner. "Gotcha!"

Before he could curse out disappointment at finding no one there, the cat skirted under his feet. He lost traction and flailed for balance. Whirling from the other side of the pillar, Josie swung the heavy, dead fish at the gangster's head, planting it square on his nose. He flopped backward and smacked hard onto the slime-coated floor. Josie dropped the fish, picked up his rifle, and whacked him in the mouth. She dropped the weapon and wound up to flee when her mind ran an instant replay. She turned back. He had a nylon holster pinning a switchblade knife to his thigh. She kneeled, reached under his leg as he groaned, yanked the Velcro loose, and took the knife and the holster.

More voices outside. "Hey, Richie. What's taking so long?" It sounded close. It sounded like Ronan.

Hurdling over the corpses, Josie made for the exit. At the broken doors, she slipped outside and scurried along the building, moving away from the bonfire. She fled, not looking back, around the next corner to the far side where the shadows were thick. She hugged the wall and, as she attached the switchblade holster to her waist and leg, she listened to the shouts of anger and demand for vengeance over Richie's busted nose. Their rage satisfied her, but she also knew they would do bad things if they caught her. One more sprint, in the darkness, to the edge of the pier.

"This way!" Ronan's voice echoed. Footfalls rounded the aquarium, getting closer.

Josie sent a thought to Loud Girl, hoping she would survive, and jumped off the pier into the frigid harbor.

# CHAPTER 16

**June 28**
**Washington, D.C.**

Shawnika pulled Tre along the sidewalk with her right hand and Melvin Tubbs with her left. They'd just turned the corner from D Street on Louisiana Avenue.

"I'm tired," Tre said, pushing the sweat around his brow with a damp arm.

"Well, we can't stop here."

"Why not?"

"You don't hear Melvin complaining."

Melvin trudged along in silence.

"But why can't we stop?"

Because, for one thing, a carload full of white girls went past a few minutes back yelling "Eat shit, niggers!" and flipping their middle fingers. If it were just her walking, Shawnika would have dared the bitches to stop and fight, and she would have taken out all four of them. But she had a little brother to protect. Best to ignore it and keep moving.

"Hey," Melvin said. "That building's fancy."

Shawnika glanced to her left. "That's the Capitol building, Mel."

"Why are all the buildings so fancy here?"

"You mean to tell me you live three miles up the road and you never came down here?"

"I don't know."

What Shawnika would have given for conversation with someone her age. All winter and spring spent hiding out with two boys, trying to keep them alive and off her nerves at the same time. Scoping hideouts during the day, moving at night. Zigging here and zagging there, waiting for gangs to move on. Sometimes they went back to old hideouts after the raiders got sick of raiding them. Sometimes she ran into kids she kind of remembered from school, and they'd chat a bit, but nobody had a good plan or a good hideout, and then gangs always came and broke things up. Staying alive meant making fast choices.

The only part of the neighborhood they avoided was around the diner. Shawnika didn't want to see her mom lying there. Or not lying there, because that meant someone took her or animals ate her. Maybe the fire burned her to ashes that blew away.

The trio found themselves on the grounds of the art museum. Ahead, the monuments still sparkled white, except for the bottom parts, which were covered in graffiti. The grass looked funny—it was up to her knees, with thick, dark-green blades a quarter-inch wide. No one had cut it for a year.

Shawnika led the boys to a tree, and they sat in the shade. She patted the sweat from her forehead. Despite the heat, she was wearing a flannel shirt with pockets she'd sewn inside for carrying water bottles. One good way to get shot was to carry a bag around and let someone with a gun see it.

She handed a bottle to Tre. She used small booze flasks to carry water because they were flat and easier to hide. "Share it."

Movement caught her eye. An orange tabby cat came strutting along the edge of the grass, stopped, and stared into the green wall, detecting something beyond the sensory capacity of humans. Then, in an instant, the animal vanished into the tall blades.

Shawnika unscrewed her own bottle and ran the lip under her nose, sniffing for the residue odor of whiskey. She did it out of habit now, always smelling things to make sure they were safe to consume.

A cluster of grass shimmied as if subject to a special breeze on an otherwise still, humid day. Then the cat popped back out of the overgrowth. Two mice dangled from its mouth, helpless, their tails swaying and their tiny hands drawn together. Shawnika's uncle Terrance used to say *It's a dog's world* all the time. She had no idea what he meant back then, but now she was wondering if it might actually be a cat's world.

She took another sip, replaced the cap, and stood. "Come on. Let's go." Sitting in one place, even partly hidden by a tree, was dangerous. "Let's find the president."

# CHAPTER 17

**June 28**
**Charleston, West Virginia**

"Shhhh. Be good," Grace said to Clucky and Pecker through the wire-thin bars. "Everything will be fine."

Rule number one of keeping livestock for food: Don't name the animals. But Grace just couldn't eat her last two chickens. What else did she have? She realized it might still come to that, but on another day. For a while now she had been living on the odd crops that grew, untended, on the Fisher farm. Nature is hearty. Things survive and grow no matter what.

Grace situated the cage in the vehicle's back seat, leaning the ten-pound bag of feed against it to keep it steady. The birds kept silent, though their swiveling heads and alert eyes betrayed fear. "Don't be scared," she said. She might have been talking to herself.

She alighted the vehicle for no practical reason but to stand in the sun one more time. Head tilted, she gazed into the cloudless blue. Sweat beaded on her brow. No hint of wind. Still. Silent.

It had to be today.

Grace sat on the warm asphalt and ran her hands over it, tiny bits of gravel sticking to her palms and then falling away. She swept her hand sideways and scooped up a handful of tiny stones. This was the world in her palm, crumbled, and it would never go back to the way it was.

It had to be today because her other choice was a pistol under her chin and really pressing down on the trigger this time. Who would take care of the chickens if she did that?

Grace stood, dusted herself off, and entered the vehicle once more. She closed and locked the door and then slid across to the left front seat, which cradled her firm and sure. Her dad had installed new seats two years ago after the others got squishy and hurt his back.

Her heart beat hard against her breastplate, threatening to break out. So much for not being terrified. She exhaled. *You've been driving tractors and mopeds and ATVs since you were four,* she reassured herself. And she had actually done this before, too. Once.

She blew out another breath and attached the seat belt. She stuck the key in the ignition. Sunlight baked the trapped air around her, staining her shirt with sweat. "You can do this."

She eyed the master switch a moment, and then her arm reached out without asking and flipped it. She turned the key. A choking sound, and then the engine roared to life, rattling the fuselage as the propeller began to whirl. Grace let out a chirping scream, sending the chickens into frenzy. Within three seconds, the silence had given way to a mad cacophony of motor noises and bird clucking and the rattling of an aged airframe.

Grace glanced at the page taped to the passenger-side windshield, a list of instructions Andrew had typed for her back when they still had power and computers weren't useless. She didn't need the list, but she had never done this without Andrew sitting beside her.

She released the hand brake and let the throttle out about one quarter, and the Piper Cherokee jerked forward. She let out another scream. *Stop doing that! Soft touch.* With a delicate movement, she guided the throttle in a notch and the plane slowed to a crawl, inching forward over the tarmac, passing a couple of Cessnas half buried in overgrown weeds. Her family also owned a Cessna, much newer than this old beater, but she had only ever handled the controls of the Piper. Dad said it was a good starter plane and was saving it for Andrew because Greg, her oldest brother, didn't care about flying. Dad said the Cherokee was slow and boring and perfect for a teenager because it was hard to do anything stupid or irresponsible with it. He said it was the Toyota Corolla of airplanes, whatever that meant.

Dad.

Images of her dad's jet breaking apart in a flaming ball filled her mind. Her mom's body lying on the airport floor. Greg's grave. Andrew being pulled apart by hungry dogs. Becca's mummified corpse. All the dead bodies. The children they left at the airport to starve...

Grace snapped to as she saw the wing of another single-engine airplane just outside her port window, its nose pointed into the tall grass beside the tarmac. The control panel of the Piper was too high to see over, but she knew the butt end of the other craft was right in front of her. In a panic she turned the yoke as if it were a steering wheel but continued moving straight toward the parked plane. Frozen, she racked her brain. What to do?

Her foot shot out and hit the right rudder pedal, and the Cherokee lurched right. She winced as the tail assembly of the other craft became visible and the Cherokee's left wing tip missed it by less than a foot.

Grace sighed and looked back at her chickens. "Sorry about that." She toggled between the rudder pedals to straighten the plane, gave it a notch more throttle, and rounded the curve toward the runway, remembering to test the flaps as she chugged forward.

Slight pressure on the left rudder pedal straightened her Piper Cherokee, which now faced straight down the runway's center line. Grace pushed the throttle in to slow the forward roll but choked out the engine and stalled it.

She pulled the hand brake, and the plane jerked to a stop.

Inhale. Exhale. Inhale. Exhale.

She looked at the empty seat beside her. The one other time she'd done this, two weeks after the world changed forever, Andrew sat in that chair. He wanted her to know how to fly, in case, as he said, he didn't make it.

Grace had sat in that chair plenty of times herself with Dad as the pilot. Once they were airborne, he often let her take the controls and made her swear to God and cross her heart that she'd never ever tell anyone, especially Mom. Later, when he moved out, Grace thought that was why they'd separated. Because Mom found out he let her fly the Piper. Grace suffered that guilt for months. On the day last summer that Andrew taught her how take off and land, he also told her what had really happened, that Dad had been kissing a flight attendant. Grace told her brother she knew what he meant by "kissing." When the world ends, there's no need to pretend anymore.

Grace took off the seatbelt, climbed across the cabin, and double-checked the latch to the plane's only door. She yanked the instruction list from the right windshield and peered down the long, gray landing strip ahead of her. She'd walked it this morning to clear debris and look for holes and big cracks. Other than a few tall blades of grass poking through, it checked out. Still, she wouldn't be able to see anything once she started her takeoff run.

She dropped back into the pilot's chair, belted up, and closed her eyes. Bowing, she placed her palms together. "Our father, who art in heaven, hallowed be the name. Thy kingdom come; thy will be done, on earth as it is in heaven."

She skipped the daily bread and trespassing part, despite it being rather more relevant to her life these days, instead saying, "Please don't let me crash."

The warmed engine started with a quick turn of the key. She pushed in the yoke, released the brake, and let out the throttle a bit. The Piper began to chug down the runway. Using the line of paint on the left edge for guidance, she tapped the rudder pedals to keep the craft aligned. "Wish me luck," she said to the chickens as she slowly pulled the throttle open. The propeller, just visible over the control panel, became a blur, and the craft lurched forward, pinning her to the seat. The fuselage rattled, and the wings jiggled as she picked up speed. Thirty mph. Thirty-five mph. Forty. Forty-five. Fifty. Sixty. Seventy. Eighty. The propeller sliced the air with a deafening whir.

Eighty-five miles per hour. Take-off speed. *Do it, Grace. You're going to run out of runway.*

Grace pulled back on the yoke, the craft lifted, and the hard vibration ceased. She looked out the left window and saw the ground dropping away, then tree tops. Idle cars in a parking lot becoming toys.

The plane bobbled, and she tapped the rudder pedal, straightening it.

She climbed. Another glance out the window. Roads threaded through a patchwork quilt of farmland. Houses were small rectangles. A cluster of buildings and a yellow McDonald's arch. She was doing it!

Grace let out an elated squeal, and the chickens echoed, though it was too noisy in the cabin to hear much of it. She leveled off with a yoke adjustment, then tweaked the throttle to lighten the fuel mix. *This isn't a race*, Andrew told her last time.

She did it. She was flying. She ruled the sky.

*Where the heck am I going?*

Grace gazed beyond the Cherokee's long white wing at the endless expanse of world. What existed out there for her? Safety? Companionship? A family?

She reached back, fumbled on the back-seat floor for her backpack, and, grabbing hold of the strap, hoisted it forward and dropped it on the seat beside her. She removed the map she had tucked in the front zipper pocket. A red circle surrounded the airstrip. She'd made dotted arrows pointing to three others. Right now she was heading north, so she kept going that way.

Pennsylvania. Maybe things were better up there. Maybe they weren't all dead.

# CHAPTER 18

## June 28
## Washington, D.C.

Across a broad expanse of overgrown lawn, appearing at once majestic and desolate, the big white mansion made Shawnika think of babysitting games. That is, finding silly activities to occupy the mind of a bored child, like making homemade play dough from salt, flour, and water or fishing for socks down a laundry chute by attaching a bent paper clip to a string.

*Let's Find the President* was her biggest babysitting game yet.

"The president lives *there*?" Melvin Tubbs said.

Shawnika scratched the back of her neck. "Uh-huh." She wondered if the president minded that crashed truck that had plowed through the iron fence or the graffiti spray-painted all over his house.

"It's fancy!"

Her head swiveled in Melvin's direction. His earnest gaze made her spit laughter. She covered her mouth.

"I'm hot," Tre said for the twentieth time.

"All right," she said, stepping onto the back bumper and into the bed of the wrecked pickup truck. "Let's go inside." Tre hopped up behind her, and, with some teetering and slipping the two of them helped Melvin up.

Shawnika climbed over the roof of the cab, walked across the hood, and slid down the front of the mangled grill. The knocked-over section of fence stuck out from under the truck tires at a low angle, but was still high enough from the ground to catch her ankle and twist it if she slipped between the metal posts. She tested it with her foot, found her balance, and turned to help Tre down. She saw, through the shattered windshield, a lack of corpses inside the vehicle. Whoever rammed this truck into the fence did it on purpose and then walked away.

After Tre was through, Melvin came rolling over the cab and plopped on the hood, denting it further. Shawnika opened her mouth to warn him about getting snagged on the broken fence, but he was already wiping out. He bounced off the grill and flipped onto the metal bars, getting his knee stuck between two posts.

"Jesus, Melvin." She kneeled in the grass and got to work prying him loose. "You test my patience sometimes."

Melvin relaxed his muscles as she turned him this way and that, as if this were part of his daily routine. "Can I marry you when I grow up?"

She shook her head and pushed down a smirk. "I think you need your mama, not a wife." At last, she lifted his knee up and out of its entrapment. Melvin took a good while to stand up, but he seemed intact.

Shawnika turned, scanning the hip-high grass for signs of danger. She didn't fancy stepping on a snake. "Stay behind me."

The first step yielded no trouble, nor the next. In a line, the three kids crossed the south lawn of the White House, kicking up little more than gnats and chasing off a mouse or two. At the other end, up close, the stately structure regained some of its dignity.

Gazing up at the imposing façade, a feeling overtook Shawnika that she had no business entering. It was the White House, after all.

"I'm hungry," Tre said.

Shawnika shook her head. "My last nerve, Tre." She approached an arched door cut into the heavy stone wall that supported the colonnade above. She pulled the handle. Darkness greeted them along with cool, stale air carrying that familiar odor of decay. She shut the door.

There had to be another entrance.

She stepped back and tilted her head up to assess the next level. The floor-to-ceiling windows spaced between the towering columns presented a more inviting possibility.

Shawnika ascended the curved staircase to her right, and the boys followed.

"Look. A dead guy," Tre said, pointing over the railing into the unkempt shrubs below. Shawnika peeked down at the skeletal remains of a man partly sunk into the ground between two bushes. She figured he must have been a Secret Service agent.

At the top of the stair was a balcony. "Stay back."

Shawnika tiptoed to the center window and cupped her hands to it. She couldn't make out many details with the sun overhead and no lights inside, but she saw no movement. Then she sized it up and down, looking for a way in. Slinking to the side, out of sight to anyone hiding in there, she reached over to rap the glass with her knuckles. It felt like steel. Of course it did. It's the White House. They aren't going to use the same stuff they used in her crappy apartment.

She poked her head around and peered inside, looking for motion once more.

"I'm hot."

Shawnika jumped. "Don't sneak up on me, Tre!" A year ago she would have given him a swat and sent him crying to Mama. A year ago they wouldn't have been breaking into the White House, either. "Stand back."

Shawnika walked to the railing, withdrew the empty whiskey flask from her inside pocket, and whipped it at the window. It clanked off without leaving a mark. She crossed her arms and furrowed her brow. "Fine. Let's go in that scary damn door downstairs. And I don't want to hear nobody complain if they get eaten by a bear."

The trio retreated down the stairway and returned to the arched doorway. Shawnika pulled the handle and stuck her head over the threshold, listening to the darkness. Despite the sour, musty odor, the cool air enticed her forward. Tre and Melvin piled in behind her, making as much noise as two boys could possibly make while sneaking around, impervious to her shushing.

"We should have brought a flashlight," she thought out loud. After hours in the high summer sun, the room seemed like a wall of murky green fog. She issued a curt, "Hey," and listened as a quick, short echo reported back. A decent-size room, but not a gateway to another dimension.

She took cautious steps into the middle of the space—as far as she could tell—until her shins bumped something. Shawnika reached down and felt for it, closing her hand around a chair leg. Sliding her other hand across, she located the padded seat, deposed vertically. The chair lay on its back. She squatted, gripped the top of the backrest, and set the chair upright.

As she stood, her head knocked something above her. It was hard, like rubber or wood, but it swayed when she made contact, like it was hanging from a…

Rope.

She reached out to steady the object, fumbling for a handhold. She felt a shoe. Shawnika ran her hand up and felt an ankle. The flesh felt cool and dry beneath the fabric of the pant leg. Skinny, like whoever it was hadn't eaten for a while. Before hanging himself.

"What is it?" Tre said.

"Nothing. Just a chair. Come on around this way." Shawnika steered them to the left, her eyes at last adapting to the darkness. She wanted to hurry them out before one of them turned and saw the hanging kid. She came to a wall and felt along its curved surface. The room was oval. This couldn't be the oval office, could it?

A door led to a second, smaller room, dimly lit, as the window was mostly covered by overgrown shrubs. "Hello?" More emptiness.

Opposite the window, another door led to a hallway, which appeared to run the length of the building. Shawnika raised an arm to stop Tre and Melvin. "Shhh."

Someone had lit candles and set them at about ten-foot intervals along the hallway. Someone lived here. Shawnika whispered this time. "Hello?"

She herded Tre and Melvin into the hall and peered from one end to the other, trying to decide the best course. Both sides looked the same in the soft, yellow glow.

"It looks Christmasy," Tre said, following his big sister's lead and whispering.

Shawnika heard a distant rumble and a crack. "Did you hear that?" The boys shrugged. She tiptoed to the middle of the hall and found a perpendicular corridor running toward the north side of the building. Two candles, set on small tables, illuminated the way.

Again, a low rumble and a crack. Thunder. But with no cloud in the sky, what caused it? She put a finger to her lips to indicate silence and herded the boys forward.

Once more they came to an intersecting hall and more candles, but with doors at the ends letting light in. From directly ahead came another rumble and a crack. Shawnika recognized the sound. Not thunder.

*They got bowling in the White House?* She figured they would have run into gun-toting gangsters by then if they were going to, so she lead her two charges through the entry into the skinniest bowling alley she'd ever seen. One kid, about Tre's age, busily reset pins at the far end of the lane, oblivious to their presence. Dozens of candles lined the room.

"Hi."

Shawnika jerked to her left, toward the sound of the voice, shoving Tre and Melvin behind her and balling her hands into fists. A girl, maybe fifteen, sat in a chair in the corner cradling a swaddled baby. "I'm Luz," she said. She nodded toward the lad carrying his ball back to the top of the lane. "That's Ricky, my cousin."

Ricky ignored them and rolled his next shot. He took out four pins.

"Hey, Ricky. Let these guys have a chance," Luz said. Like kids at camp, Tre and Melvin fell in with Ricky, trudging down to help reset the pins again.

Shawnika relaxed. "Your baby don't mind all this racket?"

"Puts her right to sleep." Luz turned the child toward Shawnika. "You want to hold her?"

Shawnika wondered how someone this trusting could still be alive. "Uh. Sure. I'm Shawnika, by the way." The girl should at least know the name of the person she's handing her baby to.

Luz stood and laid her in Shawnika's arms as Melvin rolled a two-handed gutter ball behind her. "This is Teresa, my baby girl."

Shawnika was not inclined toward goo-goo talk, so she nodded. "Hi, Teresa."

"She's six months old. You want some chocolate?"

"I could use some water if you got it. Where did all the candles come from?"

Luz reached into a plastic tub and fished around, retrieving a vitamin drink. The girls swapped baby for warm beverage. "I found two crates of them in the basement of a dollar store. They're gonna be used up soon."

Shawnika tore off the cap and took a voracious gulp. Fruit punch flavor. "There's more light upstairs, I bet."

Tre knocked down seven pins and pumped his fist in triumph.

"True, but there's also dead people all over the place, and I don't want to ever get used to that. Plus kids like to come in and run around up there, trashing shit. They come in the front. There's no basement entrance, and I blocked the doors coming down here."

"I just walked right in the back door."

The baby stirred, and Luz kissed her forehead. "Usually the body hanging from the chandelier freaks people out. How'd you miss that?"

Shawnika shrugged. "Didn't. But there's bad stuff everywhere. You gotta deal with it." She tilted her head toward the boys. "I got those two to take care of."

"Why did you come in here anyway?"

"We were looking for the president."

Luz burst into laughter, startling Teresa awake. Shawnika scowled and thought this girl was awfully lucky to be holding a baby right now. "How old are you?"

*Go ahead*, Shawnika thought. *Put the baby down for a second, and you won't be laughing anymore.* "Twelve. Problem?"

Luz reached out with her free hand and rubbed Shawnika's arm. "I'm sorry. I'm just wondering how a twelve-year-old girl managed to keep her little brothers alive for a year by herself. You don't look like no gangster."

"Tre is my brother. The fat one isn't mine. He's a hitchhiker. Anyway, I'm just doing what my mama would want me to do. Raise him as best I can."

Luz handed her the baby again and then rummaged in a paper bag. She located a chocolate bar and gave it to Shawnika. Shawnika hung onto the baby and ate the candy, staring Luz down.

"Don't be mad," Luz said. "I'm amazed what a badass you are."

"So how did *you* manage to stick around? Carting a baby and all."

"I was in a gang. I mean, Teresa's father was in a gang, then all that shit happened with the bomb, and then—"

"What bomb?"

Luz's eyebrows went up. "Are you for real? What planet are you from, Shawnika? The big bomb last winter. You didn't see that big, giant hole about six blocks from here? My god."

Shawnika remembered the explosion during the snow-storm and realized it must have been one thousand times more powerful than she'd thought. No wonder she hardly saw anyone on the streets around here. They all got blown up.

But who set off the bomb?

Luz went on. "We were never part of that big gang. We had our own identity, you know what I mean? *Los Diablos Rojos* we called ourselves."

Shawnika finished off the chocolate. "The Red Devils? That's fucking stupid." Her shifted her eyes toward Tre and Melvin. Why was this girl being so friendly and generous with the food and drink?

"So where's your gang now?" *Hiding in the shadows and waiting to kill us?*

"Dead."

"For real?"

Luz reclaimed her chair. "Our hideout got raided by another gang last week. Me and Ricky and the baby were out back and we got out in the truck when we heard the shooting. The other gang was all blacks, but I'm not blaming you for that."

"You waiting for me to apologize or something?"

Luz shifted in her seat. "No. I'm just saying those things happened, but it doesn't matter now. I don't care if…you know. The black thing."

She handed Teresa back to Luz, rather less delicately than she took her earlier. "Yeah, well, let me know if it starts to bother you." *Bitch.*

"I didn't mean nothing bad."

Shawnika strutted to her brother and Melvin and pulled them away from whatever new game they were playing. "Can my boys have two of your drinks and some of your chocolate?"

Luz produced the requested items. "Why don't you stay down here? I could use some company."

"We're going to look around upstairs. I take it no one is going to jump me out in that hall? I promise you they will be sorry."

"Come on, Shawnika. It's just us three. I swear."

Shawnika and the boys took one of the candles and searched until they found the stairwell leading to the main floor. Luz's pitiful barricade came down easily. Plenty more light up there, as expected. And piles of corpses, just like Luz said.

# CHAPTER 19

**June 28**
**Alexandria, Virginia**

Adolf Hitler. Now there was a showman.

Zane stared at the photograph: An arena full of devotees, standing in perfect, obedient rows, not a straggler out of place. Great searchlights beaming into the sky, forming ethereal towers of photons. Massive rectangular banners hanging below a free-standing metal swastika, a hood ornament to end them all. Zane could taste the electricity.

Not that Hitler wasn't a crackpot. Zane didn't understand how art could be "degenerate." Who gives a shit about a painting? And the thing with killing Jews was pretty fucked up.

Anthony stuck his head in Zane's library, which formerly served as a dressing room. "Well?"

Zane had picked this room because it lacked the stench of death. The bodies had long ago been cleared from the theater, but they left traces. He did not look away from the Hitler photo. "I'm reading."

"You're supposed to be a leader not a reader, man. Lead."

Zane waved toward the light bulbs evenly spaced around the rectangular mirrors. "This is the only building on the planet with electricity. Where do you think that came from?"

Anthony no longer displayed gratitude for his good fortune at knowing Zane. "Dude, this is all your dad's shit, and I'm getting sick of you lording it over us. We do the work and you read friggin' books and play with costumes."

"It looks bad when the emperor has to pick dirt from under his fingernails. People lose respect."

Anthony yanked the book from his hands and tossed it on the makeup counter. "Zane. You're like, seriously a waste of space anymore."

Hitler had Joseph Goebbels and Albert Speer. Zane had some dope who says *like* and *dude* all the time. Not fair. Zane motioned for him to sit. Time for some bullshitting.

"Here's the thing," Zane said. "I know I'm not that great of a leader. Not like you. I don't even know how to fire a gun."

"No shit."

"Do you remember the Queen of England?"

"Huh?"

Zane wondered if it hurt to be so dumb, or if it made life easier. "You remember the Royal Family and all that? Well, in England, people loved the Queen. They put her in an ornate palace full of jewels and the finest fabrics."

"Dude. What the fuck are you talking about?"

"I'm getting there. Do you know what a queen does?"

"I don't know. She tells people what to do. She starts wars. Cuts off people's heads. Whatever."

"Maybe in the old days. But this queen didn't do shit. She just waved and dressed nice, and people went apeshit. She was a figurehead. Someone else had the power, but they put the queen on TV for the people."

"And?"

"And, the queen was awesome. The economy could suck, there could be a war, whatever. People looked up to her, and she was the glue that held society together."

Anthony clawed the air, growled, and went cross-eyed. "So fucking what. I got shit to do. You got shit to do. Let's do it."

"Don't you understand? I'm the queen. All the kids look up to me." Zane poked him in the shoulder. "You, on the other hand, are the guy with the power who gets shit done."

Anthony hesitated. "But nobody knows that. You get all the credit."

"Right. Let them think it. Attention isn't what you need. You need power. As long as the kids follow along and do what we say, who cares?"

"I don't get it."

Zane entertained a brief fantasy about smothering Anthony in his sleep. "The queen keeps people docile...calm and well-behaved. It's better for the real leaders that she's there, because they can get shit done without people bugging them and questioning them. You understand? My actions buy you the freedom to lead without kids pestering you for shit and trying to get you to like them. I'm doing you a favor. I run interference, if you prefer a sports analogy. Praise and attention is not power. Action is power."

Action is power? Zane couldn't believe the nonsense coming out of his own mouth.

"All right," Anthony said, tentatively buying. "But we have to redo things so I make more decisions from now on."

Zane shook his hand. "Cool. How about this: Next council meeting, I'll formally hand the reins over to you, but only the council will know. We'll have a toast and everything. The kids will still think I'm in charge, but I will be giving your orders."

Anthony stood, taller by an inch. "Next council meeting."

"Next council meeting." Zane stood, and the boys exchanged a high-five. After Anthony's exit, Zane returned to his seat and began digging through the book pile. *The Real Story of Dracula: Vlad Tepes.* Read it. *Josef Stalin.* Read it. Kinda boring. Some cool ideas, but the guy's paranoia was a waste.

Beneath those in the stack sat *Charles Manson and the Manson Family Murders.* Zane had grabbed all these titles from a bookstore during a recent supply run, as the theater's library understandably went heavy on literature and scripts. All the Young Adult shit was wiped out, but no one had touched the biographies. The guy on the front of this book had a swastika cut into his forehead, and he looked like a crackhead, so Zane had almost tossed it aside. But the blurb on the back called Manson a "master manipulator," a quality Zane admired above all others.

*You can't judge a book by its cover*, he thought, smirking at the double meaning. He opened to page one.

# CHAPTER 20

**June 28**
**Altitude: 2,500 Feet**

Grace swung a slow, wide arc, just like Andrew had taught her. *You can break something if you bank too hard.* As she guided the plane around to line up with the landing strip ahead, her heart leapt. Adjacent to the tiny airport, separated by a line of trees, sat crop fields. And those fields were being tended by people. She could see the tops of their heads out her port window! They weren't raiders, either. Raiders don't stick around to work crops.

She scanned the scene again but lost sight of the farmers as she finished her turn. *Maybe they'll let me stay with them*, she thought. She knew enough about caring for the animals, and she had her own plane. She could be useful.

"Uh-oh." With the runway dead ahead, she had to fly blind. The control panel of the Cherokee, a wall of gauges and dials, rose too high. Grace didn't know what most of them did anyway, so she would just as soon not have them. It wasn't just her. Andrew and her dad used to complain about it.

She dipped the nose long enough to confirm her angle of decent and then leveled. After a quick consult of Andrew's notes lying on the right-side seat, she adjusted the throttle down and let the air currents do most of the work. Dipping, dipping, a slight wobble, but nothing serious. It occurred to her just then that this landing strip could be a disaster...potholes, debris, dead bodies. Any of these things could send her cartwheeling or drive her nose first to the pavement. She decided to trust God.

On the port side, she spotted the line of paint along the left side of the runway. She judged the wing to be a few feet inside the line, placing her dead center of the strip. *Nose Up!* Andrew had shouted the one other time she'd landed this thing. Nose up felt wrong because she couldn't see anything, but Andrew knew planes as well as any fifteen-year-old. She went nose up.

The Cherokee hopped once, but she didn't break anything and more-or-less stuck the landing. The first time she'd almost run off the runway, but this time she was calmer and managed to decelerate without incident. The vibration of the pavement jarred its way up through the yoke, the earth under her so hard and unyielding after three hours in the air.

Grace taxied to the hanger, which she was grateful to discover had been flung open as if to welcome her. She rolled into the shade, engaged the brake, and said to her chickens, "Told you I could do it." Grace was better at flying than were these birds.

When she cut the engine, the silence that followed was the quietest thing she'd ever heard, even quieter than winter nights in the storm cellar.

She pocketed the key but left the chickens and flight instructions and maps in the cabin. The latch argued a moment but finally turned. She opened the door, stepped out, and slid off the wing, landing with a spring on the concrete floor of the hanger like only a ten-year-old could after being confined to a narrow seat for hours.

First order of business: Pee. She really had to pee.

Grace made a wide berth around a dead guy dressed like a mechanic and headed down a short passage next to the check-in desk. The bathroom waited at the end behind a heavy, dark-blue door. She had to plant a shoulder to push it open, and it squealed as the bottom scraped along the cement. The windowless room offered only darkness. She held the door long enough to spot the toilet and make sure she wouldn't have to share the space with a corpse, then stepped inside and pushed it shut.

In the blackness, the ringing in her ears became pronounced. She'd have to find earplugs for next time.

Once back in the hanger, she removed the chicken cage from the Cherokee and let Clucky and Pecker out to roam. As she scooped out a handful of feed for the birds, she saw another Piper single-engine plane parked in the shadows. She might be able to fly that one if she had to, or at least siphon the fuel. Andrew had diagrammed how to do that in his notes, too. She'd have to get more juice somewhere, since she did not have enough to fly much farther. Maybe she wouldn't have to. Maybe this would be her new home.

The first cool breeze of the day swept through the open bay of the hanger and out the small door on other side, as if urging her on.

"Be good," she told the chickens, and then she exited through the side door. Hidden by the shade, she walked along the line of trees dividing the airport from the farm, the late-afternoon sunlight poking between the branches and dappling the long grass at her feet. Then a deer popped from the woods and froze at the sight of her.

"I'm not going to hurt you," she said, waving at the creature, which darted back into the tree cover.

Shortly she came upon a trail cut into the small strip of forest and followed it. She was pretty sure she was in Pennsylvania now, but this stretch of woodland looked no different from West Virginia. She could live here, she supposed.

On the other side, Grace emerged into a neglected field of root vegetables. She crouched and tugged on a carrot green until a knotty orange shaft popped out, and she breathed deep the scent of loosened soil that emerged with it. She brushed off the dirt and took a bite. The farmers wouldn't mind, she hoped. No one had bothered to till this field. Nature grew the carrot.

She found a gap between two fields and continued up the rise. At the top, she saw someone working crops and ducked behind a cluster of old, yellowed, bug-eaten corn stalks. She tossed the rest of the carrot out of sight. Maybe they would get mad if she took their food.

The sun, drifting toward the horizon ahead of her, made long shadows. She tried to peek past the stalks, but they stood too tall. Careful not to rustle them and betray her presence, she squatted and moved forward in small steps, trying to decide the best time to reveal herself. She didn't want to startle anyone and get shot.

When another gust blew, she took advantage of the dancing yellow leaves to sprint forward. At the end of the acre, where the ground became flat, she craned her head. She squinted, fighting the magic golden sunbeams exclusive to late afternoon in a cornfield, and just made out the farmer's silhouette.

He was watching her.

Of course he was watching her. She'd just landed a plane next to his field. That would be big news nowadays. Before all this happened, before the grown-ups all died, Grace would have taken off running in the opposite direction. But she had nowhere to go. No mother to flee home to or bedroom to hide in. No Disney DVDs to watch or trips to Baskin-Robbins. She couldn't fly in circles forever.

Shielding herself behind a row of ragged corn, she cupped her hands around her mouth. "Excuse me. Can I come over there?" she hollered. "I want to be friends. Please don't shoot me."

She thought maybe she heard a response, but another gust came sweeping over the countryside, drowning out the sound. She peered over the stalks one more time. The farmer waved her on. "I'm coming closer now!" she said.

She put her hands up in surrender and marched along the edge of the acre to the next field, but the sun beamed straight into her eyes now. The farmer stood amid his meager crop, watching. "Do you mind if I walk in your field?" she asked, making a sun visor with her hand.

He did not respond. He stood, staring, waving her closer whenever a breeze kicked up. Motionless.

Grace's countenance grew stern. She stepped into the field. Another step closer to the farmer. And another. She positioned herself in his shadow, inching closer but eliciting no reaction other than his intermittent waving.

She drew up on him and stopped. His burlap face stared down, dumb and wordless. His hand, suspended from a wire so as to simulate life, ceased its wave when the breeze moved away.

A decayed human adult, skeletal but for the hair, lay at the scarecrow's feet, partly absorbed into the soil. The dead man's hand still gripped a rusty wire cutter used to fashion the figure standing before her. He had just clipped the wire and tested it to make sure the arm would swing free in the wind. Then his life ended, leaving his body to rot where it fell. It happened on June

10 of last year at 9:27 in the morning, the exact moment Grace's mother did the same thing.

The scarecrow continued to gaze brainlessly.

Despite the still, warm air, a chill ran over her. Not for the dead man at her feet but because she knew. She replayed the moment she looked down from the air, and she realized she knew. When she followed the trail from the airport, she knew. When called out from behind the rotted old cornstalks, she knew. She knew it was a scarecrow the whole time.

She waited for it to start laughing at her. She'd talked to it! What if it had answered? What if it had wanted to be her friend? What if, right now, it grabbed her and dragged her down into—

*Stop it!*

Grace let out a scream of rage and leapt at the scarecrow, digging her hands into the burlap face and ripping it off. She tore at its clothes, yanked on its arm until it broke free, and jerked the post back and forth, pulling it loose. She wrapped her arms around it, twisted it from the soil, and threw it down on top of the corpse.

She stared down, huffing, her hands frozen into claws. "I'm not going crazy."

Then she used the scarecrow's hat as a string-bean basket, picking the hearty ones that decided to grow anyway this year, and carried them back to the Piper. She sat on the floor of the hanger, eating string beans and talking to Clucky and Pecker, who didn't answer, and reading her brother's notes on how to siphon fuel from an airplane. The she unfolded her maps.

She would find a home yet.

# CHAPTER 21

**June 28**
**Washington, D.C.**

In the Rose Garden, bathed in the glow of a full moon, Shawnika strolled along the perimeter, her mind too busy to permit sleep. A half hour earlier she had put Tre and Melvin on exam tables in a doctor's office that opened into the White House's central corridor. The medical supplies were long-since ransacked, but the space was quiet and out of the way. Too many dead bodies and trashed rooms made the upper levels unsuitable. She didn't tell Luz they had come back down. The less that girl knew the better.

Shawnika ceased her pacing and listened to the night. A gun pop sounded in the distance every so often, and cars would race by now and again. Cackles arose near one of the monuments, then shouting, then fighting, then kids trying to stop the fighting. All of this audible thanks to the absence of white noise that had once dulled everyone's senses.

The gunfire and fights reminded Shawnika of her old neighborhood during a power outage, except no police sirens followed anymore.

She heard tires screeching, and then a car full of drunken revelers sped past, its occupants tossing bottles that shattered on the asphalt in the vehicle's wake. Shawnika had enough and headed back inside.

In the oval room with the hanging body, she ran her fingers along the wall until she located the exit and then slipped into the hallway, where she retrieved a candle and checked on Tre and Melvin, who pretended to be asleep. She decided to explore.

Near the end of the corridor, past the stairs, she stepped through an open doorway on her left and held the candle aloft. A library! A small one, but a lot nicer than the one at her school.

*Of course it's nice*, she thought. *It's the White House.*

Shawnika inched along, holding the candle to the spines, reading titles and admiring the fancy bindings. Many were biographies and big, weighty historical tomes with hundreds and hundreds of pages. Nineteenth-century British literature ran along one shelf, and American twentieth-century on another. She withdrew *Of Mice and Men* and placed it on the table in the center of the room with the satisfying thump only an old hardcover can make, and then added a collection of Sherlock Holmes short stories and *Fellowship of the Ring* to the pile.

She returned to the hall and absconded with three more candles, leaving one in the middle for Tre and Melvin if they came looking for her. Back in the library, she set them up on the table in a semicircle, pulled up a chair, and cracked open book one of Lord of the Rings. She skipped the five million pages of notes and preface and began chapter one.

Her young eyes were pleased to read by candlelight, for it fit the flavor of Tolkien's prose, and she allowed herself one of those uncomfortable acknowledgments: Mom was not here to nag her about reading in the dark, and she didn't mind this one time.

In minutes, Shawnika fell into the story of an ageless Bilbo Baggins of Bag End, of the Shire, of wizards, of magic. She could see it all, and she had never watched the movies. She forgot the fall of the Earth, the dread of starvation, and the kid who'd hung himself in the oval room halfway down the hall. Instead, she cavorted with Frodo and Gandalf the Grey. Subconsciously, she sensed movement in the corridor behind her, but the book held her rapt. Wizards, elves, and magic filled her head, except for that tiny, quiet corner of her mind that still paid attention to the space around her.

She closed the novel.

Someone was in the hall.

"Tre?"

Shawnika picked up a candle and took silent steps toward the door. "Tre?"

A muffled cry echoed from down the hall. Her brother's voice.

"Tre!"

Shawnika flew into a sprint, the flame of her candle vanishing into a wisp of smoke as she arced to the right and into the corridor. She had no time to react to the husky figure blocking her way. A fist hammered into her sternum, sending her to the floor. Her arms curled up in front of her chest, and she rolled to her side, grimacing and sucking for air. She heard her name called from far away, high-pitched, spoken by a young boy.

She remembered a video of her dad getting knocked down in the ring a bunch of years ago. The ref was counting. Dad had ten seconds to get up. Five. Six. Seven. Get up!

Shawnika pushed herself upright, to her knees, the one candle in the hall enough to show three people in black; one carried Tre with a hand over her brother's mouth, and the other two struggled to wrangle Melvin, who was doing a job of squirming. Finally, the one who had punched her bear-hugged Melvin and hoisted him up. The abductors disappeared though a doorway on the left.

Forcing her legs to move, she launched herself forward in pursuit. Before she could reach the door, one of the figures leaned into the corridor and tossed what looked like a soup can toward her. It began to hiss and spew a fog, and at once her eyes seared and her throat closed. The remaining candle flame extinguished.

Shawnika dropped to the floor to crawl away from the homemade gas bomb but barreled into the wall. Feeling her way, pinching her eyes shut, she found an open doorway and rolled through. She tried to orient herself, but the stinging vapor pushed her eyelids back down. Stumbling forward, she crashed into something. A table. She reached up, and her hand landed on a book. She was back in the library. Her mouth tasted like bug spray.

Squinting through her lashes, her eyes opened long enough to locate a side exit. She stood and staggered toward it, falling through to the other side and then into a smaller room behind that one, where the air was clear. Shawnika sat on the floor, catching her breath as a flood of tears washed her eyes. She ran her fingers in a circle over her sternum, the pressure sending a jab of pain in across her chest.

Those motherfuckers. They took Tre.

How did they know?

Shawnika hauled herself up, shook out her arms, and leaned against the wall until her vision returned. As the gas vapor dissipated, she backtracked to the library, moved the candles, and turned the table over with a loud crash, sending her books flying. She stood in the center of the table's underside for leverage and kicked until an oaken leg broke free. Gripping the table leg's narrow base and laying it across her shoulder like a baseball bat, she marched back into the hallway.

The chemical taste filled her mouth again, but the gas had been spent. It was dark anyway, so she closed her eyes and stormed down the corridor, running her left hand along the side until she found the doorway, made a left, and then made another left into the oval reception room. On the way past the hanging body, she took a swing with the makeshift bludgeon and landed a blow square on its ass.

Outside, she scanned the south lawn for signs of motion but saw none.

"Tre!"

Shawnika marched across the expanse of tall grass, climbed over the crashed pickup truck, and peered down Pennsylvania Avenue. "Tre!" she called once more.

She turned right, arbitrarily, and marched to the corner of 17th Street. She shouted her brother's name again and heard a drunken "Shut up!" coming from the window of a nearby building. She ignored it, climbing over the security barricades and storming down 17th, her club at the ready.

Her dad won that fight after being knocked down.

She traveled north to K Street, across to 15th, and back down to Pennsylvania Avenue, making a box around the White House, but saw no sign of her brother or his captors. Adrenalin spent, tears of frustration and panic came. What if she was moving in the wrong direction? What were they doing to Tre? Were they at least telling him not to be scared? How could she have let this happen? How could she have let Mama down so?

Shawnika dropped the club in the grass and reentered the White House, stepping around the hanging corpse without feeling her way. She knew it well enough by then in the dark.

Luz, wearing a white nightgown, was relighting the candles in the hall, her hands shaking and her face streaked with tears. She stood and turned as the younger girl approached. "My god! What happened?"

Shawnika's fury exploded. She took three long strides toward Luz, grabbed her by the throat, and slammed her against the wall. "Where's my fucking brother, you stupid bitch?"

Luz slapped and kicked, but Shawnika only tightened her grip. She pressed her forehead to Luz's. "I'm going to fucking kill you."

Luz mouthed, *I can't breathe*, and tried to squirm free, prompting Shawnika to twist her arm. "Where's your gang hiding?" Shawnika could not see the girl's face turning purple.

"I can't breathe!" Luz hissed, and finally Shawnika relented. The older girl slid down the wall, cowering. Shawnika stepped back and paced, waiting for her to recover, never looking away.

After two minutes, Luz said, "They took Ricky and Teresa too."

"Bullshit. You set us up. I knew you were too nice. If they hurt my brother, you're gonna pay. You're gonna wish you was never born."

Luz turned and gazed up at her pleading eyes. "Shawnika. They took my babies! They took my babies too."

Shawnika clasped Luz's hair and yanked her head back. "Why would your gang steal your own baby?"

Luz pressed her hands together as if in prayer. "*Por favor!* I swear."

Shawnika pulled her to her feet, keeping a grip on her long black hair, and shoved her forward. "Show me."

Luz led her through dim halls and around shadowy corners to the north side of the building into what looked like a small shop with two sleeping mats on the floor.

"They came in here and took my baby right from my arms. I woke up and screamed, and they wrapped me up in a blanket so I couldn't move. It was so fast."

Shawnika processed Luz's words for a moment and then listened to the silence. If Teresa was nearby, someone was doing a good job keeping her silent. Maybe Luz spoke the truth. Maybe she lied. There was one way to find out.

"Get dressed," Shawnika said. "We're going to your gang's hideout."

"Shawnika. Please don't do this."

"I'm making a trade: You for Tre and Melvin. You take me to the wrong place, you die. If Tre is harmed, you die. You fucked with the wrong bitch tonight."

***

Shawnika and Luz walked east by moonlight, heading away from the monuments and federal buildings, Shawnika brandishing the table leg for a weapon. She knew Luz had no chance fighting or fleeing from her, but, to preclude an attempt at the latter, she made her go shoeless.

"My feet hurt. I think I stepped on a piece of glass," Luz said as they passed a burned-out hotel.

Shawnika shoved her forward and told her to shut up. She did not know who made her do these things to Luz. She felt like a spectator in her own body as she egged on the cruelty.

With every step, she felt farther from Tre. What was she doing, tormenting this girl, making her walk barefoot over sidewalks and gravel? Forty minutes into their march, she thought of turning around and walking the other way, letting Luz wander aimlessly in the night, to hell with her. But then what? How was she going to find her brother in a world with no phones, no transportation, no police, no nothing? If Luz's gang kidnapped Tre, at least she had an answer.

They came upon a massive pile-up of cars in an intersection, a particular curiosity she had noticed over the past year. One intersection full of wrecked cars; the next one empty. One store littered with corpses; another as if the clerk had simply run off to the stock room. One house burned to cinders from something greasy on a lit stove, and the neighbor's intact because they had had Cheerios for breakfast. A million snapshots of a random yet specific Friday morning in June.

"Help me find a flashlight in one of these cars."

Luz made a pleading gesture. "They're picked over already. Believe me. I don't want to crawl over no dead guy's lap."

Shawnika shoved her against the side of a van. "Get in there and start looking, or I'll fucking kill you." Again the words came from her mouth of their own volition. Luz hunched in resignation and made her way to the passenger side, Shawnika following inches behind. Luz yanked the door open, the creaking echoing up and down the block. She opened the glove box and fished around, throwing papers to the foot well.

Luz looked back over her shoulder. "Nothing. I told you."

"Check under the seats then." It occurred to Shawnika that the next thing Luz touched could be a gun. "And if you find anything, you best tell me about it instead of acting stupid, because that will be the last thing you ever do."

Luz swept her right arm under the seat and found only an empty Tic Tac container. "I want to find my babies too. Why are you doing this to me?"

Shawnika wasn't sure. Maybe Luz was simply being nice to her this afternoon by giving her food and inviting her to stay. Maybe they should be working together.

"Keep digging," her mouth said.

While Luz dug through glove boxes and rummaged under armrests, Shawnika peered through windows as best she could with the grime and grit that had accumulated on the glass. She didn't tell Luz about the mummified infant in the baby seat of the Subaru outback.

The eighth car they checked, a compact Hyundai, produced nothing of value in the front, but Shawnika noticed the right rear backrest was not snapped in place. She tugged on the door. It was locked. "Look out," she said, two-handing the table leg. She swung, shattering the back window. A dog barked in the distance.

She poked the crinkled glass through with the end of the club and unlocked the door. Then she turned to Luz, who stared back. "Go on."

Luz opened the door and pulled the backrest forward. Shawnika peeked over her shoulder and saw the faint glow of a white emergency kit. "Take it," she said.

Luz kneeled on the seatback and reached into the trunk, then let out a scream and jumped back, brushing at her arms. "There's a spider nest. You get it."

Shawnika pointed the club at her. "Don't try any stupid shit." She backed in, sat on the seatback so she could watch Luz, and reached blindly into the trunk. She shook her head. "Ain't no spiders."

Her fingers probed for the box. *There it is.* She located the handle, just as the fine hairs on her arm began to register the soft flutter of a hundred tiny legs skittering up toward her head.

With that, she issued her own scream and popped out of the car as if launched by a catapult, hitting her head on the top of the doorframe. She flung the club and the plastic case. "Get them off!" she shouted, spinning and slapping at her arms and shoulders.

"I'm trying," said Luz, swatting at her. "Stop moving around."

Shawnika peeled off her top and shook it.

"What are you wearing a bra for? You don't need one."

"Shut up."

Convinced she was clear of crawly things, she slipped her T-shirt back on and retrieved the emergency kit. Inside she discovered a pack of plastic reflective triangles, a bottle of water, a box of adhesive bandages, and a small LED flashlight.

Shawnika pocketed the flashlight, tossed the reflectors on the ground, and closed the box, handing it to Luz. "Carry that."

The two girls walked for twenty minutes, sometimes with Luz in front and sometimes side by side. Once they took a detour around the block to avoid drunken boys holding a bonfire, but not before doing reconnaissance. This particular pack of revelers did not suggest the wherewithal to run an organized kidnapping raid, nor were they likely to want a baby around.

Soon it grew quiet and dark again; clouds swept through to swallow the moonlight.

"Promise me this isn't a trap," Shawnika said, walking beside Luz with a grip on each end of her club. She would not hesitate to swing at heads to rescue her brother, but what could she do against an armed gang?

"Why would I go through all this to trap you? We could have attacked you this afternoon."

Shawnika shot her a glare. "We?"

"Shawnika, you know what I mean. If I was part of some conspiracy, it don't make sense."

Clouds now filled the sky, and the night became one big shadow. Shawnika grabbed Luz by the arm and pulled her into the street to walk, away from the invisible ridges, humps, and missing sections of sidewalk. "You don't seem too upset they took your baby."

Luz walked silently for a minute. At last, she said, "Teresa's not mine. I found her last month in the park just lying there in a baby carrier."

"I knew it. Everything you say is a lie."

"I did it for a reason. I lost Tito's baby for real. I mean he was stillborn, and I so wanted us to be a family. For what it's worth, I'm sorry I took Teresa. I regret it now more than ever."

Shawnika didn't know a thing about stillbirths, so she didn't get why that would make Luz steal a baby. She figured Luz was full of shit about all of it, but she also heard pain in her voice. "You think Teresa's mama came back for her tonight? Sent her crew in?"

"That is what I think. Look, I promise my gang didn't take your brother. My gang is dead. My Tito is dead. My cousin Ricky is gone. Teresa is gone. I got nothing left."

Luz led her around a corner and froze.

"What is it?"

The older girl pointed. "That's it. Our hideout."

Across the street and down half a block, a limousine agency, two floors high with a long, attached garage, radiated silence. Shawnika withdrew the flashlight and directed the beam. She turned it off and waited. No one came outside.

"Come on," she said, tugging Luz, who began to resist. "We're making a trade."

Luz shook her head and began to cry. "I can't go in there." She pulled free of Shawnika's grip and backed away. "Please."

"If you think you can get away from me, think again. Stay put."

Luz sank to her knees, praying. Shawnika let her be and darted across the street. She inched up beside the entrance, club raised in her right hand. She reached out and felt for the handle of the metal security door. A slight pull told her it was unlocked. She withdrew the flashlight again, clutched the door handle once more, and flung it open.

She leapt before the opening, flashed the beam on and off, and spun away, replaying a mental photograph of what she saw: Bodies. Four or five. Young. Crusted with dried blood. A gun on the floor?

She glanced across the street to see Luz watching, wringing her hands as she leaned forward. Facing the street, holding the flashlight backward, Shawnika reached across the door opening and shined the beam inside. No response.

She pivoted and stood in the doorway, and the odor of rotting flesh blasted her like heat from an oven. It smelled like last summer. Steeling herself, she buried her nose into her arm and stepped inside.

More than five bodies lay strewn. Five by the door, the first to die, were riddled with bullet holes. Even their clothing was shredded. Two more lay to the side on the couch in a little lounge, their heads tilted toward the door, mouths open in the moment of shock. Another corpse rested face down on a flight of stairs leading to the second floor.

Shawnika figured this place had been swarming with a million flies just hours ago. Around when she was drinking her vitamin drink and the boys were bowling.

The boys. Tre. She didn't want him to end up like this, shot up in a gang war.

Ahead, in the kitchenette, more bodies were sprawled behind a table shot to splinters. They had hidden behind the particle board, as if it could somehow stop automatic weapons.

A roar of anguish rang out behind her. She whirled around and found Luz standing in the doorway. With a choking cry the girl called her dead lover's name. "Tito."

Shawnika killed the flashlight beam and guided Luz onto the sidewalk, away from the stench and the gruesome tableau. The full moon had found a gap between the clouds, and it bathed them in ghost light. "Shhh," she said, dropping her club. "I'm sorry."

Luz buried her head into Shawnika's shoulder and began to wail. "Everything is gone."

Shawnika held her. "We'll find them," she said. Tears flooded her own eyes, her heart empty and her spirit lost in a black void. Tre could be anywhere, moving in any direction. "We'll find them."

At that moment, Shawnika Williams felt like the world's oldest twelve-year-old.

# CHAPTER 22

*Where:* Bryce Center for the Performing Arts, Arlington,
     Virginia
*When:* July 1, 8:00 p.m.
*What:* Bart "Zane" Barzán's greatest performance yet

And this one would not take place on a stage. Rather, in the table-read room, where the Council of Elders, aka Council 13, held their meetings.

Eleven elders filed into the room, finding the other two, Zane and Anthony, at the far end of the table. Curious glances were exchanged. Nagesh's terrible poker face betrayed his suspicion as he stared at Anthony.

Zane soaked it in. Nagesh and Anthony used to be tight as spandex. They were the first two he had recruited, and they consulted each other before they ever talked to Zane about anything. Now here was Anthony standing shoulder to shoulder with Zane.

Once everyone took their usual places, Zane smacked the gavel (prop rooms rule!) on the table. "This is Zane calling the

Council of Elders together for a special meeting. Please put your asses in a chair."

Silent expressions of disapproval circled the table. It was supposed to be: *Please be seated.* Zane and Anthony remained standing.

Zane waited for all the shuffling and nose scratching and chair adjusting to finish and then allowed three seconds of silence for dramatic buildup. "Thank you for coming on short notice. You're probably wondering what the heck is going on, and I'm sorry I have not been one-hundred-percent transparent, but I think you'll be happy."

Twenty-two eager eyes gazed up at him. Cool. Sometimes it was hard to focus a bunch of teenage boys. He made a mental note that changing up meeting times fosters intrigue, which seems to increase attentiveness.

"This council has been together for over ten months. We've recruited close to seventy-five kids. We need to start expanding their responsibility."

So far, so good.

"I am aware that not all of you are on board with the babysitting club I've got going, but a gang of thirteen boys is just that: A gang. Nothing more. With these kids, we're going to get the place running again. We're going to get the power back on. We're going to get roads cleared. We're going to own Washington, DC."

A few shifting butts. They'd heard variations of this before. But the good part was coming next.

"And we're going to own Fairfax, and Baltimore, and eventually Wilmington and Roanoke and every other big town in the middle Atlantic. It might take ten or fifteen years, but if we stick with it, we're going to build a kingdom. Every city is going to need a governor. And where are these governors going to come from? From right here on this council."

Zane pointed at the fourth boy on his left. "Geno. How old are you?"

"Fifteen."

"Before all this shit went down, did you think you'd ever be the governor of your own city by age of twenty-five?"

Nagesh opened his mouth. "Dude. Cities have mayors."

Zane never liked Nagesh, he had to admit. "In the old world, yes. But think of them as city–states. Territories. Do you know anything about colonialism?"

"No. But I suppose you're going to tell me." Nagesh tilted his head back to stare at the ceiling.

"Well, maybe now isn't the time. Basically, a governor gets to bang all the chicks he wants and kill people who piss him off. Are you on board with that?"

Anthony elbowed him.

"Right!" Zane said. "Anyway, getting these kids trained is going to be a project and a half. They all worship me—"

"No shit."

"They all worship me, so it makes sense that I lead that initiative. Which requires full-time dedication. That means...I am stepping down as council head, effective in about three minutes. Taking charge of the council will be, as you can probably guess, the one and only Anthony."

The most popular kid in the room drew a loud applause, except from Nagesh. "Aren't we supposed to vote on this shit?"

Zane chose a fatherly demeanor for his response. "And who do you think they would have voted for? Anyway, I have more good news and changes. Effective in two minutes and forty-five seconds, Anthony will have the title of Captain. Nagesh will be Alternate Captain. Cool?"

Nagesh leaned back into his chair, shrugged, and nodded reluctant acceptance. "I guess that'll work."

"My last act as council head, before I have to start asking Anthony for permission, is a swearing-in ceremony. Now don't do anything until I speak."

Zane held his hands aloft and clapped twice. Thirteen children, all young boys in tuxedos, marched in holding silver platters. On each platter was a shot glass filled with caramel-colored liquid. Each boy reached over and placed the drink before a council member, except for the two who stood behind Zane and Anthony. They waited while the leaders turned and retrieved their drinks. Jorge, the boy to whom Zane had given the candy bar, served him his shot glass.

Nagesh manufactured a laugh. "Where did you get the penguin suits and the trays?"

Zane manufactured a more convincing smile. "You guys are all into raiding hunting stores and supermarkets that have been ransacked fifty times over. Meanwhile, you can go to a tux shop or a wedding hall and take brand new shit right off the racks."

Nagesh, seemingly content with his new role as Alternate Captain, shrugged again.

"Okay," Zane said to the group as the children tucked their trays in unison and stepped back. "Are you guys boys or men?"

The council members shouted, "*Men!*"

"Good. What you have here in your shot glass is scotch. Rare scotch. A bottle of this particular rare scotch would have cost you three hundred bucks back in the day." He held it up to the light and peered through the amber fluid. "Normally I'd give it to you in a proper glass because you don't take shots of scotch, but we have no ice, and it tastes weird without ice."

"It smells like gasoline," one of the elders said.

"That's what a boy says. You're a man, remember. You just told me so."

Anthony patted him on the backside. "I think you're going over your two minutes and forty-five seconds, pal."

Ah, camaraderie. How quickly it leads to a love fest. "I'm getting there. Anyway, I'm going to give a toast, and together, we all gulp it down in one shot, then slam your glass on the table upside down like they did in the movies. And if you're not a man yet, you will be after this. Okay, so…"

He winked at Anthony, who couldn't contain his grin.

"So…I, Zane Barzán, hereby step down as council head and pass the role to your new captain and—don't clap 'til it's all done—council leader, Anthony Donaldson. One, two, three, drink!"

Zane poured the warm scotch whisky down his throat, and the others followed suit. He slammed his glass upside down, and the others did as well. Clack clack clack, echoed thirteen times.

"Holy shit, that is nasty," Nagesh said. "I think it spoiled."

Zane didn't bother. "Trust me, it tastes better with ice." He scanned the group. They were all making the same expression that suggested nausea. Geno rubbed his gut.

Anthony, looking a tad gray, pointed to Zane's glass. "How come yours has a red dot on the bottom?"

Zane picked it up. "Hmmm. Good eye. The red dot is the one without the cyanide."

Anthony stared at him, baffled.

"Wait for it," Zane said. Several of the boys began to clutch at their guts, faces twisting into knots as they turned blue.

"You fucker," Nagesh hissed, then slid out of his chair to the floor.

By then the boys were dropping and writhing, their flailing arms knocking shot glasses across the table, reaching to the children in desperate pleas for help. The children remained at attention, silver platters tucked under their right arms, staring ahead and ignoring the gurgling and foaming mouths and bulging, terrified eyes.

Anthony, who had tumbled to the floor, grabbed Zane's ankle, but Zane kicked his hand away. Zane turned to Jorge. "Well done, young man. I'm so proud of you. You have pleased the Lord." The he took the gavel and banged on the table four times.

Twenty more children, not wearing tuxedos, entered the room.

"Okay, boys. The evil ones...the deceivers have been vanquished." Except that they were still writhing around, and a couple were crawling. Zane handed the gavel to Jorge. "Go on, son. Go give those two a whack on the head as hard as you can. It's the Lord's will, and you will never be punished."

Jorge stood over the two crawlers and methodically gave each four or five blows hard enough to slow them down.

"As I was saying, the deceivers have been vanquished by the grace of the Lord. Now I want you guys to cart the dirty devils out front and cut their motherfucking heads off. For real. Stick their heads on the spikes of that black fence. If you can't reach the top of the fence, get a stepladder or ask one of your taller friends. And if any of these deceivers tries to stop you, you may beat them with clubs or whatever. You can't beat a devil hard enough."

The boys gathered around the feet of the council members, most of whom had stopped squirming, and dragged them into the hall to the waiting flatbed carts. It took three to drag Anthony, who was bigger than all the others. His arms flopped back, and his mouth fell open, frothy saliva dripping down his face.

"You guys did great," Zane said. "Just try to get them out before they leak shit everywhere." His obedient followers complied without a word.

The room emptied, Zane walked around the table tucking the chairs back in place. At the door, he turned and took a silent bow.

# CHAPTER 23

## July 4
## Baltimore, Maryland

Crawling in basements can be hard on the knees and often attracts enough cobwebs to make a hat, but it offers rewards. Food missed by raiders for one. Storage rooms with handy supplies and a decent place to sleep for a night. And crates and wood scraps, at least in the fried chicken joint Josie had been exploring all morning.

The chicken was long gone. That had been taken in the first couple of days. But oil still sat in vats, and, though it had turned to lard, Josie figured she could scoop some of it out into a pot and build a fire to heat it. She also found bags of uncooked French fries in a storage locker. They were inedible, but they weren't for her. They were for the birds.

Josie watched from just inside the restaurant's entrance, her hand gripping a string tied to a wooden stick. In the old times, not a soul would have noticed the little wooden rod lying under a storage shelf, much less bent over to inspect it. Today it was perfect for propping up one end of a crate on the sidewalk. A handful of fries lay underneath.

Josie didn't like to be this visible. Not after the pier, when Ronan and his gang of killers came. Since then she'd remained in the shadows, alone.

A pickup truck bounced past, weaving around crashed vehicles. Any slower and the driver might have become curious about the crate and the stick. Maybe he would have gotten out and chased her, and she'd have had to seek yet another dirty hole or grimy nook in which to wait out a killer.

But this particular driver had other concerns, leaving Josie to her task. For twenty minutes she waited. Her leg numbing, she shifted positions and leaned against the checkout counter, halfway into the shadows. A motorcycle zoomed past, vibrating the floor.

She shut her eye and rested. She didn't sleep well these days, for she worried about being discovered by Ronan, though since that day at the pier she mostly ran into kids just like her. She noted their grimy faces and matted hair and their tattered clothes and weariness. They acknowledged the same in her. Her clothes weren't as tattered, though, because she had no problems taking garments off a corpse or rifling through drawers in a house while a dead body rotted behind her.

She heard fluttering, and her body stiffened. Josie turned slowly, trying not to startle, and saw it: A large, white gull standing next to the crate, poking its beak in and bobbing its head around. Josie got this idea from all those times in the Burger King parking lot with Cara when they'd tossed the extra fries for the seagulls and laughed as the birds grew increasing aggressive about getting more.

*Come on. Go on in and get that french fry. You know you want it.*

The bird stepped back, scouted for competition, and peered into the shadow cast by the crate.

*Come on.*

It slipped halfway under and pecked a fry. Another peck, this time tossing it around in its beak for a second before dropping it. Another step into the shadow...

Josie yanked the stick, and the crate fell over the bird. She bolted into the morning sunlight and dragged the crate to the door as the bird flapped and tried to stay upright while being knocked along. She slipped the edge of the crate over the ridge at the bottom of the doorframe and ducked into the darkness with her quarry.

"Don't you give me any shit," she said. She counted to three and flipped the crate on its side, flailing at the bird in search of a grip. She decided the best plan was to smother it, so she dived onto the animal and wrapped her arms around it. The bird went into a flapping frenzy, and Josie turned her face to the side, waiting for it to tire, imaging herself as a constricting snake.

The bird exhausted itself, and she sat upright, cradling it, feeling its gasps and drum-roll heartbeat against her chest. As her eyes readjusted to the darkness, she noticed the gull shooting glances around the room, frightened, as if it didn't understand that Josie was the thing scaring it. One quick flap or two and it settled in her arms.

"Shhhhh," she heard herself whispering. "It's okay."

Now all she had to do was break its neck, and she was halfway to frying a bird. Just one hand around its throat, a twist, and then she'd have a nice breakfast. Her first one in three days. She had vomited that morning when she realized the date: July 1st, the anniversary of her sister's murder. Only today had Josie's appetite returned.

She caressed the bird's head and sighed. She couldn't do it. "Come on, now. I'm not going to hurt you."

After cradling the gull for a few minutes, she stood. She carried it outside, glanced up and down the street, and then entered the door beside the restaurant. A long, narrow flight of stairs stretched up before her. The bird squawked, and she hushed it again. Up she went.

Josie carried the creature up five creaky floors to the roof. Her stomach growling, she set the gull down on the pebbly surface and gave it a nudge. "Go on."

The bird limped and tried a weak flap. The left wing complied. The right, twisted to the side and bleeding where the bone poked through, did not.

Josie had broken its wing.

As she watched the helpless, maimed creature stumble and make another feeble attempt to become airborne, the grit on the left side of her face was moistened by a fresh, warm tear. The creature took a step and settled, broken right leg jutting out sideways from under its body. It let out an agonized squawk and began breathing in gasps and jerks. Josie scooped the animal up one more time.

"I'm so sorry," she said, petting the gull twice and then sliding her hand down its neck as she went blind with tears. Her body heaved in torment as she twisted.

She heard the tiny bones snap, and the bird went limp.

Josie carried the animal to the ledge and held it to her breast, the way she wished she could have held and comforted Cara's dying body, as she waited for the river of tears to cease. She hadn't cried like that since she saw her own mutilated face in that mirror at St. Agnes nearly a year ago. Another anniversary coming.

Gazing toward Center City, she thought those towering office buildings and hotels looked the same now as they had before, shiny and silver-black. Far from those skyscrapers sat her old, crummy neighborhood where, as far as she knew, Hector still rotted in the rubble of her apartment building. To the left, silent factories and construction sites waited to be animated once again. Way down yonder, Interstate 95 met the big bridge. If not for the motionless cars and the rotten and burnt odors, Baltimore looked the same as before.

Josie felt something sticky on her forearm. She looked down at the dead bird seeping blood from its broken wing. Just then, another gull, not so foolish as this one, raced past her on its way to the Atlantic Ocean.

How she wished for wings of her own. She would fly to the sea and never come back.

# PART TWO

---

## WHAT HAPPENS TO ANGELS AT THE END

**Two years and three months later**

# CHAPTER 24

## October 10

From the corrugated rooftop of the construction vehicle hanger, Josie Revelle watched the yellow, motionless dust hover over Baltimore's streets like a fog of sulfur. Skyscrapers in Center City poked up from the powdery mist like crystalline granite, no longer reflecting sunlight, for the windows that hadn't fallen out or been broken were coated with soot and grit.

She took another bite of rat, tearing away a strip of charred meat.

When at ground level, she couldn't so much see the dust as taste it. If she were lucky enough to find food these days, she took her breakfast up here, away from that cloud. She didn't mind getting a break from Carter, either. He wasn't the worst companion, but she might not have picked him from a crowd. Peter Cottontail, she called him sometimes, because he jumped and skittered like a bunny rabbit.

She finished the edible parts of the rat, including the tail, flung the bones over her shoulder, and began nibbling on another. Last night, after the shit that went down with the snipers and hiding in the sewers, she'd been too ravenous to prepare a proper meal. Gut. Skin. Grill. This morning, the first one in a week she hadn't felt chased by starvation, she spent time cleaning the animal and cutting away the gristle.

Once full, she stood and stretched and wondered for the hundredth time how she would survive the coming winter. Gone were the days of finding overlooked food in the back rooms of nail salons and dollar stores or in the offices of car dealerships and furniture outlets. She'd hit all of them, or someone like her had. In the spring, she'd finally gotten over her fear of the waterfront only to find the inner harbor thick with shiny sludge from a ship that had busted open and spilled fuel everywhere. So much for crabbing.

She scanned the horizon for a place she hadn't explored, a store of food that somehow everyone missed, for signs of life. Her gut full for the first time in ages, she felt lucid.

*Why am I still here?*

That must have been how her mom felt every time she looked at Hector, her repugnant white-power boyfriend who made eyes at her daughters. Or whenever she paused for a gander of their shitty apartment. Or at herself in the mirror.

*Why am I still here?*

Josie could easily have taken a step forward and gone headfirst to the asphalt thirty-five feet down, saving herself a lot of worry. Like all the other times she could have, she didn't, instead turning and heading toward the covered ladder that led into the vehicle depot below.

Then, on instinct, she dropped and pinned herself to the roof.

Like a bird or a bug or another prey animal, she had learned to act first and let her brain fill in the details after. Flat on her chest, her brain told her that something to her left, on the street below, had moved.

She slithered until she faced the other direction and then peeked over the edge.

Two boys wearing combat fatigues and holding military rifles had taken position behind a derelict truck in the intersection. Josie got lucky. Their adventure, playing out at street level, did not factor in the possibility of girls on roofs. She realized these must be the snipers who wiped out that gang yesterday. Making Josie doubly lucky, because they could have easily picked Carter and her off first.

Carter. He was below, asleep. The snipers surely saw the smoke from her fire and followed it. They were going to march right into the hanger and kill Carter.

*Shit.*

Her weapons included the switchblade strapped to her leg and her canvas bag with the flashlight they'd found the day before. Cool. Maybe she could shine it in their eyes. Who needs an assault rifle when you've got a three-watt bulb?

Josie slung the canvas sack over her shoulder, scampered to the rain cover, gripped the sides of the latter, and began sliding down. She'd learned to escape from trouble quickly this way, though now she seemed to be moving toward it.

Once on the ground, in the shadows, she crouched and listened. Feet scuffed along the smooth cement floor at the other end of the hanger. Josie crawled under a wheel loader and then another. She zigzagged between rows of diggers. Finally, she slithered under the dump truck and reached their nest. She listened again but only heard Carter's slow breaths.

She crept forward on her knees, laid a hand on his mouth, and put her lips to his ear. In the softest whisper she could produce with adrenaline pumping through her system, she said, "Carter. Wake up, but don't move or make a sound."

Carter's eyes popped open, wide and confused. His hand came up to pull hers away, but she whispered a soft, "Shhhhh."

His pupils locked on her face. She removed her hand. "Snipers. We have to go *now*. Are you awake enough to get what I'm saying?"

He nodded and then turned over onto his knees. Josie pointed to the back exit, and he nodded again. They'd have to sprint into the open, but once outside could zip through the abandoned warehouse next door and put three blocks between them and the snipers in less than a minute.

The pair wriggled around various buckets and scoops attached to mechanical beasts of another age. They pressed their backs to the big tire of the last wheel loader in the line. Josie fixed on the door twenty-five feet away and then nodded at Carter. He returned the gesture. With her fingers, she counted one, two, three, and they bolted.

"Hey!" came the voice from halfway across the hanger.

Carter threw his shoulder into the door's release bar, and they spilled into the sunlight. He put his arm across his forehead and squinted but was jerked forward when Josie yanked his other arm. "Come on!"

In through the broken door of the empty warehouse, derelict long before any global catastrophe destroyed civilization, and down the long, debris-strewn corridor they ran. Once outside again, they cut left and trotted along the front of the building. Across the street rose an unfinished office tower, all girders, piles of dirt, slabs of this and that, and heaps of pipes. Josie figured they could hide there until the snipers got tired of looking. Then she glanced over her shoulder and saw the two killers already circling the warehouse and heading for them.

"Go!" she hollered, and she and Carter leapt over a pile of white PVC pipes and into the forest of steel beams. She looked back again and saw the snipers standing still. They were taking aim.

"Watch out."

A round clanged off a post to their left. Holding hands, they veered toward the densest section in the middle where supplies had been stored three and a half years ago, never to be touched again.

Josie and Carter continued straight for a quarter mile, leaving the construction zone behind. The landscape opened up to reveal a vast rail yard perhaps twenty lines of tracks across. Engines, freight cars, and passenger coaches sat alone or coupled on one pair of rails or another, some pointing east and some west. A hearty layer of grime had glued itself to everything.

"What do you wanna do?" Carter said, his back to the stone wall of the station house separating the two of them from their pursuers.

Josie fought to catch her breath. "Are they still coming?"

Carter peeked around the side of the building and jerked back in a hurry. "We gotta move."

A chilly breeze danced across the rail yard in loops, kicking up old plastic bags and a tornado of powdery dirt. Josie took Carter by the hand and charged into the yard, swinging left around a desolate, graffiti-covered boxcar to screen out the shooters. She spotted a diesel engine and hopped into the cab.

Carter, taller by ten inches, bounded on board behind her. "What are you doing?"

Josie eyed the multitude of gauges and levers, trying to make sense of them. "My dad was a train engineer," she said, and then thought about it. "Well, maybe."

"Seriously. This thing is not going to start in a million years."

A silver switch! Josie pushed it left, then right. She toggled it. Nothing happened. Outside, the wind moved away, and the dust and quiet settled around them. "Shit. It's got to be one of these." She flipped every switch she could find and began turning levers. The old locomotive slept on.

Josie stepped back and stared, one arm across her chest and the other holding her chin to aid concentration. Then she dropped her hand away and craned her neck, her attention caught by something new.

"Dude," Carter said. "This thing ain't gonna start. The tank is probably full of water, and the plugs are soiled. It's been three fucking ye—"

Josie held her hand up to silence him. "Do you hear that?"

"What?"

"That noise."

"What noise?"

She stuck her head outside the open cab. "A train. An engine I mean."

"Bullshit."

She glared. "I can hear it. There's an engine running out there."

With Carter unconvinced, she climbed out of the cab on the opposite side, forcing him to follow. She sprinted straight and then left around a coupling of idle tanker cars. Carter followed, swiveling to look out for snipers.

The sound grew louder as they moved across rails and around engines and cars. By then Carter heard it too, and they began to pull each other along by hand.

Squeezing between the middle coupling of a long train of freight cars, they emerged to find a diesel engine idling on the far track, trailed by a passenger coach and a string of boxcars and flatbeds, clean in contrast to the rusting metal hulks behind them. And operational. The engineer, a slight boy in a clean blue polo shirt, looked as surprised by them as they were by him.

"Uh, hey. Are you guys looking for a ride? This is really more of a test run."

Josie didn't bother with formality. She jumped up and into the cab, and Carter pushed his way in after her. "Go."

"I'm Cristobal," the engineer said, extending a hand. "And you are?"

Josie stared, baffled by his behavior as much as by his existence. "Cristobal. Does this thing actually work? Because we need to start moving immediately. Like, now. There are two guys right behind us who—"

"Wait a minute." Cristobal said. "How old are you? I can't take anybody over ten."

Carter's hands started to jitter. "Jesus Christ, Dude. Is this a fucking kiddie ride? Go before we all get shot."

Cristobal's raspy voice sounded too low for his age. "I'm not really supposed to take anyone over ten. You guys have to get off."

Josie scanned the control panel. "Then I'm going to drive it."

"Hey. I said you have to get off. Those are the rules."

With that, a bullet clanged off the doorframe about two inches from Carter's left shoulder. He and Josie shouted in unison, "Go!"

Cristobal fumbled to release the brake and then moved the throttle from idle to the first position. The train chugged a moment before beginning to inch forward. Another shot rang out, this time pinging off the frame of the cab and denting the metal.

"Faster!"

Cristobal shifted to the second position. "This isn't a motorcycle. Even an empty freight train weighs several hundred tons. Give it a minute."

Thirty seconds passed with Josie and Carter pinning themselves against the back of the cab to keep out of the line of fire. All the while, Josie watched Cristobal's motions, trying to get a feel for the operation in case the kid caught the next round in the back of the head. But by then the train was moving at a speed faster than any sniper could follow.

Cristobal glanced over his shoulder. "As soon as we get far enough away from Baltimore, I'm stopping and letting you off. Sorry, but you're too old."

A slow terror built up in Josie, way different from being shot at. This was already the farthest she'd been away from town since everyone died. Since before that. Since her mom took her and Cara to Ocean City five years ago.

Ocean City. That would be a place to go. Better yet, North Carolina.

"Where are we going?"

Cristobal monitored the tracks ahead, the throttle now in the middle position, the train rolling at safe, steady pace. "*We're* not going anywhere. I'm going. You are going to get off in about five minutes. I just want to get a safe distance from your friends back there."

"What if we don't get off? What are you gonna do?" Carter asked, trailing off when Josie gestured for him to be quiet.

"Why do we have to be ten to ride with you?" Josie asked.

"I said ten or *under.*"

"But you're not ten. You're my age. Why do *we* have to be ten or under?"

Cristobal kept his eyes fixed forward. "Because you have to be. That's all I can say. And I don't have to be ten because I don't."

Josie and Carter shrugged at each other.

"I'll stop the train and let you off somewhere safe. That's all I can do."

Josie, now thirteen, the age her sister was when murdered, lacked Cara's sultry appeal and curves, partly from genetic chance and partly from a diet of dead rats and Slim Jims. That and her sister had two eyes in her head instead of one, which probably helps with sex appeal. But she was old enough now to understand a least a few of the maneuvers in Cara's playbook.

She stepped closer to Cristobal and leaned her shoulder against his back, pressing into him as she peered over the control panel at the perpetual vanishing point in the distance.

"How fast are we going?" she asked, adding a lilt to her voice.

He maintained his stance. "About thirty-five miles per hour. These rails aren't in great shape, so it would be dangerous to go faster."

She nodded. "Can you drop us off somewhere near the beach?"

Cristobal frowned. "We're going south. There is no beach. Seriously? Have you ever seen a train at the beach?"

She avoided the temptation to shove his head into the control panel. Instead, she placed her hand on his shoulder and caressed the back of his neck. "Silly me. Thanks for letting us ride with you. How did you get so good at being an engineer?"

Josie felt like a fraud trying to manipulate him with flirtation. Still, she didn't want to get dumped in the middle of a field with nothing but a canvas bag, a switchblade, a half-dead flashlight, and silly old Carter. If she had to flash a cute smile or show some leg, maybe—

"Can you take your hand off me? It's grimy, and this shirt is new. Don't be disgusting."

Josie dropped the singsong voice. "Fine. But I'll fucking stab you if you let us off next to a garbage dump."

Scowling, she retreated to the back of the cab and leaned against the metal wall next to Carter. She felt his jealous glare and ignored it, instead watching the erstwhile engineer manipulate the controls. On curves, he adjusted the throttle down and applied the brake; on straightaways, he throttled up, sometimes jerking and rattling the train from inexperience. If searching for a place to kick them out, he didn't show it. Maybe he thought she was serious about stabbing him.

Then he dropped the throttle, and the train slowed to a crawl.

She leaned to Carter's ear, using the low chug of the diesel's engine for cover against being overheard. "He can't make us get off the train. He can either take us all the way to wherever, or he can stop, but if we don't get off, what can he do? It's stupid."

"Or he's full of shit and has a gang waiting to shoot us when we get there."

Josie was tired of running from people trying to shoot her. She had never started any of this shit. "Or we throw him off the train and take it ourselves." She liked that option best.

A final scenario she did not anticipate presented itself at once, rendering the others meaningless. It involved a high-powered assault rifle.

The snipers, having climbed onto the last flatbed car of the train back at the rail yard in Baltimore, crawled their way up, car by car, taking advantage of the low speed to race through the passenger coach, straddle the coupling, and inch along the foot rail of the diesel engine. With the train nearly stopped, the lead shooter hopped into the open cab and took aim at Cristobal's head. "Keep driving."

The second squeezed in behind him and targeted Carter. "Stay right there, punks."

Josie recognized him. The curly hair. The long, skinny, neck. It had been over two years, but she knew him, all right. She had sat next to him in the back of that Nissan Maxima the day Cara died. She had beaned him on the head with a frozen fish at the aquarium.

Richie the rapist. That meant...

She glanced at the lead sniper's face, and her heart leapt into her throat.

Him. Again. Cara's killer.

Ronan.

Ronan was the goddamned sniper turning Baltimore into a ghost town.

Ronan, oblivious that he was in the presence of a girl he'd already shot once, said to Cristobal, "I said keep driving."

"I can't! We're coming up on—"

Ronan jammed the barrel into his neck. "I'll tell you when to stop." Then he motioned to Josie and Carter with his rifle. "You two, next to Chicken Chow Mien over there. Face me."

Josie and Carter slid around and put their backs to the control panel while Cristobal throttled up. The train lurched and accelerated.

Cristobal spoke without taking his eyes off the track. "The station is just ahead. We're going to miss the stop if I don't slow down."

"This is the express train today, kid," Ronan said. "We'll stop when I say stop."

"But—"

"Are you from Baltimore, Chicken Chow Mien?"

"My name is Cristobal."

Ronan smirked. "Okay, Chinaman. You from Baltimore?"

"I'm Filipino. And no, I'm not from Baltimore."

"Then this is your lucky day. These two punks, not so much."

Carter's hands jittered. "What did we ever do to you?"

"Nothing, really, sport, except you got away yesterday, and I don't let my prey escape."

Josie leaned an inch to her right, then another, wedging between Cristobal and the control panel just a bit.

"I have to stop!" Cristobal said. "We're at the station."

"In a minute, Chinaman. I'm looking for a nice, dramatic location to execute these two los—"

Josie, her right hand obscured from view by Cristobal's leg, yanked the brake as hard as she could; the engine's wheels issued an outraged squeal in response. The two snipers were flung forward, barreling into Cristobal. G-forces pinned Josie and Carter to the control panel, but not with such force that she couldn't turn her head and see four or five young kids with rifles standing on the platform.

Ronan was halfway to his feet when the locomotive hopped the rail, hurtling him headfirst into Cristobal once again. Josie smacked Carter's chest to get his attention as the train wheels rained sparks on them and the engine careened against the platform. Fighting momentum, she pulled herself toward the door of the cab, grabbed the side of the doorframe, and jumped. She failed to clear the platform, cracking her shin on the concrete edge. Carter came fast behind, landing on his feet and grabbing her by the arm to scoop her up. They bolted past the Union Station sign, stumbled up the escalator, and fled into the gloom.

Ronan, his forehead gashed open and blood smeared across his lips, charged up the steps, growling, "You're going to die, you fucking bitch."

# CHAPTER 25

Grimacing anew with each step, Josie held on to Carter's arm as they moved through the vast hall of Union Station, her staccato footfalls echoing off the barrel-vaulted ceiling. On instinct, they headed for the shadows, plowing through the sea of skeletons once belonging to the late rush-hour crowd passing through a June morning long ago. Kicking them aside was easier on Josie's damaged leg than stepping over.

Across the hall, the snipers charged through the entrance in pursuit. Josie and Carter cut sideways down a hallway, which, without electricity to light their way, could have been a mine shaft.

"Watch out for bodies," Josie whispered, trying to deny the throbbing pain in her shin.

"What's that 'M' for?" Carter nodded toward the sign on the wall.

"The subway, I think. Metro."

Carter came to a stop and grabbed her by the arm to pull her back. "We need to get the fuck out of here. Now."

She'd heard the stories all the way up in Baltimore. No one, not even people with guns or in gangs, went into the subway anymore. And if one of those people with guns or in gangs chased you down there, you never came back up.

But that was everyone else. Not her.

She limped on, following the signs, and soon came to a row of turnstiles. She hiked up her dress to climb over, glad Carter couldn't see her in the dark. Despite his earlier admonition, he followed, and they found an escalator. The remaining few light photons hinted at steps. Beyond lay a black abyss.

Carter whispered. "Come on. Let's get out of here."

Behind them, the echoing footfalls of the snipers grew louder. "Get ready to die, punks!"

Josie stood at the ledge of the first step, staring into the pit.

Ronan bellowed again. "I see you!"

Josie placed her left foot on the first step like she was getting acquainted with a cold swimming pool. With deliberation, her right foot followed, her banged-up shin protesting.

"I got my site trained on you, and I never miss," Ronan said from somewhere in the shadows. Then, quieter, he said, "Tell her, Richie."

"He don't miss!"

Josie lowered herself to the second step. Then the third.

Carter looked back over his shoulder. "They're climbing the turnstiles." Josie reached the fifth step. "Aw, fuck it," he said, following.

Josie descended step after step, imagining herself as a mouse moving through the tall grass undetected. Up top, Ronan continued to shout taunts, but she could tell he did not know where she was.

Carter patted her on the shoulder. "Hey. Let's just wait here until they leave."

"No," she whispered. They could both get picked off if Ronan decided to start firing into the darkness.

"I can't see."

"No shit."

Josie's foot rolled over something that lay across the step, and she slipped, smacking her elbow on the metal step. She scrunched her face to suppress a cry of pain. Feeling around, her fingers wrapped around a skeletal arm. She gritted out "loose bones" as a warning to Carter.

That didn't make sense. The body of an adult who died on this escalator that day would have been carried to the bottom. That mean this arm belonged to a—

Carter reached around her chest and hoisted her back to her feet. She reached over the handrail and dropped the child's arm on the other side.

In total blackness now, the pair continued to descend what seemed like a bottomless stair. After each step Josie expected to find floor, only to discover yet another step. Was it possible someone had built a never-ending escalator and she hadn't heard of it?

As last, with triumph and relief, her toes met concrete. She shuffled her way onto solid ground, Carter following blind with his hand on her shoulder. She led him away from the escalator using her right foot to feel around the dead bodies piled at the bottom. Away from the sun and airflow, these corpses retained more of their mass.

She stopped and reached into the canvas shoulder bag.

"What do we do now?"

"This," she said, turning on the flashlight they'd found in the Toyota the day before. The beam reflected off the bright surfaces and curved ceilings, setting the room aglow. The dead bodies littering the platform would have filled her young soul with pure terror four years ago. Today, it was a relief not to discover something more deadly.

"I see you!" Ronan bellowed from the top of the long escalator. Josie turned off the light.

Sensing agitation and perhaps a hint of fear in his voice, she returned the volley. "Oh yeah? Why don't you come down here and prove it, chicken shit!"

Carter threw his hand over her mouth, and she could feel his head shaking in disbelief.

Two rifle rounds sliced the air, the report reverberating up and down the subway tunnels with a crackling echo. Josie pulled Carter's hand away and waited for the noise to stop bouncing around. "You missed, asshole!"

More rounds fired, harmless but for the noise.

Once again, Josie waited for the echoes to subside. "I thought you never miss, *Ronan!*"

He remained silent, and she figured he was wondering how she knew his name. At last he said, "Go ahead and hide down there. You'll be dead either way."

*Maybe*, she thought, *but you'll never know.*

Josie inched her way to the edge of the platform, sweeping her toes out until she reached the ledge. Then she sat, flashed the beam at the tracks below for a moment, stowed the flashlight, and hopped down, grimacing at the jolt of pain in her right leg. She retrieved the light and made a circle on the ground as a target for Carter.

He slid on his butt, dangled his legs, and jumped down. "We aren't seriously going down that train tunnel, are we?"

"What else can we do?"

"Even that crazy asshole with the rifle is too chicken to come down here. What the hell, Josie? No one who goes down here ever comes back."

She shrugged. "We lived this long." She turned the beam toward the tunnel and started walking.

Carter looked behind, the space already enveloped in shadow. "Why not this way?"

"Because this way said 'Metro Center.' I like the way it sounds."

"I wish I never met you," he said, but Josie could tell it wasn't true.

She swept the beam around the tunnel to make sure they weren't being watched. She couldn't help but think that tangy scent on the air smelled a bit like blood.

# CHAPTER 26

Metro Center subway station did not exist. In its place was a scorched-black cave carved out by a massive explosion. The first two stations they had passed were carbon-scored and partly collapsed, with the remaining walls and platforms scarred by twisted hunks of metal, train wheels, and broken masonry that had come hurtling through the tunnels.

"Holy shit," Josie said, sweeping the flashlight beam along the piles of crumbled stone and metal that used to be the ceiling. Only a mangled crisscross of steel beams kept the immense collection of shattered stone and earth above from dropping onto their heads. Wherever the exit topside used to be, Josie saw no evidence.

She pressed her foot against a broad slab lying diagonally over a knot of metal and started to scale it, careful not to drop the flashlight and extra careful to secure her footing. The pain in her shin had faded to a dull throb, and she hoped to keep it that way. Once at the top of the debris hill, she shone the beam down the other side.

Carter called up to her. "Maybe we should turn back." His words bounced through the chamber.

"And then what?"

He shrugged and grabbed on to the slab, pulling himself up with a jerk. In moments he was beside her atop the twelve-foot high pile.

She aimed the light to the left, toward the opening of another train tunnel. "Looks like we have to go that way."

"What if it goes nowhere? We should turn back."

"I'm not going back to Baltimore."

"Yeah. I meant that train station back there. Those shooters probably gave up by now. We've been down here for, like, an hour."

Josie worked out a path and began her descent, testing each metal rod or chunk of masonry with her toes before putting her weight down. "I'm not giving that fucker the satisfaction of shooting me. You can to go back if you want."

Carter sighed again and followed. His long, gangly legs enabled him to catch up in moments. "You know we're totally fucked if you drop that—"

Josie let out a high-pitched chirp as a chunk of stone shifted under her. She sank into the empty space beneath it, instinctively grabbing for the slab next to her. The flashlight bounced free and rolled away. She watched in frozen horror as it accelerated toward a yawning gap in the debris. It caught on a bent loop of metal.

Carter gripped her by the arm and started to pull.

"Get the flashlight!"

He huffed and released her. Spreading his legs to straddle the wobbly slab, he leaned forward, holding himself up with a metal rod that jutted from a giant block of stone above. With his free hand he reached down for the flashlight. His fingers brushed the rubber grip, jarring it.

"Get it!"

"I'm getting it. And I'm not the one who dropped it, so cool your jets."

Carter dipped his right shoulder, supporting himself with his left arm, and looped his index finger and thumb around the flashlight. "Got it." He clawed his way to a standing position. "I'm holding it from now on."

Josie opted not to argue, instead using that energy to extricate herself from the crevice.

Once at the bottom and on solid ground again, Carter ran the beam over her. "Jesus Christ. Are you all right?"

Josie did a self-appraisal. Both arms were streaked with blood. Her shin was torn open anew, fresh blood mixed with the dusty paste made from old blood and bits of crumbled masonry. Her dress was torn. Somehow, her knife harness and blade were intact.

"Hey, look!" she said, reaching into the debris pile and withdrawing a cylindrical object from a gap. "Ginger ale!"

They consumed the can as they walked, Carter burping every few seconds until he got tired of being slapped. They soon came upon another station, destroyed and collapsed like the others. The sign above the platform, or what remained of the platform, read FEDERAL something, the second half too scuffed to decipher.

Carter circled the room with the flashlight beam. The path for the escalator had caved in. "We gotta find a way out of here soon."

Josie became aware of the blood running into her boot. She also noticed the flashlight had grown dim. "The next station," she said, the somberness in her own voice alarming her. Suddenly, she missed the sunlight as much as anything she had ever missed.

They trudged along the subway line for ten minutes, weary, agreeing to turn the flashlight off to save the batteries. In the dark, they used the rails for guidance.

Carter flicked the beam on and off.

"Turn it back on."

He did. "What?"

"What's that?"

Carter slapped his thigh. "A dead end. You're fucking kidding."

*Please no*, Josie thought. As they drew closer, though, she realized it was not a termination but the back end of a subway train, cold and dark and coated with powdered concrete. She inspected the space between the outer skin of the passenger coach and the tunnel wall. She might be able to squeeze along the outside, but not Carter.

"We have to go through."

"Whatever. I just want to get the hell out," Carter said. He hopped up, turned the handle, and yanked the door open. Then he pulled Josie up, and in they went.

The floor was a rumpled sea of mummified bodies in moth-eaten business clothes. Decayed, shriveled adults occupied the seats, some wearing hats, some leaning on strangers' shoulders. Some still holding tabloid newspapers dated June 10, others clutching tablets and smartphones with knotty, gray fingers. Josie knew that people sometimes fell asleep on buses and trains and wondered of any of these folks dozed through the end of the world.

Neither she nor Carter had moved. Perhaps it was the stillness. She imagined this place to be quite like the inside of a grave, no light and no air and untouched by anything resembling life.

The light flickered, and Carter slapped it against his palm. It brightened. "Can we keep going please?"

In all that had happened, with all she had lived through, Josie had never had to use deceased humans as a floor. Sure, what kid hadn't tripped over a corpse or put her hand in a maggoty mouth by accident, but she never had the time to think about what it meant. Now, with each foot pushing down on desiccated flesh, the feel of dry tissue compressing under her, the way the bones and joints rolled and shifted and popped, she began to fear the dead. She thought of her blood dripping off her fingertips and into their mouths, making them hungry. Her blood giving them just enough taste of life to resent her. The ones in the seats... maybe they were keeping so very still on purpose, waiting until they were between her and the door.

Such stillness.

Carter slipped and shot his arm out for balance, knocking a corpse's head off, which plopped at their feet. They both shrieked and sprinted for the other end of the coach. Josie fumbled for the handle, pushing it, unable to budge it until she realized she should have been pulling. She yanked. The door opened, and they scrambled through to the next coach.

Once across, she leaned on her knees, gasping, and forced a laugh. Carter fell against the door and took a deep breath. Then he shone the beam down the center aisle. "This one isn't so bad."

This time they had room to weave around the corpses, and the third car held fewer bodies still. Some even looked flat. Josie kicked at one, pushing around a suit jacket with nothing in it. "That's weird."

Carter flashed the beam on a leather jacket. He scooped it up, inspected it, handed the light to Josie, and put it on. "What do you think?"

"I think it's weird there's a bunch of clothes on the floor."

The next car was free of corpses, as was the fifth.

"Where did they all go?" Carter wondered aloud.

"I don't know," Josie said, "but we have to get going. These batteries are going fast."

Carter opened the door at the end of the car. "Sounds like a plan." He stepped into the motorman's cab. Josie, feeling the darkness creeping up on her, slipped in behind him.

"Where's the engineer?" The seat was empty.

Carter shrugged. "Dunno."

Josie sensed something odd about the sound of their voices. In such a tiny space, the noise should be close. She stuck her hand out, over the control panel, and felt air. "Windshield's gone."

"Well, that makes it easy," Carter said, stepping on the empty chair and climbing through the opening to the front of the train.

Once on the ground, he shone the light up for her to follow. She climbed through, gripped the window frame, and lowered herself, still disturbed about the missing glass. "Something strange is going—"

"Dude. Shut up." Carter pointed the flashlight. "Look."

Josie followed the beam. Along the side of the track, piled against the tunnel wall, were hundreds of human bones cleaned of meat. She crouched, running her fingers through the stack, feeling for a heavy one.

"What are you doing?"

She stood, clutching a man's femur. She tapped Carter's shoulder, put her finger to her lips to order silence, and motioned forward with the bone. She took a tentative step, then another, and her companion followed.

On the third step, the flashlight went out.

Josie took Carter by hand, and the pair inched forward with stifled breath for twenty-five feet, when Josie's keen ears told her to stop. She held her breath and reached up with her left hand to cover Carter's mouth.

She still heard breathing. They were not alone.

Carter whapped the flashlight against his palm. The beam popped to life.

Two figures with bluish, vein-webbed skin, shaggy hair, and gnarled fingernails crouched against the tunnel wall, gnawing on hunks of raw meat. The fresh crimson blood around their mouths and dripping from their chins seemed so stark beside this blue and gray underground world.

The section of flesh being devoured terminated in a human foot. A young human foot.

The light went out again. Carter smacked it one more time. The beam flickered to life, illuminating three more blue-skinned tunnel dwellers charging at Josie and Carter, gnarled hands outstretched, hissing and baring their teeth. Carter shined the light straight into their mad gray eyes, causing the cannibals to recoil.

Then the flashlight died for good.

Josie, with all the strength she possessed, swung the femur blindly in a wide arc, striking the lead attacker and sending it tumbling into the others. One of the monsters clawed at her boot. She brought her weapon down on it like a bludgeon. Then she gripped the leather sleeve of Carter's jacket and yelled, "Run!"

# CHAPTER 27

Shawnika Williams did not believe in ghosts. She really didn't.

If anyplace should be haunted, it would be this world cluttered with billions of corpses, where the dead sleep in every shadow, along every street, inside every house and apartment building. In cars and trucks and hot dog stands. Yet not one had ever emerged from a crack in the wall or caressed her with an ethereal finger. No ghosts, and no monsters, either, except for the human kind. She had given up on supernatural things.

So why did she hesitate? The machete in her left hand and the industrial flashlight in her right ought to be everything she needed for this excursion. Then again, what good would a machete be against ghosts?

She reminded herself: Shawnika Williams does not believe in ghosts.

Shawnika stood with the sun on her shoulders, staring into the gaping black hole. She'd ventured into thousands of dark places across the city looking for supplies, for food, for people.

For Tre.

But not the Metro. Kids said the subway was haunted. Kids said that if you went down, you never came back. Shawnika wanted nothing to do with the subway and stayed far away from it. But kids also said that ghosts came out of the subway in the dark and stole children. She'd looked everywhere for her brother, and she'd looked every day for over two years, but she'd never gone to the one place that made the most sense.

Shawnika meditated all week to prepare for her adventure. First she decided to hit the station closest to the White House— or at least the massive crater where it used to be—because that's where they were when Tre was abducted. Two stations east were caved in as well. Yesterday, she'd headed south to Federal Triangle station, and the entrance there was a pile of rubble. Whoever set off that bomb way back sure did a number.

Today, Smithsonian station had its turn. And here she stood, staring at the dark shaft cut into the earth, not caved in one bit. That meant she had to do it. She had to go down and look for Tre.

She chopped the air with her machete to get a feel for its weight and how it moved. She took a breath and thought about her brother needing her. "Now or never, kid," she said and marched down the stairs to the first landing. That's where the shadows began, cutting a clean line across the concrete. Beyond, the light gray steps faded to back.

Shawnika exhaled and planted her foot into the shadow. Another step. Another. Now no sunlight touched her.

"Tre?" she whispered, shaking her head at her own silliness. Somehow, if he were hanging out on the stairs at Smithsonian Station, he would have at least poked out to say hi once or twice in the past two and a half years.

She walked down to the next landing, the glow of sunlight now yards behind her. She listened, but a sudden breeze blowing down from above obscured any sound that could be vibrating up to her from below. At last, the wind died down, and she walked halfway to the next landing. She listened again. Silence.

"Ain't no ghosts," she said, taking three more steps. Then... something echoed up from the depths, like clapping. She backed up one step. "Hello?"

The clapping got louder.

Then it appeared.

For a moment, she remembered those times from her childhood when she believed Dracula or the Wolf Man to be hiding in her closet. Mama would check, and one hundred percent of the time, the scary monster pulled a no-show. Now, at age fourteen, she knew there were no monsters. So why was she seeing one?

The figure, long and gangly and powder white with a gaping maw and beady, mad eyes, bounded upward. Her heart pounding, Shawnika stumbled backward and crab-walked up the stairs, unsure whether to turn her back to it and run or to claw and punch and tear at the beast to at least give herself a fighting chance.

It ran right past her.

Shawnika jumped back to her feet and turned as the creature hit the sunlight and covered its face like a vampire. Then, more clattering from below. She faced the darkness once more to see a second phantom, even more horrible, coming at her, its long, gray hair pasted to its face, its arms and legs and ghostly dress streaked with dirt and blood.

Shawnika turned and ran up to the first landing and into the sunlight, next to the vampire, which she now realized was a dust-coated boy in a leather jacket and a pair of ratty Levis. As the ghost girl drew upon her, a third creature appeared from below in pursuit. Its skin was blue and covered by a network of veins, its mouth dripping with bright blood and its hands terminating in jagged yellow talons.

A real, honest-to-god monster.

The ghost girl held out her hand. Shawnika tossed the flashlight and reached for her, but the beast jumped and snatched a clump of the girl's hair in its clawed hand, yanking her back.

The ghost girl caught Shawnika's eye, pleading. Shawnika took two steps closer, grabbed hold of the monster's wrist, and pulled. It resisted, dragging the ghost girl down a step.

Shawnika remembered the machete in her left hand. She thought of the bastards who took Tre. She felt the snarl take over her face. Tugging the creature closer, she brought the blade down, cleaving its forearm in two. Emitting an inhuman wail, the monster tumbled into the black shaft.

The ghost girl ran, leaving Shawnika to stare at the blood dripping from her machete.

Up top, the boy shielded his eyes from the sun. "Goddamn it's bright up here."

Shawnika guided the sun-blinded ghost girl the rest of the way to the surface to her companion's side. The girl reached back, detangled the creature's severed hand from her hair, and whapped the boy across the back with it. "Thanks for leaving me down there, asshole." She tossed the hand away as if it were an empty bottle.

The boy threw his arms up. "It was fucking dark. I thought you were in front of me."

Shawnika wiped her machete on the withered, brown grass and sheathed it. She placed a gentle hand on the ghost girl's shoulder, turning her. The poor kid was cut to shreds and coated with powdered concrete. "Are you okay?"

"You have no idea," the ghost girl said, fingering the grit from below her left eye and flinging it. "It's been two fucking shitty days, let me tell you."

"Girl, you look a damn sight. We gotta get you and your friend cleaned up."

"Thank you, by the way," said the ghost girl. "I don't know what you heard, but that 'cannibals in the subway' shit is true."

Shawnika didn't want to think about what might have happened to Tre. "Why why why were you in the subway of all places?"

The ghost girl leaned on her knees to catch her breath. "Okay. First we got captured by a gang, then snipers killed them, then we hid in the sewer—"

"Don't forget to tell her about how you cooked rats for dinner last night," the boy said, trying to rub the cramp out of his side.

The ghost girl ignored him. "Then the snipers followed us to our hideout, and I saved *his* dumb ass for the hundredth time, then some weird Filipino kid gave us a ride on a train—"

Shawnika smelled bullshit. "A train."

The ghost girl gave her a look with one eye peeking out from under all that scraggly hair. "Yes. A train. You think I'm making that up after what you just saw? Anyway, the snipers hijacked the train, I crashed it on purpose, and they chased us, so we went into the subway because we knew nobody is bat-shit crazy enough to follow us down there."

The boy pointed at her. "I can vouch for everything she just said. That is by far the most insane chick you've ever met in your entire life."

Shawnika did not doubt that. "All right, then, crazy chick. Let's get you guys washed off. I'm Shawnika, by the way."

"I'm Josie. That's Carter."

The boy swiveled his head around. "Holy shit. The capitol building! We're in DC."

# CHAPTER 28

Josie didn't know a thing about this ten-foot-tall black chick, but she was too exhausted and hungry to do anything but drop dead on the spot or follow her. They walked for a good while in the blazing sun, and Josie had to find reserves to keep up with the girl's long strides. If school still existed, this girl would have killed it in volleyball.

"Your shin looks pretty bad," the girl said.

Josie took a gander. It did look bad. "I jumped off a crashing train."

"That you made crash."

"Well, some asshole had a gun pointed at me, which was about the third or fourth time that's happened in the past twenty-four hours, so I felt like it was his turn to eat a shit sandwich for once." Josie realized this was the first girl she'd spoken to in probably a year. "What's your name again?"

"Shawnika."

"It's pretty."

"Thanks!"

Shawnika lead them across a road and down a path to the side of a river. "Hop in and rinse all that grit off," she said. "Don't drown. My place is about five blocks from here. I'll be back with some towels and clothes and shampoo in ten minutes."

Josie frowned at Carter. "Turn around."

Shawnika asked her why she wore a dress instead of jeans. Josie hiked up the tattered bottom and revealed the switchblade. "So I can hide this and get it when I need it."

She laughed. "You are the hardest bitch I ever met. I thought I was tough, but you're half my size. What's with the boy's drawers?"

*How did this girl live so long being that blunt?* Josie wondered. "They're boxer briefs. I wear them so the knife harness doesn't slip." She glared at Carter one more time, and he turned away for real. She doffed the dress, crumpled it, and threw it into some dried-up bushes. Then she removed the knife and laid it close to the water's edge. To Shawnika she said, "You're really going to bring back clothes, right? Carter doesn't want to spend the rest of the day naked while I wear his stuff."

Shawnika waved. "I promise I'll be back in ten," and darted up the embankment.

Josie turned and put her foot in the water and then recoiled at the cold. The sun had cooked up a hot day, but it was October nonetheless.

"Just jump in," Carter said, grinning.

Josie growled, covered herself, and hopped into the soft current. The chill stung her wounds, but it also shot a jolt of energy into her body. She surfaced, spit the dusty water from her mouth, and took a fresh gulp. She went under again, rubbed her hair, and popped up in time to see Carter's pale white ass sticking up out of the water. She spun away. "Gross."

"Hey, there's fish down here," he said.

"Uh-huh."

As promised, Shawnika returned within the quarter hour carrying folded towels and clothes. She tossed Josie a bottle of HEAD AND SHOULDERS.

Josie hadn't used shampoo in six months, and it was awesome to have it again. She washed twice. In the middle of that, the current carried Carter closer to her, or he let it carry him more likely, and she shooed him away. He swam back upstream, where Shawnika had laid out a towel and some clothes for him on the withered grass along the bank. Shawnika retreated back to where Josie was washing off. "I got my back turned, Carter," she said, "so go on and get out when you're ready."

The two girls faced the bridge downstream as he dried off. After a few minutes, he shouted, "Hey. These are girls' clothes!"

Josie and Shawnika laughed. "Sorry, man," Shawnika said, hollering over her shoulder. "That's all I got. You're lucky my mama was a giraffe and gave me her DNA. At least they fit you."

"You can shout around here without getting shot at?" Josie asked, getting a sudden fit of the shivers.

"I ain't heard a gunshot in two months. You two are the first people I've seen in a week or more."

"Baltimore sucks compared to this. The water's all full of oil."

Shawnika shouted back to Carter. "You turn around now, you hear? Josie has to get out before she gets hypothermia. I'm watching you!"

Convinced Carter was behaving, Josie climbed out, leaving the boxers to drift downstream. Shawnika threw a towel around her and handed her a second one for her hair. Josie began to pat it dry, then lost patience and raked the towel over her head. "Well, look at that," Shawnika said. "You're a blondie. I thought you were gray haired all this time."

200

"Well, that's the subway for ya these days." Josie became aware Shawnika had gone silent and was staring at her face. "Yes, I only have one eye."

"I…I'm sorry. I wasn't sure with all the grime and blood."

"Don't worry. I know it freaks people out. You can have a big scar or a missing leg and people are like, 'oh,' but if you don't have an eye, it's this dramatic thing all of a sudden."

Shawnika handed her underwear, sweats, and a sweatshirt and placed a pair of running shoes beside her. "I'm sorry to look at you like that."

Josie slid into the bottoms first, figuring Carter was getting ready to sneak a peek, and then the pullover. "Don't tell Carter this, but that asshole who tried to shoot me today? That's the same asshole who shot my eye out three years ago."

"No wonder you train-crashed his ass."

Josie retrieved her switchblade and reattached the harness. Now that she was out of the cold water, the throbbing in her shin returned. "I think I got the worst of it, though."

\*\*\*

Shawnika's west DC hideout did not qualify as a hideout. With its floor-to-ceiling windows on the second floor and attached police station, it was the most obvious building on the street.

"You live in a library?"

Shawnika unlocked the door and held it for them. "Why not? The bottom half is like a brick fortress. I got plenty of books to read, and there's a courtyard for my greenhouse."

"You have a greenhouse? Me and Carter live under a dump truck."

Shawnika locked up. "No kidding. My dad drove one of them."

She led them to the second floor, where the bookshelves had been rearranged to block out a living space that was hidden from the outside. "I get plenty of light up here for my reading, and if things get crazy, I can hide in the police station. It never gets crazy, though. This is the nice part of DC, even still."

A small shelf near Shawnika's sleeping mat held a row of about twenty books. Josie scanned the spines. "*Introduction to Zen Buddhism. Principles of...Tay-oh-ism?*"

"It's pronounced *Dowism*. It's a Chinese philosophy about finding and flowing with the energy in the universe instead of resisting it."

"Like *Star Wars*?" Carter asked.

"I guess."

"You never saw *Star Wars*?"

Josie had read nothing but comic books for the past three years. Her and Carter's only common interest. She withdrew a book with a skinny bald dude on the front. "Who's Gandhi?"

"You don't know who Gandhi was? He was a pacifist who helped end British colonial rule in India and—"

"I'll take your word for it," Josie said, shoving the book in place. Just her luck to get saved by a future social studies teacher. "You got any food?"

"Have a seat at the table." Shawnika opened a cabinet and brought out cucumbers and tomatoes in a small basket. Josie and Carter dove for it, and she pulled it back. "Like humans, not like baboons."

Josie sat at the table across from Carter and folded her hands until Shawnika placed the basket in the center. Carter pursed his lips and took a cucumber with his pinky extended. Josie opted for a tomato. "I haven't had vegetables since...ever." The first bite sent a glob of tomato innards down her chin.

202

"Gandhi figured out how to get what he wanted without violence, and that's what I study. Passive resistance, nonviolence. I used to be like you, Josie, always ready for a fight. Someone pissed me off, I took her down. I'm looking for a better way for the future."

Carter took another bite of cucumber. "You just cut somebody's arm off with a machete."

Shawnika shrugged. "I didn't say I'm successful every day."

Josie glanced at the bookshelf. "You a Buddhist or something?"

"I'm working on it. Keeps me sane."

"No Jesus or whatever?" Josie didn't remember meeting a Buddhist before, except maybe that Filipino kid on the train this morning. *God, was that only this morning?*

"I used to be a Christian, but it doesn't make sense anymore with everything that happened. What about you?"

Josie didn't know anything about any of it, but she did know that a lot of dumb kids hid out in churches in the beginning, and they got robbed and beaten pretty fast. A church full of scared kids was a free-for-all if you were a gangster. "So how come you have four chairs around this table? Where's everybody else?"

Shawnika ignored part of the question. "The other chair belongs to Luz. You're wearing her clothes."

"She get shot or something?"

Shawnika's eyes became downcast. "No. She lived with me for a while, but she ran off with some gang that came through a few months back. Left all her shit here. She came from that gang life and had to go back, I guess. She lost everything else."

Josie didn't feel a rush of sympathy. "We all did. Fuck her."

"I almost killed her one night, a little over two years ago. She was at the lowest moment of her life, and I was accusing her of shit. She needed me, and I was being my bitch-ass self. But she forgave me without a word. I kinda miss her now."

A tear rolled down Shawnika's bronze skin. Josie opened her mouth and then hesitated. She didn't know what to say to crying people. "Hey. How about a tour?"

Shawnika wiped her face and stood. "Okay. What about him?"

Josie twisted backward. Carter had found a book on Marvel superheroes, and he munched a cucumber as he flipped pages. "He's fine." She took a cucumber for herself and bit into it. Pretty good for a vegetable.

Shawnika led her along the bookshelves, the backs of which faced the windows. Books filled the upper and lower shelves, and the middle held Shawnika's clothes and supplies. "Here's my shampoo and toothpaste and stuff. I'm trying to read up on how to make my own, because eventually all this shit will dry out."

The next shelf held feminine products. Josie yanked out a cardboard box filled with tampons and started fishing around. "Whoa! Where did you get these?"

"Public restroom. I smashed the dispenser open."

Josie put them back. "I actually haven't needed one in, like, three months anyway."

Shawnika nodded toward Carter. "Did you guys…"

Josie waited for the second half of the question and then realized what Shawnika was asking. "Ew. No!"

Shawnika stifled a laugh. Carter sighed without looking away from his book. "I'm right here, dude. I can hear you."

The shelf above the tampons held books on world history. Josie recognized the swastika on the spine of one and took it down. She scanned the cover. "*The Nazis. A Complete History of the Third Reesh.*"

"It's pronounced *Rike.*"

Josie flipped through and recognized many of the symbols and imagery. "My mom's boyfriend was a white-power Nazi."

Shawnika's voice rose a half octave. "What!"

"He had all this stupid Hitler shit tattooed all over his chest and neck and arms."

"Why on Earth did your mom date a Nazi?"

Josie replaced the book. "Because she was a white-trash idiot."

"Don't say that. She's your mom."

"She used to fuck Hector with the door open while I watched TV. She married my dad, who went to jail for stabbing somebody. For all I know he got out already, and I trampled over his dead body a dozen times without knowing it. And this is the first fresh cucumber I've ever had."

"Aw, honey. I'm sorry." Shawnika tried to hug her but backed away when Josie stiffened. Hugging made Josie feel like her arms were pinned down.

Still, something about this girl made Josie feel like talking. "Can I tell you something? That day—the day they all died—I watched Hector drop dead right in front of me. You talk to kids and they all tell you how horrible it was, how they cried and freaked out when they saw the grown-ups die. You know what I thought when Hector face-planted? '*Good*.'"

Shawnika stared, breathing it all in. Then she looked to her left to the third bookshelf, which held the combs and spray bottles and lotions. "Say. I got an idea."

# CHAPTER 29

Shawnika moved a chair closer to the window to make the most of the remaining sun. She set a spray bottle, a comb, and a tube of hand lotion on a library cart. Then she dragged Josie over by the arm and sat her down. Carter half watched over the top of his book like a kitten peeking through the leaves of a houseplant.

"What are we doing?" Josie said.

Shawnika gathered up Josie's long, tangled clumps of hair and hung them over the back of the chair. "I'm going to make it harder for cannibals to grab your hair."

"Don't cut it. I want it long."

Shawnika pumped a fine mist of water over Josie's head. "I'm not. Just relax." She squeezed out a blob of lotion on her index finger and rubbed it into a knotty clump. "Sorry. I don't have hair stuff right now so I gotta use lotion."

Hair prepped, she began to work the comb up from the bottom, stroking out the little tangles. Josie sat motionless. Shawnika moved the comb sideways, breaking up the big knots bit by bit, working herself around to Josie's left side, the side with vision. Here she looked like the most apple-pie American kid anywhere: High forehead. Wispy eyebrows. Petite, upturned nose. Thin, childlike mouth. Delicate chin. Freckles across her cheeks.

Shawnika had never seen anything so hard and cold in so unlikely a package. So much pain hiding behind that singular eye. An eye so unlike the rest of her face: deep green with dark lines in the iris, dense and mysterious and impenetrable like an ancient forest. A portal hidden by a heavy jungle canopy to keep everyone else out of the black and lonely place inside.

She teared up again and swung to the back so Josie couldn't see. Sometimes Shawnika got tired of all the suffering. Sometimes she got tired of feeling like she'd lived a hundred years already.

She sniffled. "You hangin' in there, kid?"

"I'm thirteen."

"Ooh. I'm sorry. You hangin' in, Grandma?" Knots removed, Shawnika moved to Josie's right. She always started on the right. A neurotic thing, like putting a certain shoe on first. She ran the comb through Josie's hair, parting a small section away from the rest, following the line of her ear down to the nape of her neck.

Carter put down his book and came over to watch.

Shawnika applied another dab of lotion and further divided the little section of hair into three smaller clutches. "Wow. Your hair is a dream for this. So straight." Then she set to work.

"What are you doing?"

"Cornrows."

Shawnika's long, thin fingers began a waltz, weaving one narrow length of hair over another over another. One two three, one two three, one two three. With precision and speed she ran the pattern down Josie's scalp, finishing off with a tiny French braid that landed on her shoulder blade.

"Holy shit," was Carter's contribution.

"I thought this was going to hurt."

"Not if you do it right it doesn't," Shawnika said. "I did this for my cousins and friends about a million times, and none of them ever complained once." She stood and started partitioning the next section of hair. "So what's your last name, Josie?"

"It doesn't matter."

*This girl must have come from a womb full of ice*, Shawnika thought. "Carter. What's your last name?"

"Glass."

Josie laughed and started to turn her head, but her stylist pushed it back in place. Staring across the room at the book-shelves, she said. "Carter *Glass*?"

"So what? What's your last name?"

"Revelle."

Shawnika shook her head. "Carter Glass and Josephine Revelle. You two did not know each other's last names until this very minute?"

"No one calls me Josephine anymore."

Carter leaned over the back of his chair. "I'm totally calling you Josephine from now on."

Josie flipped him the middle finger.

Shawnika started weaving the pattern again, her fingers dancing without effort. "I'm Shawnika Williams, since none of you asked."

"Shawnika," Carter said. "How come so many black people are named Williams?"

"I don't know. Ask the slavers who brought us here in chains and erased our history, destroyed our culture, and took away our identities."

Carter mumbled something unintelligible and returned to the comfort of his superhero book.

"Nice one, Peter Cottontail," Josie said.

Shawnika failed to stifle a smirk. "Where you from, girl?"

"Baltimore. I was born in North Carolina, but I don't remember it. Except for visiting relatives a couple times." She hesitated and then asked, "You?"

*Now that's how you have a conversation,* Shawnika thought. "Born in Philadelphia, moved to DC. Atlanta for a bit, chasing work. Then DC again, where we got really poor. Mom lost her job and ended up working in a diner. My dad worked in...eh, you don't care about all that."

"No. It's fine," Josie said, but she didn't ask for more. "I want to leave the city. It's dead. I'm sick of scrounging for food all the time."

Shawnika stopped braiding. "Yes. That is a problem. Pretty soon there will be nothing left to scavenge. Ain't no trucks with milk and bread coming in."

Josie tilted her head back. "I want to live on a beach. A good one like in North Carolina. That's where I want to go."

Shawnika pushed her head back in place and resumed weaving. "I don't like sharks."

Josie laughed. "There aren't any sharks. We can catch all the crabs and fish we want, though. We can steal a boat."

Shawnika thought about the beach. Maybe that would work. Because as much as she was okay living in the library, winter was coming again, and her greenhouse would collapse under a heavy snow. The city was dying, the earth slowly swallowing it. Josie was right about it coming time to leave. The only thing left to do was...

Find Tre.

Shawnika finished the cornrows in silence, racing the fading sunlight. She lit a tray of votive candles and handed Josie a mirror. "What do you think?"

Josie stared, angling her head left and then right. Her face bloomed.

Carter shuffled over. "Dude. I have never seen you smile before."

Shawnika, standing behind her, leaned up to her left ear. "I think someone just fell in love with you."

Josie swiveled toward her. "Let's move to a farm. We'll find a car somewhere in a garage and drive west. Or south. I want to grow vegetables."

Carter took a step closer. "Can I come?"

"No, dummy. You have to stay here and make sure no one steals the Washington Monument."

Shawnika wasn't quite sure what to think of this new, improved Josie. "You want to live on a farm. What happened to the beach?"

"Farms are awesome. We can have steaks and potatoes and cucumbers whenever we want."

"I don't know."

"Come on. What could go wrong on a farm?"

# CHAPTER 30

Grace stared down the double barrel of Tucker's shotgun while the cows stood by and did nothing but chew their stupid cud. *Creeps! I fed and brushed you today!*

"I repeat, and I hope Mr. Remington here helps clarify, you *will* marry my brother tonight."

Mariel, Tucker's underdressed wife, wrapped her hands around his waist from behind and laid her head on between his shoulder blades. "You can't point a gun at the bride and expect her to be all in for a wedding, dear. Girls want to be excited on their wedding day. Let's just do it tomorrow morning."

Lucas, the groom, stood against a support beam some ten feet away, his hands fidgeting. "She doesn't have to if she doesn't—"

"Shut up! Both of you. We're having this wedding right here and right now." Tucker lowered the ancient shotgun, clamped a hand around Grace's arm, and shook her to get a feel for her weight. "This young lady is good stock. We're gonna rebuild the Earth, and we're starting right here by getting a wife for Lucas."

Grace gave up on the cows uniting to save her. She also opted not to say, *I'll guess you'll just have to shoot me, then* because she didn't want to get shot. She glanced sideways and sized up Lucas. At least he seemed nice. "If I have to, I have to."

Tucker leaned on the rifle as if it were a cane and smiled. "That's more like it! Mariel, go get Grace here a nice dress. Not one of those whore outfits you wear, either. My brother is not going to marry a slut."

Mariel rolled her eyes and sashayed toward the barn door. "You don't seem to mind my whore outfits any other time."

Up until fifteen minutes ago, Grace loved nothing more than the smell of a barn full of hay and animals. That was before she found out the chicken dinner Mariel cooked was made from *her* chickens. They killed Clucky and Pecker, and when she said *I hate you* a dozen times through tears and spit at them, that's when Tucker said it was time Lucas took a wife.

Grace got scared and tried to run, but Tucker dragged her out to the barn. Then she refused the marriage, and Mariel yanked her around by the hair while Tucker retrieved his shotgun from on the workbench.

He pointed it at her face and said what he said, and now she hated the smell of hay and horses and cattle more than anything.

They all stood there in the center of the barn, not talking, until Mariel returned from the house with a frilly yellow Easter dress. "Best I got," she said, holding it up for Grace's approval. "Sorry it ain't white. You're still a virgin, ain't you?"

Tucker laid the rifle across his shoulder. "Beggars can't be choosers."

Grace did not appreciate being discussed in this way. She glared at Tucker, who mocked her expression with an exaggerated mirror of it.

Mariel held the dress against Grace's shoulders, eyeballing for fit. "This was mine. I wasn't much older than you are now when they all died. I think it'll go on fine."

Grace sagged. Why were people like this?

"Well, put it on," Mariel said.

"Why did you kill my chickens?"

She shrugged. "They was just chickens. Who cares?"

"They were *my* chickens!" Grace felt her face heat up, and her vision clouded over with tears once again. She didn't even get to say good-bye.

Mariel turned to Tucker. "This girl is in no condition to get—"

Tucker swung the rifle around and unleashed a round into the side of the barn. The girls screamed and jumped back as the report echoed around the room, and the animals sent up a chorus of alarmed moos and neighs. Tucker cocked the rifle, sending the shell casing flying. "Put her in that motherfucking dress right now. I'm tired of fucking around. The wedding happens in exactly one minute."

***

"Dearly beloved," Tucker said, standing at the west end of the barn, surrounded by a semicircle of flickering beeswax candles shaped sort of like Christmas trees. "We are gathered here today to witness the union of Lucas McLevy and Grace...what's your name?"

Grace muttered "Cavanaugh" between gritted teeth and did her best to stare at nothing. She failed to notice Lucas doing the same.

"Between Lucas McLevy, my brother, and Grace Cavanaugh in holy matrimony. We're sorry, Lord, that we're doing this in a barn, but you saw fit to burn the church down last year, so we gotta make do."

Grace doubted that God approved of people being forced to marry at gunpoint.

"But we thank you, holy father, for sending us this beautiful angel. We was pretty down last week when we realized that Mariel was cursed with a barren womb—"

Mariel cut in. "Hey! My womb is fine. You're firing blanks."

Tucker gazed toward the crossbeam and shook his head. "Anyway, we were down, and then, by the miracle of your grace, no pun intended, this angel fell right out of the sky on Thursday—"

"It was Tuesday."

Tucker blew a jet of air out his nose. "Jesus, woman! Shut. The. Fuck. Up. Anyway, brave little Gracie here fell out of the sky just in time to lift our spirits and to become the devoted wife to my dear Lucas, who…"

Tucker began to ramble on about his brother, but Grace didn't hear it. She did not fall out of sky. She *landed*, and she stuck the landing like a pro. And now she felt sorry that she had. That long, wide stretch of road, free of smashed cars and debris, next to a field of real, live cows. A farmhouse with a barn beyond the tree line. She had to land. She'd dreamt it so many times. And they were nice at first.

"So, if anyone objects to this union, speak now or forever hold your peace."

Grace blurted it out. "I do!"

Tucker stared straight ahead, holding open a bible from which he had yet to read a word. "Save that line a minute, Gracie. You're gonna need it." He turned to his brother. "Lucas, do you have the wedding bracelet?"

Lucas faced Grace. Tucker reached over and nudged her. She pivoted, her heart hammering at the inside of her rib cage. She tried to swallow.

Mariel sniffled. "So beautiful." She lowered the six-shooter she had pointed at Grace's back, stowed it under her belt, and wiped the tears away.

"Lucas. Do you, Lucas, take this little angel here, Grace Cavanaugh, to be your wife? Do you promise to cherish and all that?"

Lucas's head dropped, and his chin pressed into his chest. His looked like he just lost a baseball game 12–0. "Sure. Whatever."

Grace's arms hung like dead snakes. Panic decayed into numbness. She rolled her head in Tucker's direction, wondering what the hell was going to happen when she told him to go jump off a bridge.

Tucker cleared his throat and shifted his weight. "Gracie already said 'I do' a second ago, so that's good enough. Lucas. The bracelet?"

*Hey, wait a minute!*

Lucas removed a rainbow-colored friend bracelet, woven from shiny embroidery thread, from his shirt pocket. He offered a disinterested glance at Grace. "Well?"

She stomped her foot, huffed, and held out her left hand. Lucas tied the bracelet on.

"I now pronounce you man and wife!"

Mariel bent down, picked up a bucket, and heaved a fountain of dollar-store confetti paper. She jumped and hooted as it rained down around them.

"All right then. We've had enough for today. Gracie can come out and clean this tomorrow morning first thing, right before she starts milking the cows." Tucker pinched out the candle flames and then put one arm around Grace and one around his brother

215

and guided the couple toward the barn doors. Mariel led the procession facing backward, smiling and clapping and vocalizing the *Wedding March* melody.

At the door, Gracie turned back to get a look at the site of her wedding, a cow barn illuminated by a propane generator. Not exactly her fantasy.

*****

Upstairs in the farmhouse, Tucker opened the door to the spare bedroom and pushed Grace and Lucas inside. "Now don't come out 'til you make a baby!" His laugh resonated down the hallway. "Seriously, I reversed the doorknob today. That means it locks from the outside, and I put some old boards full o' rusty nails under the window. It's a twenty-foot drop. Don't get funny ideas about running away. If you behave for a week, I'll extend your privileges."

Lucas, whose despondent gaze had not changed for the past twenty minutes, shoved the door closed in his brother's face. Tucker pounded once on the door and said, "Start making a baby," his voice muted by the heavy oak. Grace heard the click of the lock cylinder.

The newlyweds stood there, not moving or acknowledging each other. Grace searched for the right words to tell him she had no interest in baby making when Lucas said, "Don't worry. I'm not going to touch you."

She sighed. "Really? 'Cause I'm just not ready for that kind of—"

Lucas sat in on the edge of the bed. "I said don't worry about it. I fucking hate my brother's guts, and if I had somewhere to go I'd leave right now."

"I could drop you off somewhere. I've got a plane."

Lucas didn't respond. Grace sat next to him, feeling the texture of her bracelet. "Thanks for the bracelet anyway. Where did you get it?"

"I made it."

"No kidding! It's pretty. You made it for me?"

"No."

Grace shrugged. "Oh."

"I made it for my ex."

"You have an ex-wife?"

Lucas laughed, but without humor. "No. Tucker didn't approve and ended it. With a shotgun, which is his modus operandi for getting his way."

"That's horrible. What was her name?"

"Joshua."

Grace's brain backtracked to see what she'd missed. "Hold on a sec. You said…" Then it clicked. "Ohhhhhhh."

Lucas slapped the tops of his thighs. "Welcome to paradise."

"Do they have a lot of gay people in Pennsylvania?"

"How should I know? This is West Virginia."

"It is? Crap. I thought I was flying north. I never wanted to come back here." Damn it. She'd had enough surprises for one day.

"Man, when we saw that plane land a couple days ago, we thought Armageddon was over and adults were here to take us away. Then some teenage girl climbs out. I admit I had a non-romantic crush on you for a minute. That's some shit, flying around like that."

"I told you. I'll take you away from here. I'm a good pilot."

"You also told me you were flying in the wrong direction. I'm not sure that qualifies as good."

He said it like a gentle tease more than an insult. She crossed her arms in mock disapproval. "Let's see you get that thing off the ground. Whatever direction I go, I can still get us airborne. It's not exactly like riding a tricycle, you know."

Lucas laid a brotherly arm on her shoulder. "Grace. Tucker is not going to let us leave. We're prisoners."

Grace nodded. She liked Lucas, but she thought it best not to tell him about the gun that had fallen out of Mariel's shorts in the barn and lay covered in homemade confetti.

# CHAPTER 31

"They have no idea what the hell happened here. We're still the same old twinkle as far as they're concerned."

Josie reclined in the deck chair, gazing at a patch of stars. A dry breeze swept over the roof of the police station. She pulled the blanket up to her shoulders.

Shawnika angled her own backrest to get a better view. "Sometimes I see satellites circling over. We never saw 'em before because of all the lights. Now they serve no purpose, but they keep going 'round and 'round."

Josie sat up. Low on the horizon, many miles away, a pink hue reflected off the haze in the atmosphere. "What's that? A fire?"

"I don't know. It's been like that for a while. I can't get high enough to see past the tree line." Shawnika took a sip from her water bottle. Over her right ear, two cornrows meandered this way and that, too thick in some spots and too skinny in others. Josie did her best on Shawnika's hair but gave up when the light got too low and her fingers started to ache. Shawnika told her it was normal to get sore hands the first time. "So what's the deal with Carter? He's totally in love with you."

Josie shrugged. Carter was...whatever. "I'm not interested. Anyway, look at me. I'm a walking scab." More than once, recently, it occurred to her that Cara had already had sex a bunch of times at thirteen, Josie's age. Cara also used to talk about the Breast Fairy, who as of yet had not intervened in Josie's life. "I think there's something wrong with me."

"I read this psychology book, and this researcher, I forget his name, came up with this thing called the Hierarchy of Need."

Josie couldn't get over that Shawnika read books like that without being made to by teachers. "Yeah?"

"It's like, if you think about a homeless guy—"

"We're all homeless."

"I'm talking about before. You might think he's lonely. But his brain don't care about being lonely because he has no food. He doesn't even care about living in a cardboard box. Once he gets food, then he cares about living in a box. Then, he moves into a shelter. Now he has food and a roof. Then he starts feeling lonely. In other words, you only care about the next level of need, not the levels over that."

"Great. I'm a homeless guy."

"So maybe you can stay here. Then you'll have food and shelter, and then maybe Carter starts to look more cute to you."

"Carter's a dork."

Shawnika waved her off. "How often do you meet a boy who you can trust like that?"

"Yeah, well, he's still a dork. Anyway, why are you trying to hook me up with Carter?"

"I want you to have some happiness in your life. You're carrying around way too much pain."

"Okay, Dr. Williams. But I don't think we can stay here."

Shawnika turned toward her. "Why? You got a place that's dry with a roof, and there's no snipers, and you got books and good company."

Josie felt a queer melting sensation. No one had ever wanted her around before. "I mean 'we' as in you, me, and Carter. We should leave."

Shawnika sank back into her chair. "What's wrong with here?"

Josie didn't feel cold anymore. She sat up again and put her bare feet down on the tarred roof of the police station. "My mom and my sister died over three years ago. I stayed in Baltimore for no reason except I didn't know I had a choice. I grew up by myself. I've been running from snipers and eating cat food and crawling around in basements like a rat for no reason. Baltimore is dead. DC is dead. There's no food. There's no reason to be here. We could live on a farm and have a well and cows and grow tomatoes. What the hell are we doing trying to live in a concrete graveyard? It hasn't even rained for three months. You see all the dust everywhere."

"My. Those cornrows have you wound up."

Josie glanced up at the patch of stars, looking for the right words. "All this time, I ran and hid because I didn't want to die, not because I cared about being dead. Know what I mean? It's instinct, like when you poke at a bug and it circles around in a panic trying to stay alive, even though it doesn't really understand what's happening 'cause it's just a bug. But today, when me and Carter were coming through those subway tunnels...I had to walk on dead people. The whole floor was dead bodies. And the way they crunched under my feet. It was like they were nothing. Just some dried-up nothing, lying on the ground in the dark, like it didn't matter that they were ever here. I don't want to spend my time running and scrounging and being covered in dirt and blood and then just die in a corner and no one will ever know I existed. I want to be something. Start something. With you and Carter. But a dead, dried-up city is not the place."

Shawnika leaned over and hugged her. Josie let her this time. "I'm glad I met you, Josephine Revelle. I want to go, but I can't."

"Why?"

"Because of my brother, Tre. He's out there, missing. He might be dead, but he might not, and I can't leave until I find him. And if I leave, every day I'm going to go to bed wondering if he came looking for me and I abandoned him."

"Where do you think he went?"

"I don't know. I've looked everywhere in this city but one place. And it's the place that makes the most sense. Everybody says they come out at night and steal children, and that's how it happened."

Josie patted her shoulder. "There was nobody who looked like you hanging out with those cannibals, if that's what you're trying to say."

"That's the only place left, though. Those tunnels. And I'm too scared."

Josie still had one eye to stare with. "I'm not scared of anything anymore. Look at my face. I survived getting shot point-blank. I was trying to save my sister from being raped, and she ended up getting killed because of me. So, when I die, I at least want to die for a reason. Tomorrow, you, me, and Carter are going into those tunnels and finding your brother. And if he's not there, we'll look until we find him. Then all four of us are going to start a farm."

Shawnika dabbed her eyes with the corner of her blanket. "Tomorrow?"

"Tomorrow we are going to find your brother."

# CHAPTER 32

**October 11 (The Last Day)**
**9:15 a.m.**

Grace's eyes fluttered open to the sound of a door being unlocked.

She inhaled the scent of clean sheets and a soft down pillow. As the space around her came into focus, she saw powder-green walls with white crown molding and an antique night table painted white, chipped in spots.

*Where am I?*

The door opened. "What the hell is she still doing in her wedding dress? I thought I told you to start making babies."

Tucker.

"Hey. Girl on the bed. Get the fuck up. It's after nine for Christsakes. You are not exempt from chores."

Grace rolled onto her back and sat up in time to see Lucas pop out of a reading chair positioned in the corner near a tall, narrow bookshelf. "Don't talk to my wife that way," he said. He thrust out his narrow chest but stayed more than an arm's length from his brawny older brother.

Tucker smirked. "Okay, baby boy. You're right. I shouldn't have disrespected you. But…those cows aren't going to put themselves to pasture. So get your lovely wife out of bed and put her to work."

With that, he left.

Lucas turned to Grace. "Sorry about him. I should have said sorry about him a dozen times already, but I was preoccupied."

Grace wriggled off the bed. "That's fine. You probably wanted to marry me even less than I wanted to marry you."

He laughed. "Well, if I am forced to marry a girl, I could do worse than you. Although thirteen is kinda young when you're almost sixteen."

"Let's not go there."

"Let's not."

After a breakfast of potatoes and homemade tea, Tucker led Grace outside, still in her yellow Easter dress but with sneakers on and a pullover sweatshirt over top for protection against the crisp, dry October morning. Mariel followed behind holding a butcher knife.

The dust of parched soil danced in swirls as they kicked up loose driveway stones on the way down to the barn. Tucker glanced eastward, between the house and the empty horse stables, shielding his eyes from the morning sun. "If we don't get some rain soon, that well is toast."

"What about the cow's milk? We can drink that," Mariel said.

Tucker snorted. "Woman, if the cows don't have water, they aren't making any milk."

"Well, I don't know. I didn't grow up on a farm."

Grace thought Mariel must be some kind of idiot. And then she shuddered at the thought of sympathizing with Tucker McLevy.

They arrived at the barn door. Tucker unlocked the padlock, removed the chain, and swung the door open. "Follow me."

Inside he pointed to the old heifer in the first stall. "Since you live here, you might as well know their names. That's Bessie."

"How original," Grace muttered.

"Yeah, well, that's Bessie, and over there on that half wall is a plastic container. Make sure there ain't no hay in the container, and then milk Bessie. Don't spill it, or I'll give you a whooping, because Lucas sure as hell don't have the stones for it."

"She's just a kid, Tuck."

"Exactly. She's just a kid, so she gets a whooping for spilling milk just like I did when I was a kid. When she's eighteen, no more whooping because she'll be a woman, and I don't hit women."

Grace moved to retrieve the bucket. At least spending time with the animals would be okay. Maybe she'd have time to brush Katydid, the sickly nag in the last stall, later. If there was a later.

Tucker wasn't finished. "After you milk Bessie, I want you to clean up all that confetti on the floor. Then take these other cows out of the stalls and line 'em up. I'm gonna show you how to take them out to pasture all neat and tidy, but first I gotta go take a dump."

Mariel heaved a sigh and shook her head.

"What? You know this morning air makes me have to shit."

Grace placed the bucket under Bessie and pulled up a short milking stool, but then she caught the animal's eye. She leaned on her and began to stroke her flank. "That's a good girl."

Tucker looked on with approval. "That's right. She'll like you." He turned to his wife. "You guard her while I'm in the toilet. If she tries to run, shoot…Goddamn it, Mariel. Why are you carrying a knife?"

"I can't find the gun."

"Jesus Christ almighty. Where is it?"

She waved the knife around. "Do you know what 'I can't find it' means?"

Tucker dragged her outside and locked Grace in the barn with only two small windows for light. She heard his muffled voice ordering Mariel back to the house to look for the six-shooter and demanding to know where Lucas was hiding. Something about having to work on a tractor, but the sound faded before the sentence ended.

"I'm sorry, Bessie. Maybe another time," Grace said. Then she hurried to the confetti pile, kneeled, and started running her hands through it.

***

Tucker returned to the barn with Mariel at his side and the old Remington slung over his shoulder. "I swear, girl, you'd better find that thing. You have until noon." He handed her the rifle and unlocked the chain.

"Or what?"

"Or something," he said, swinging the doors open. Just as the wood smacked against the cinderblock stopper, three rounds from a six-shooter fired in rapid succession. An explosion of moos followed, and Tucker got knocked on his ass by a stampede of cattle.

He rolled over and leapt to his feet, letting out a roar, his head swiveling back and forth between his escaping cows and the thirteen-year-old girl sitting atop a bareback Katydid. She trained Mariel's gun on him.

He growled with rage and stomped. "You little fuck! Mariel, shoot that bitch while I get them cows rounded up." With that, he tore off after his animals.

Mariel took step inside the barn and hoisted the Remington up. "You get off that horse, or I'll shoot you dead, girlie."

"I'll shoot you first," Grace said. She had no intention of shooting anyone. She already felt as low as she could for shooting those cows in the rump, but Mariel didn't know that.

"Honey, there were only three bullets in that pistol, and you spent all of 'em. Now get down off the horse before I blow your head off."

Was she bluffing? Grace hadn't thought to inspect the cylinder before. But as she mulled over whether to surrender and take the punishment that would no doubt follow, she noticed the shotgun's barrel sway. Mariel jerked it back up into position and fought to hold it there. That side-by-side double barrel surely weighed a lot.

"Last warning. I said get down."

Grace realized the butt was against Mariel's right boob instead of her shoulder. The barrel was drifting high. If Mariel squeezed the trigger now…

"Yah!" Grace shouted, throwing the gun away and pounding her heels as hard as she could into the nag's flanks. She threw her arms around Katydid's neck and held tight as the horse charged.

Mariel recoiled at she fired, and the shotgun's stock hammered into her chest and threw her against the door jam. The shot missed the horse by a foot, tearing up the underside of the roof instead. Grace glanced down as she sailed past, catching a glimpse of Mariel writhing on the floor and clutching at her sternum.

Onto the stone driveway the nag carried her, straight into the cloud of dust kicked up by the stampede. The wretch of a horse still had some life, galloping so hard Grace began to slide down the animal's smooth back. She pulled tighter, her arms beginning to ache.

As she was moments from sliding off the back, the ground dipped, and Grace was slung forward, almost somersaulting over the animal's head. She dug her face against Katydid's ragged mane and let gravity hold her. In a moment, the ground leveled off. The dust cloud having moved off in a different direction, Grace took a peek. The Piper! It was just a quarter mile ahead through a line of trees.

The old horse slowed to a trot. Using the mane for a grip, Grace looked back but only saw a wall of brown dust. Within a few more paces, Katydid was spent and came to a stop. "No!" Grace kicked the animal's flank but got no response other than a snort.

She jumped off, kissed the horse on the neck, and sprinted for her airplane. She was halfway there when she heard a buzzing noise rise over the still air. A dirt bike.

She slowed, whirling to locate the rider. Nothing. Just sickly Katydid, standing in the gravel path. Still, the sound grew louder. Was it Lucas, hoping to get away from his crazy brother for good?

Grace fled into a gully, probably a stream before the drought, and clawed her way up the bank. Darting between two maple trees, she stumbled onto the asphalt. She used her momentum to roll back onto her feet, circled the Piper, and hoisted herself onto the wing. She fumbled to open the door and fell into the craft once she did. The smell of chickens swirled around her like a ghost.

From under the seat she retrieved the key, shoved it in the ignition, and hit the master switch. One…two…three. Turn.

The fuselage shook like mad. "Come on!"

The propeller kicked into motion. She sighed and started to give it throttle. The Piper inched forward. Then she cut back.

What if Lucas was trying to reach her before she left? What if she could help him get away?

She stood up to peer down the empty highway before her. Then, from a break in the trees yonder, the dirt bike popped in the air, bounced once, and circled to a stop. The rider alighted, carrying the Remington. Tucker.

He pumped it in the air with aggression. He aimed it at her, sure and steady. He was not going to miss.

Grace heard nothing over the engine's thunder, but something caught Tucker's attention. His head swiveled just as Lucas burst from the trees and brought a shovel down over the shotgun, knocking it to the road. He swung his arm toward Grace, a gesture that said, "Go." Tucker, enraged, grabbed his brother by the shirt and brought a heavy fist down on him.

Grace wanted to run him down, but hitting Tucker and the dirt bike would be the end of the Piper. So she hit the rudder pedal, adjusted the throttle, and swung the plane the other way. "I'm sorry, Lucas."

Twenty-five seconds later she pulled the yoke, and the Piper Cherokee lifted her into the sky.

She left the throttle out, roaring over the countryside at full speed with nowhere to go. As long as she was away from Tucker and Mariel and all those cows and that stupid barn. Tucker called her an angel who fell from the sky. Unlikely he would ever say that again.

Once she caught her breath and the adrenaline flow faded, she remembered she was piloting a damn plane. She checked her gauges. Shit. Less than half a tank.

She pushed the throttle in and slowed to minimum airspeed to save fuel. Somehow in the next two hundred miles, she had to find an airstrip at a real airport and hope another Piper Cherokee or something else that used the same fuel was parked there and hadn't gotten water in the tank. And right now, she had no idea where she was. Somewhere over West Virginia.

Grace cruised for a half hour, checking her altimeter, monitoring the fuel level, and gazing out the port window for an airstrip. She passed over small clusters of houses, a main street, a highway with a Target, and a McDonalds. After all this time, cars and trucks still lay scattered across every road. Millions of them, rotting in the sun for three and a half years, useless yet preventing her from setting down.

The flat ground gave way to hills, and the hills became the Appalachians. Not exactly the Alps, but just as useless for landing a plane.

Maybe she should have stayed on the farm. Milked cows. Picked tomatoes. Dug up carrots. It wouldn't have been the end of the world. Tucker would have softened up if she had cooperated. Too late now.

Grace craned her neck to see over the cockpit controls and get a sense of what lay ahead. And she saw something she hadn't for months: Rain clouds. No good flying into that. She banked left. Twenty miles ahead, a massive storm had begun to roil. She banked again, now going back the way she had come. More heavy clouds. The weather system was closing in around her.

She banked one last time, the only direction left to her, and let out the throttle, heading full speed for the patch of blue sky ahead. She prayed to the Almighty for a place to land before the storm caught her. Or she ran out of fuel.

# CHAPTER 33

**11:45 a.m.**

"In the spring, you couldn't even stand here," Shawnika said. "The grass came up to your knees, and it was full of snakes and mice."

The three of them had come down Virginia Avenue and were cutting diagonally across the mall past the Washington Monument. After a rainless summer, the brown grass lay flat, half covered in powdery dirt. Carter pointed toward the Air and Space Museum. "You ever look for your brother in there?"

Shawnika laughed. "Of course. Up until recently, there was always boys running around in there, climbing on the planes and everything." The scariest place she ever searched: the art museum. All those eyes following her.

Josie, wearing a clingy blue evening dress with full sleeves she and Shawnika had discovered in a locker at the police station, flipped the machete as they walked, catching it by the handle again and again. "Carter just wants an excuse to play in there."

"When I was a kid, I was terrified I would somehow end up in one of those rockets or planes and it was going to take off by accident. My mom had to drag me in there." *Now I'm about to climb over a bunch of dead bodies and crawl through tunnels full of cannibals*, she thought. *Times change.* She squeezed the nightstick in her hand.

Shawnika wore a police uniform they'd found in the same locker as Josie's evening dress. She had said something about them being a walking metaphor for the complexity of modern womanhood, to which Josie replied, *if you say so.* Shawnika made a mental note to get the girl some reading material.

Meanwhile, seduced by comfort, Carter still wore the pink jogging outfit Shawnika had given him the day before.

Josie fell back alongside Shawnika, leaving Carter to lead the march. "The only thing missing is the word SASSY across his ass."

Carter shook his backside. "You betcha." The holster he wore, taken off a dead cop, held a cheap pistol he'd found in plastic bag inside a padded envelope. It did nothing to offset his comical appearance.

"He's still riding the high of finding that gun after I told him the place was picked clean."

"Yeah," Josie said. "Five bucks says he shoots himself in the foot before the end of the day."

Carter mooned her.

"Uh!"

\*\*\*

"I can't believe we're doing this," Shawnika said as they approached the glass shell covering the escalators to the L'Enfant Metro station on 7th Street SW. "You two are either the craziest or bravest lunatics I ever met."

Carter marched over the top of a crashed taxi, jumping from the roof to the hood and back down to the street, for the heck of it.

"I can't believe we're walking down the middle of the street without getting shot at," Josie said as she spun, taking in the view from the center of the wide intersection. "It's not that bad down here."

She was used to broken windows and a thick layer of grime back home. Aside from all the faded graffiti, this part of DC almost seemed livable. "Too bad all those trucks and plows are back in Baltimore. We could use those to clear all these cars away."

Carter nodded. "Hell yeah. That's would be insane. We should go back and get one of them big ones and just plow a path down the highway. All that equipment is sitting there getting rusty."

"What equipment?"

Josie answered. "We lived in a construction depot full of all those big yellow trucks and plows and stuff for digging. It sounds weird, but it was the only place where you could sleep in peace. It was just a big old ugly dump that looked like an abandoned factory with a scratched-up little white sign that said BARZÁN INDUSTRIES. No one dreamed it was really a five-star ho—"

Shawnika grabbed her arm. "No shit? My dad worked for Barzán up there. Just part time, but he drove a dump truck. It wasn't much. He used to be a heavyweight boxer."

"For real, or is that some bullshit your mom told you? Like how my mom told me my dad was working on the railroad when he was actually in prison?"

"No, he really was a boxer. You could have looked him up on YouTube back in the day. Andre Williams."

Williams. The skeleton in the dump truck who watched over them. Josie shot a warning glance at Carter.

He bounced like an eager rabbit. "Hey! We knew this dead guy na—"

Josie kicked a chunk of asphalt toward him and mouthed *Shut the fuck up*, glaring as best she could with one eye.

His face sagged. "Uh, we knew this kid named Andre, I mean. I *didn't* mean to say 'dead.' He was fine. I think he had a ruptured spleen, though, which kept him out of school a lot."

Shawnika's face turned curious. "You guys went to school together? I thought you just met a few weeks ago."

Josie offered a curt, "He's drunk," and shoved him toward the sidewalk. "There's the subway."

They did an inventory check: One flashlight, one machete, one night stick, one rickety gun that would probably blow up in Carter's hand, and two bottles of water on Shawnika's belt. "Ready?" Josie asked.

Shawnika gazed down the steep escalator tube into the darkness. "No."

Carter said, "If it makes you feel better, neither am I."

Josie took her by the elbow and guided her to the first step. "We'll stay as close to the escalator as possible. If we run into cannibals, we come back up. They can't stand bright light."

Shawnika tilted her head back and let the sunbeams warm her face. "Don't go anywhere, sun. I'll be right back."

Josie took the heavy-duty flashlight, switched it on, and inspected the escalator as far as the beam shone. Looked good. With a silent step she had perfected these past three and a half years, she began her descent.

*\*\*\**

L'Enfant station went deep. Shawnika thought of the elaborate tunnels and caverns in *Journey to the Center of the Earth* and imagined they were halfway through the planet's crust.

Josie swept the beam across the vast curved ceiling. "Whoa!"

Shawnika pushed her arm down. "Stop drawing attention to us."

"I thought we were trying to find your brother. He can't get to us if he doesn't know we're here." This time, Josie ran the light across the expanse of the concourse at eye level, birthing shadows that existed for but a second. She shone the beam across a newsstand kiosk; two skeletons in rumpled business suits lay at its base. Newspapers were scattered around them.

"*TRE!*"

Josie's voice ricocheted across the complex, chasing ghosts of a million subway runs through the tunnels beneath them.

Shawnika clung to her. "What are you doing? Those cornrows don't make you invincible!"

Josie made for the kiosk and aimed the light down into it.

"What is it?"

"I'm looking for soda. Ooh!" She handed the light to Shawnika, scampered over the narrow counter, and dropped in on top of the dead cashier. Shawnika leaned over to see. Josie popped up with an AriZona Tea. "I gotta come down here more often."

She exited through the side door, twisting off the cap and taking a gulp. She handed it to Shawnika, who shook her head, took a swig, and offered it to Carter.

"Man. It's warm," he said in mock irritation. He and Josie huddled together and giggled.

Shawnika tried to focus on her Zen lifestyle and her meditation, but it worked so much better in the library with all her books around and her vegetables and sunlight streaming in the tall windows. Down here, she began to feel unnerved by the blackness at her back, as if it were wrapping itself around her. Were those ethereal fingers tickling her neck after all?

She spun and shone the light behind her, jerking the beam this way and that, over peeling ads on the walls and an abandoned janitor's bucket and mop, and…a face! A face in the information window!

Josie placed a hand on her arm and pried the flashlight away. Leaning as close as she could get to the taller girl's ear, she whispered, "Shawnika. You can't panic. You have to *be* part of the darkness."

Shawnika pulled her close and took a long, deep breath. "But it's so dark down here. It's like a giant coffin. I can't take it."

Josie guided Shawnika to the middle of the concourse and trained her beam on the escalator that led down to the subway platform. "Listen. Me and Carter survived all this time by learning to be one of the ghosts. By crawling into the holes that no one else was willing to crawl into. Big, tough jerks twice my size got killed because they didn't want to get dirty."

Josie led the way down the escalator to the platform, a space as cold and dead as any Shawnika had ever witnessed.

She gave it a shot. "Tre?"

Silence.

\*\*\*

Josie kept the light aimed higher than she should have, but she had already seen a few gnawed bones along the side of the train track and didn't want the others to freak out. They'd been in the tunnel for fifteen minutes. If Tre had ever been down here, he was long since dead.

"Are we almost out?" Shawnika asked, the quavering of her voice betraying her efforts not to panic.

"Next station should be just ahead." Josie didn't tell either of them they were being followed, either. She became aware a few minutes earlier when the echoes of their steps sounded wrong, like one extra set of feet was involved. "Maybe we should walk a bit faster."

Minutes later, the space opened around them. Shawnika climbed onto the platform and helped Josie. Josie swept the beam around. They'd been here before. She shoved Carter toward the escalator. "Up. Up. Up."

"What is it?"

More clandestine footsteps, now coming from both sides. "Just go up. *Now.* This is the same station from yesterday."

Carter bolted for the escalator. Shawnika shot a look at Josie, her eyes wide. Josie said: "Go."

The girls sprinted. Behind them, the sounds of bare hands and feet, once human, slithered across concrete. The sound grew closer. Fleeing up the escalator, Josie felt it shake from the weight of their pursuers.

On the concourse level, Josie whirled and shone the high-powered beam. The horde of cannibals cresting the escalator recoiled and hissed. Carter nudged Josie aside, pulled out his gun, aimed, and squeezed the trigger.

Click.

Jammed.

"Fuck!" he said, flinging it at them.

Josie kept the beam trained. "All we have to do is back our way out. I'll shine this in their eyes. They can't take it."

The trio backed away as the wide beam kept the creatures in sight. One of them kneeled and began to crawl with its head tucked. The others followed the example, their jagged nails clicking on the dirty floor as they creeped along like humanoid insects.

Shawnika moaned. "Aw, that's messed up."

"We can still move faster than them," Josie promised.

Then an eerie wail sounded behind them, reminding Josie of a frightened cat. *What the hell could be making* that *sound?* She turned and shone the light. Three more cannibals blocked their way, the one in the middle holding in its gnarled fingers...a live cat.

"That's fucking *IT!*" Carter said, taking the machete from Josie's hand. He charged at the creature, swung, and brought the blade down on the side of its head. The cat jumped free and sped up the last escalator.

Josie started forward but was slammed from behind and fell. The flashlight tumbled away. A cannibal wrapped an arm around her neck and began crushing her windpipe. She jammed her thumb backward into its eye but it held on...until she heard a resonant whack and it rolled away, gasping. Shawnika took Josie's arm and hoisted her to her feet. Her other hand held the nightstick.

Josie grabbed her hand to pull her along when two of the creatures leapt from the dark onto Shawnika, knocking the baton loose. As Josie dove for it, she landed on her side and saw, in the spotlight cast by the flashlight, Shawnika plant a roundhouse right on one cannibal's nose, snapping its head back and dropping it cold. She blasted the other in the throat with a left jab and then brought an underhand right into its gut. Then she shoved it down, jumped on its chest, and began raining punches.

A third charged from the darkness, but before Josie was on her feet, Carter stepped into the circle of light and hacked its face with the machete. "Come on!' he said, pulling Shawnika away.

The trio stumbled toward the last stairway, sucking oxygen and pushing each other upward. Josie growled at herself in disbelief that she was running up the same exact stairs being chased by the same exact cannibals for the second time in twenty-four hours. Except why did the escalator seem longer this time? Shouldn't she see sunlight by now?

The trio burst forth from the hole in the ground once known as Smithsonian Station and straight into a tempest. Low, violent gray clouds roiled and churned above them while an agitated wind roared across the surface, turning over leaves and bending branches and whipping the dry dirt into a frenzy.

Shawnika and Carter stopped, gasping. Josie spotted the chopped-off hand from yesterday, carried it to the top of the stairway, and threw it down. "Lose something, fuckheads?"

She did not get the answer she hoped for.

The cannibals, at least twenty, came galloping up, some of them on all four limbs. Mr. Sunshine was not here to stop them this time.

Josie shoved her companions. "Keep going!"

The three of them aimed for the Washington Monument and ran. The creatures hit the surface and hesitated, unsure of the strange goings on in the atmosphere. Shawnika looked back and stopped running. "They aren't following."

One of the cannibals shoved the two in front of it to the side and lurched forward.

"Oh my god," Shawnika said. "He's only got one hand."

The creature somehow recognized Shawnika, either by sound or scent, for his one hand held a bone sharpened into a knife, and he pointed it straight at her, issuing a grunt in some weird language no longer English. *En masse*, the cannibals charged.

Shawnika, with her long legs, sped ahead of her new friends. Josie would have fallen behind further, but Carter took her hand and pulled her. Her right leg began to throb again. Her feet couldn't move fast enough to keep up with him. "I can't Carter. Just go."

A bolt of lightning blasted the top of the Washington Monument, followed a millisecond later by an explosive crack of thunder, so startling them that all three fell to the dirt. Josie glanced over her shoulder to see the cannibals cowering and crawling backward. She got back up, sucking deep for air. Shawnika circled back, and she and Carter tugged Josie along.

"They following?"

Josie looked again. "Yes."

The trio rounded the top of the mound from which the monument projected, huffing and panting as the first scattered drops of rain began to pelt them. They crossed the 17$^{th}$ Street traverse and approached the dried-up reflecting pool, a long, shallow rectangle that terminated on the other end at the steps of the Lincoln Memorial.

Josie glanced back the way they had come once more. The cannibals were advancing again but with hesitation and fear. Maybe the three of them had time to get some air in their lungs. Maybe they had time to escape.

Shawnika took Josie by the wrist. "We should go."

Josie noticed the blood on her friend's knuckles. "Remind me never to get in a fist fight with you."

"I told you. My dad was a boxer."

"Yeah?" Josie said after a deep breath. "My dad was a stabber. You don't see me going around stabbing people."

Shawnika patted her on the shoulder. "The day's not over. Now let's get moving before they get any closer."

Carter, facing the other way, said, "What. The. Fuck?"

The girls spun. "What?"

He pointed across the reflecting pool. "That."

Six lions were fanning out, forming a semi-circle around them, shoulders crouched.

Lions.

Big ones.

# CHAPTER 34

**2:25 p.m.**

Grace gripped the yoke, fighting to keep the Piper from flipping backward and breaking apart in the air. The wind came at her in pulses, tossing the plane up and then letting it drop as if it were a plastic toy floating in the ocean.

She had maybe twenty-five miles to go before she ran out of fuel, and right now, she couldn't see the ground.

The wind cut from the side, shoving her right wing up thirty degrees. A scream escaped her lips, and she plummeted fifty feet until she slammed into the cross current. A shudder ran through the craft.

"Please, God."

The Piper plummeted again, dropping out of the gray mist. In desperation, she stared through her port window with pleading eyes.

"Yes!"

Buildings. Tall ones. Hotels. Crisscrossing streets and traffic circles. Bridges over rivers. A city. There had to be an airport!

Grace stood up to peer over the control panel. Her eyes widened.

Less than two miles ahead, something she would have visited on a school trip this very year: The U.S. Capitol building. She had flown right into Washingto—

A dagger of lighting stabbed the air right in front of her. She screamed, and her dashboard lights flickered. Then she hit the wind shear. The Piper nosed down and began to roar as it picked up speed, hurtling toward the ground. Grace wrestled with the yoke, the flaps groaning. The plane leveled off, but she doubted the airframe could stand any more stress.

The altimeter read fifteen hundred feet. She had no choice but to set down. She dipped each wing in turn, peering out the side windows to look for any stretch of open road long enough to take a landing roll. As far as she could see, every single block of city street was a cluttered mass of crashed vehicles, as if someone had taken a bucket of Matchbox cars and dumped them over a play village.

Unless…

That long stretch of land with all the memorials. There were too many cross roads by the Capitol, but the far end…What if she could squeeze the Piper between the Washington Monument and the tree line and set down on that narrow stretch of grass. Could that work?

Another blast of lighting cleaved the sky in front of her, leaving a dark-green afterimage on her retinas. *It has to work.*

Grace banked left, away from the Capitol Building, circled, and came around. Now she was in a line with the Capitol just ahead and the Lincoln Memorial at the far end, half lost in the haze. She let out a breath. *Here goes.*

She dipped the nose and eyed a stretch of ground ahead. It would be a tight squeeze to avoid that white shaft sticking straight up without clipping the trees on the left of it. She tweaked the throttle and inched the yoke, dropping the plane to one thousand feet. Nine hundred.

A hard current shoved her from below, lifting the Piper and dropping it twice as far. She cleared the Capitol building. Seven hundred feet. Another bump, this time lifting her right wing and pushing her off course. She tapped the rudder. Six hundred feet. Over another building, a street, and more buildings. Museums. She dropped hard. Three hundred feet. Over another street, and another. Seventy-five feet. Past the Washington Monument, clean.

The Piper bobbled, its right wing dipping, and for a moment Grace saw the ground out her starboard window. A crosscurrent straightened her.

It took a millisecond for her brain to deliver a message: *You just saw three kids running for their lives down there. Can't be.*

Grace nosed up, and the Piper's landing gear pounded the ground. If that had been asphalt, she would have blown the tires. But she didn't. She stuck it. She could also see the pediment of the Lincoln Memorial through her windshield. Too close. Way too close.

"Poop!"

She yanked the hand brake and jammed the throttle, stalling the plane. She coasted to a stop, flung off her seatbelt, and tossed her earmuffs. "Damn, I'm good."

Grace crawled across to the passenger seat, unlatched the door, and opened it, stepping out onto the wing. That's when she saw quite possibly the strangest sight in her entire life, which was saying something when a person has lived through the End of Days: Indeed, three kids about her age were running toward her...a tall, skinny African American girl dressed like a police officer; a tall, skinny, shaggy-looking boy in a pink jogging suit, holding a machete; and a skinny, pale girl in a sexy evening dress. They were being chased by a bunch of naked people with the bluest skin Grace had ever seen. All of them were being chased by a curtain of rain and lightning bearing down fast, against a backdrop of the most famous buildings in the world.

"Come on!" she hollered in her best, loudest farm voice.

Movement on the left caught her eye. From across the field, width-wise, charged two lions, closing ten feet of ground with each muscular stride.

Did they know about the lions?

"Hurry!" she bellowed, jabbing her index finger toward the open door of the Piper. *I can save them*, she thought. A flood of hope surged through her body. "I can save them!"

She hoped they weren't afraid to fly.

# CHAPTER 35

**2:31 p.m.**

For a second, Josie thought a giant hawk was dive-bombing her. The sudden growl of the plane overhead sent her to her knees, but Carter yanked her back up without slowing. Every other step felt like a hammer on her shin, and her body begged her to stop running. But the lions circling them, and the cannibals behind, mad with fury, were not interested in a time out.

The three of them sprinted for the plane. It had an inside; reason enough to call it salvation. Then, as if flying in from an alternate universe where the world still existed, a girl in her Sunday best stepped out onto the white wing and shouted at them to hurry.

Then the girl looked to her left, Josie's right, and her eyes doubled in size. Whatever she saw on Josie's blind side, it impressed her more than naked cannibals running across the national mall in Washington DC.

Josie was five feet from the wing when she heard the huge cat's feet pattering across the bottom of the empty reflecting pool beside her. Perhaps, if she turned and charged at the animal,

Shawnika and Carter could reach the plane. Josie promised Shawnika last night, in inexact words, that she meant to go down fighting, not as some meaningless pile of bones in a hole. What better way than to save her friends?

She leaned right, ready to cut behind Carter and face the beast head on. Then she felt hands under each armpit, one belonging to Carter and the other to Shawnika. Without breaking stride, they flung her upward, her momentum carrying her onto the wing. The pilot caught her in a bear hug and redirected her through the opening. Josie, from years of practice, dove for the farthest corner in the back. Shawnika stumbled in next to her. The pilot crab-walked to the left seat. Carter whipped the machete toward the lion and then swung himself in like a monkey just as the beast hit the wing and began clawing at it.

"Close it!" the pilot shouted.

Carter pulled the door shut, and the pilot reached across him to turn the latch.

At once, all sounds became muted. Raindrops began to ping off the roof, making Josie feel as if she were in the back seat of her mom's car on a rainy morning.

The second lion reached the aircraft, smacking the tail section of the fuselage with its massive paws. The vehicle shifted by a foot.

"Put your seatbelts on," the pilot said.

Shawnika leaned forward. "Why?"

The pilot turned the ignition, and a shimmy ran down the body of the craft.

Shawnika punched the seatbacks in front of her. "Stop. I want to get out! I gotta look for my brother."

Josie reached across Shawnika's lap, took hold of the lap belt, and attached it for her. "Shawnika. He's not here. You're never going to find him."

"What if he comes looking for me?"

Josie leaned up to her ear. "He's not here. It's time to go."

The plane lurched forward, heading straight for the steps of the Lincoln Memorial. That didn't seem right. Josie fumbled and attached her lap belt. No way could they get off the ground without hitting—

"Hold on," the pilot said, yanking the hand brake. The plane spun a hundred and eighty degrees, knocking Josie into Shawnika. Now she could see the Washington Monument through the windshield. The pilot pulled a stick on the control panel, and the propeller blurred.

Shawnika leaned forward again, shouting over the roar. "Can't we just wait down here?"

The pilot poked her head into the gap between in the seats. "This field is about to turn into mud, and your friends out there don't look too friendly. This thing is not a tank. It's made of aluminum. They'll rip it apart."

With that she turned and let off the brake. The plane began to barrel forward. Shawnika hugged Josie again, burying her face into Josie's shoulder. Josie said, "If it makes you feel any better, I'm kind of scared that this thing is only made of aluminum."

Shawnika cried over the noise. "I thought you weren't scared of anything."

"I lied," Josie said, maybe not loud enough for Shawnika to hear her.

The pilot pulled the stick out more, and the plane lurched. Josie watched the lions circle away in momentary fear, gather themselves, and charge, running not at the plane but alongside it, interested in some other target. The lead animal threw its paws out and wrapped them around one of the cannibals, who was smashed down under the beast's weight. The attack vanished from

Josie's line of sight. The plane was barreling fast over the ground, bouncing and rattling and sounding like it would shake to pieces. Then she closed her eyes, held onto Shawnika, and breathed deep at the ground dropped away.

\*\*\*

Fast running out of room, Grace pulled back the yoke the second she hit takeoff speed. The plane bobbed and shimmied side to side, and the wipers were unable to wick the raindrops away fast enough. She winced as they sailed past the Washington Monument, bracing for a wing clip that would send them fluttering back to the ground like a falling leaf, but none came.

The Piper shot up, clear of the obelisk, and Grace banked to put the rain at her back.

"Can you see over the dashboard?" she asked.

The boy craned his neck. "Uh. Yeah. Kind of."

"Do you see an airport anywhere?"

"Not so far. I see the Pentagon. Why?"

A bolt of lightning arced in front of them. The control panel went dark, and all the gauges bobbled. *Not now!* Grace slammed the panel with the side of her fist. It flickered back to life.

"Because we're out of fuel."

The boy nodded. "That sounds bad."

The girl in the party dress, who Grace first thought bald but turned out to have blond cornrows, leaned between the seats. "What's bad?"

"We're out of gas," the boy said.

The blonde told the African American girl, and the African American girl looked at the ceiling, shook her head, and slapped her thighs. "Wonderful."

"Not totally!" Grace said, sounding as cheerful as she could. They looked scared.

"I'm Carter," the boy shouted over the engine and the rain, extending his hand.

Grace wrestled with the yoke. "Hi, Carter. Grace. I hate to be mean, but I can't really shake right now because I've never flown in a storm before and I need both my hands."

Carter nodded. "Every time you say something, I feel a little bit worse."

He had a point. "At least you're not getting eaten by lions. Now look for an airport."

Carter twisted back to face the two girls. "Hey. The pilot's name is Grace."

"Race?"

"*GRACE!*"

The blonde in cornrows said, "Carter, how come you're scared of your own fucking shadow on the ground, but up here you're Mr. Cool?"

For a petite thing, her voice cut. In other circumstances, Grace would have asked her to please not cuss in the plane, but the girl appeared to be under a lot of stress.

Carter turned back. "That's Josie. She's my girlfriend."

"*AM NOT!*"

"The black one is Shawnika."

Grace twisted and peeked into the back seat. Shaniqua or whatever her name was had her arms around the blonde, but she opened one eye and caught Grace watching. She waved. "Sorry. I'm just a little terrified of dying right now."

Then Carter said, "What the fuck is that?"

Grace stood up and peered over the control panel. About ten miles ahead, a bright glow emanated, from what she couldn't tell through the rain. But she knew one thing: it was made by electricity.

She plopped back into the seat. "I sure hope it's somewhere to land." She tapped the fuel gauge. "We're out of fuel. For real."

Grace lightened the throttle, and the Piper pushed on toward the strange glow. She eyed the fuel gauge again and again. "Please hang on." She prayed in her head. She prayed for a hand to hold them up. She prayed for a strip of flat land just long enough to bring her Piper Cherokee in one last time.

"Check that out," Carter said.

She dipped the nose. Ahead, glowing like a star, a massive oval building sat bathed in its own spotlights. The sign read MORGHEN BANK ARENA. Parking lot lamps radiated white across a vast field of asphalt. No cars in the lot.

"Woo-hoo!" A place to land.

No one else had time to celebrate. They sailed straight into the eye of the storm, the wind shear yanking the yoke from Grace's hands and sending the plane into a dive. She pulled back and banked left out of the sheer, the Piper groaning under the g-force. Screams ran through the cabin.

"I got it," Grace said, but they hit a current, punching the plane up and then dropping it one hundred feet. More screams. She banked right and then straightened again, eyeballing a lane between two rows of parking lamps below. She adjusted the yoke, and the plane bounced three times, as if it were careening down a flight of stairs.

"I think we're too high," Carter said, as if she didn't know.

She nosed down and dove two hundred feet, fighting crosswinds that threatened to flip the Piper on its back. The plane began to shimmy, and Grace worked the rudder to keep her ersatz runway in line. She nosed out of the crosscurrent, into a pocket, and dropped another one hundred feet in two seconds, sending her stomach into her throat. The turbulence ceased, and Grace sighed. "We're out of it."

The propeller coughed twice. Then stopped. Out of gas.

An eerie silence fell over the cabin. Grace checked her altimeter. Nine hundred feet. Now that parking lot seemed awfully far away. She pulled back on the yoke for lift, but without thrust she only got an extra quarter mile before the Piper began to sink.

Carter pinned himself against the seat and turned his head.

The piper dropped. Three hundred feet. Two hundred fifty feet. Two hundred feet. Grace settled back into the seat and held the yolk steady. She had nothing else to do. One hundred fifty feet. One hundred feet. The Piper cleared an overpass. Fifty feet. Forty. From her port window, Grace saw the high fence surrounding the complex slide just below by a few meters.

The towering parking lot lamps become visible through her windshield. The Piper was in line but angled too low. She tried to nose up. Nothing.

"Hold on!"

The front landing wheel hit first, snapping off. The nose slammed, shattering the propeller and flinging its spokes away. Grace squeezed her eyes shut, grimacing as the aluminum underbelly of her Cherokee screamed across the asphalt. The plane began to drift sideways. The tail section whacked a concrete lamp support, and the Piper jerked in the opposite direction. The left wing hit a lamppost on the opposite side and was torn away from the airframe, sending them spinning. The cabin filled with screams.

One. Two. Three full spins, all the while hydroplaning across the fresh-soaked asphalt. At last, the Piper came to a rest.

Grace opened one eye. Rain spattered across the cracked windshield. She opened the other eye. A glance out her port window. No wing. She released her seatbelt and poked her head between the seats. Behind the blonde and Shaniqua, where the tail section ought to be, she caught view of wet asphalt and the white lines of empty parking spots. The Piper was destroyed.

Her plane was destroyed. She didn't want to say it, but she had no choice.

"Fuckity! Fuckity! Fuckity! Fuck! Fuck! Fuck!"

Seatbelts unclicked around her. People began to breathe again.

"I have nothing! All I had left was this fucking plane and two fucking chickens, and now I don't even have that." She jerked the yoke in and out and then slammed it with her palms. She turned to the girls. "I have nothing."

Shaniqua squeezed between the seats, embracing her and kissing her on the cheek. "You did it! You saved us!"

She did.

Then the blonde reached through and shook her hand. "That totally kicked ass."

Carter pushed the blonde back, leaned over, and kissed Grace on the lips. She blinked, unsure of what to do next.

The blonde said, "Carter. Open the damn door already."

Though they could just as easily have exited out the back, the quartet climbed through the doorway in turn, sliding off the remaining wing and onto the wet asphalt. Grace surveyed the destruction. "It's a good thing we were out of fuel, or this baby would have gone up in flames." She tried not to think about her piloting days being over.

Shaniqua said to the blonde, "Does every day with you end in screaming and running?"

"Pretty much."

Carter tapped the blonde on the shoulder. "Guys. I don't think the day is over. Not by a long shot." He pointed toward the sports arena.

Grace turned. A high concrete wall surrounded the building. Through an open metal door, at least twenty kids in uniforms marched toward them in formation carrying rifles affixed with bayonets. They stopped about twenty feet from the wreckage of the piper and, in unison, trained their weapons on Grace and her new friends. The oldest soldier, no older than ten, said, "Come with us."

"Oh my god," Shaniqua said.

Grace followed the taller girl's eyes to the top of the concrete barrier. Her throat closed. Across the structure's entire visible length stood black metal spikes about six feet apart. Atop each spike was a human head.

# CHAPTER 36

**3:03 p.m.**

Shawnika tilted her head back as they approached the door, horrified but unable to look away. Those heads were not mere decorations pilfered off the bodies of dead grown-ups. Many were fresh and from kids no older than her.

*What kind of people do this?*

Surrounded by child soldiers, the four of them were marched along a grooved vinyl runner and through the door built into the concrete wall. A fine mist sprayed sideways across the asphalt in advance of the heavy rain they had momentarily outraced. Lightning ripped across the sky like gods in battle.

The sports arena glowed with electric light, as if a rip in time let it slip through from four years past.

A service entrance large enough for delivery trucks punctured the curving wall of the structure. The vinyl runner led into the tunnel beyond. To its right, a wide oval staircase terminated at a series of doors with metal detectors, where eager ticket holders had once entered. Before each door stood an armed guard. The guards held formation, staring straight ahead, disciplined. Not acting like the children they were.

Shawnika and her friends entered the service tunnel, and at once she became mesmerized by the illuminated florescent lighting fixtures running down the center of the ceiling. She had forgotten how bright the world used to be.

They were led through another door and down a series of hallways to a holding cell once reserved for unruly or drunken spectators. The soldier who spoke to them outside motioned with his bayonet. In silence, they entered. "The Lord is coming," he said.

Shawnika eyed his name tag. Jorge.

He backed out without lowering his weapon. The cell door, operated electronically, slid shut and latched with a reverberating click. Jorge exited, leaving another child soldier outside the cell to watch them.

Carter sat on the bench along the back wall. "What was that supposed to mean? 'The Lord is coming.'"

"I think he was talking about Judgment Day," the pilot said.

Josie sat on one of the benches. "I'm pretty sure that already happened."

Shawnika got her first good look at the pilot. Her light brown hair hung flat, too fine and limp to stand away from her head, but the rest of her said she ate well, from her muscular calves on up to her wide shoulders. Her Easter dress had suffered damage for sure. Parts looked new and bright yellow, but the fresh grass stains and dirt streaks suggested this wasn't the first trouble the girl had gotten into today. Shawnika forgot her name. "So…"

The girl seemed to read her thoughts. "I'm Grace. Don't feel bad. I forgot your name too."

The kid had an honest face. "Shawnika."

"Hi, Shawnika. You're probably wondering why I'm in this dress."

"You're probably wondering why I'm in a cop uniform. I have no good reason, but I bet you do."

"I got married last night, and this was the closest thing they could find to a wedding dress."

Carter sat up. "Seriously?"

"Long story. I didn't want to get married, let's just say that. That's actually how I ended up meeting you guys. I ran away."

"We're glad you did," Shawnika said. "We were in a spot. Although I think we might be in a bigger one right now."

Grace leaned forward. "Do you think we should we pray?"

Carter leaned back against the cell wall. "To what?"

"I'm sorry, Grace. I'm a Buddhist, but you go ahead. And I think Josie over here is a heathen."

Josie ran a finger over her banged-up shin and did not look up. "She means that I think God is bullshit."

Grace's mouth fell open. "That's blasphemy. Why?"

Josie pressed the big purple blotch two inches below her knee and winced. "Well, I never gave it much thought, but, since you asked: if God is all powerful and can make anything happen, then he made all this bad shit happen. Which makes him a total asshole. If he's not all powerful and this shit was going to happen no matter what, then he sucks. Either way, bullshit."

Grace crossed her arms, turned, and gazed into nowhere, processing.

"I think what Josie's saying," Shawnika said, "is that we all had a difficult time lately and that prayers don't seem to do anything. Maybe God's busy with another planet somewhere."

Josie wasn't done. "What I want to know is why people eat Jesus at church. I went once when I stayed with my aunt because my mom was declared an unfit parent. Which was definitely an accurate statement. Anyway, at that church they passed around grape juice and bread and said it was Jesus's blood and body. What the hell? I've seen cannibals up close. Trust me, you don't want that. And what's with those statues of Jesus nailed to a cross? Gross."

Grace sat next to her. "I'm not Catholic, but Jesus died for us so we could be redeemed. For *us*. You and me and everyone. God sent his only son to die because he loves us so much."

Josie pointed to where her right eye should be. "When you meet him, tell him I said thanks."

The conversation ended when Jorge returned with several more young soldiers. Beside him stood a boy dressed in civilian clothes with his arm in a sling.

Josie rose. "Hey Carter! It's my buddy, Cristobal. Sorry about your arm, dude."

The boy she called Cristobal glared at Josie and pointed with his good hand. "That's her! And him too!"

The cell door clicked and slid open. Jorge entered with another soldier. "You come with me," he said to Josie.

"No," she said and turned to face Carter. "Dude. I'm tired of taking shit from—"

Jorge lurched forward and rammed Josie in the back with the butt end of his rifle, sending her piling into Grace. Carter leapt to his feet and took a swing, but the soldier dodged it and planted the rifle into Carter's gut, dropping him to his knees.

Shawnika stepped forward, balling a fist and getting ready to snap the motherfucker's neck with one punch, when Josie held out a hand and said, "Shawnika, don't!"

Shawnika froze in midstride. Josie gazed up at her, gasping for air and grimacing. "Don't." The one green eye was ablaze. "Shawnika…I'm ready."

"Don't say that." *Please don't say that, girl.*

"You made it worthwhile."

Shawnika's eyes blurred with tears. *Don't.*

More guards flooded in and picked up Josie and Carter by the armpits, hoisting them to their feet. Cristobal walked out first, followed by the soldiers dragging her friends. Jorge, the son of a bitch who attacked Josie, ordered one guard to stay while the rest of them exited. The cell door closed.

Shawnika slumped to the bench and blotted her eyes.

Grace huddled close to her and wrapped an arm around her shoulder. "What did she mean by, 'I'm ready'?"

Shawnika exhaled. "It means she's going down fighting. And that she plans to take at least one of those fuckers with her."

"Where?"

"To hell."

Grace let go of Shawnika and pressed her back the cell wall. "We're going to die, aren't we?"

It seemed rough to say it to such a sweet girl, but what was the point anymore of deception? "Yup."

"I should have stayed on that farm."

Shawnika let out a tired laugh. "A farm girl? Josie would have loved you."

Grace waved to the solitary guard. "Can you let us go please? We're good people. We didn't mean to crash in your parking lot. Please?"

The guard remained at attention.

Shawnika cocked her head so she could see him between the bars. "What's the matter? They cut off your tongue for talking around here?" She leaned over and whispered to Grace, "Just so you know, if this clown lets us out, I'm not escaping. I'm going after that bastard who hit Jo—"

The guard's face.

Shawnika stood up and tiptoed to the bars. She stared, peering deep into him, past the child soldier and into his soul. That face. Changed, so much thinner, but…A swarm of butterflies took flight in her gut.

"Melvin?"

No response.

"Melvin Tubbs, don't you dare ignore me. It's Shawnika Williams. Melvin, look at me! Where is Tre? Where is he, goddamn it?"

The guard stared straight ahead.

"Listen. Your name is Melvin Tubbs, not whatever brainwash bullshit they told you. Talk to me!"

His eyes gazed into nothingness. "The Lord is coming."

# CHAPTER 37

**4:00 p.m.**

Gods and saviors spent little time occupying Josie Revelle's thoughts before The Fall or after. But limping through this maze of corridors beneath the sports arena, the pain in her shin jolting her with each step and her ribs echoing the child soldier's strike with her every shallow breath, she hoped Grace was right.

All Josie ever had was Cara. Her sister, with a grown-up girl's body and a flirtatious smile that drew boys like kittens to milk, hardly seemed to have come from the same womb. Yet Cara stood alone in seeing Josie as a real person. Josie wondered, now, if her own existence since Cara's murder had been nothing more than an afterimage slow to fade.

If Grace knew some truth about life, Josie didn't mind being wrong. Soon, she would be with her sister again. Or she would be nothing.

As the soldiers' unison footfalls echoed around her on the concrete, she regretted not telling Shawnika what it meant to know her for a day. She got to have a sister once more, and that made this march so much easier.

Shawnika and Carter and Grace would be killed too, of course. That's why Josie intended to take at least one of these fucks with her. *Sorry God, if you exist.*

After walking for what seemed like half a mile, Josie and Carter were led through a double door with THEATER written across the lintel. Beyond, a soldier stood beside an extra-wide service elevator. He pressed a button, and the door opened. Four soldiers, including the bastard who hit her, entered with them along with Cristobal, and the rest remained outside. The door closed, the floor shook, and Josie took her first elevator ride since who knew when.

Up top, they were marched down a hallway, through swinging doors, and Josie smelled theater. Until then, she'd never realized that theaters had their own scent, but one whiff and she was transported back to Cara's school plays.

She and Carter and the soldiers formed a single line, walking past lighting and electrical equipment—much more elaborate than anything at school—and then past a heavy curtain onto a stage.

To her left, a runway at the edge of the stage extended into the seating area for singers to get up close to their fans. A boy dressed like a Roman emperor stood on the runway watching their entrance. Maybe she was too used to seeing dirt and grime on people, but he looked like a movie star with his perfect haircut and flawless face. More than simply handsome, he qualified as beautiful, perhaps the best-looking boy she had ever seen. For a moment, he seemed transfixed on her, like he knew her. Then he broke his gaze and moved toward them. The soldiers fell back and pointed their bayonets at her and Carter's backs. Cristobal positioned himself near the back of the stage.

"Welcome," the beautiful boy said. "My name is Zane, and I am the director of this operation. I understand you are the little monster who wrecked my train."

Josie had never met someone with such a penetrating stare. At once, she understood the obedience of the child soldiers. Since she had only one eye, though, he would have his work cut out trying to get into her head. "That was not my intention. My intention was to escape from the sniper that had a gun pointed at me. And pointed at that kid over there that was driving your train, by the way."

Seriously, why was Cristobal giving her such a pissy glare? She'd saved his life.

Zane pressed his fingertips together. "Thing is, we worked really hard to get those tracks cleared and that diesel engine working. I'm really mad at myself, though, for letting a little monster like you screw up my hard work so easily."

Josie shrugged. "Blame the snipers."

Zane stepped back and projected in a stage voice. "Ah, 'the snipers,' she says. Snipers! Enter stage right."

Josie peered across, her breath catching. Ronan and Richie stepped out onto the stage from between two curtains, still in their combat fatigues. Her heart began to race; images of Cara lying naked on the floor of that locker room reared up in her mind. As vivid as ever, Richie pinning Cara down as she screamed, Ronan on top of her with his pants down.

Josie vowed to throw herself onto a soldier's bayonet before they could do the same to her. Before Carter could be beaten to death for trying to save her.

Then she realized the two rapists were handcuffed. Eight soldiers followed holding their bayonets close, respecting the danger Ronan and Richie posed. Those two were far bigger than anyone else in the theater.

Zane spoke. "Are these the shithead snipers you were referring to?"

Josie's glare seemed sufficient as an answer.

"Great. I love how this stuff works out. These shithead snipers had the audacity to hijack my train and point guns at my people, which is punishable by death, naturally, as if you couldn't tell by all the heads on the barricade outside. That's how we roll. Anyway, they got their stupid asses captured, and here they are."

The bruise on Ronan's jaw suggested he had already mouthed off once and learned the value of silence.

"Being a lover of theater," Zane said, "I am bored by workaday executions. Therefore, I have decided on this afternoon's entertainment. Young lady, what is your name?"

Is every boy a sadist at heart? "Josie."

"Okay, Josie, shitheads. What's going to happen is a fight to the death. Josie versus the shithead with curly hair, Josie's friend versus the shithead with the big muscles. To make things fair, the snipers will stay handcuffed for round one of the battle."

Josie changed her mind. She hoped Grace was wrong about God. Otherwise, God would be casting Josie into hell very shortly.

"Josie and curly shithead go first. Now, Josie. You have a distinct advantage here. Make it worthwhile. If you stand there bitch-slapping him like a toddler, I'm going to call time and take his handcuffs off early."

Josie stared at Richie, and she felt grateful Shawnika had been left in the cell. She didn't want her to see this. She wanted Shawnika to remember her as a human being.

Zane retreated to the runway flanked by two of his soldiers. The soldier who'd hit her, Jorge, moved to center stage, facing the audience of three, to serve as referee. Zane said, "Before you guys go at it, you should know that if either of you attempts to move in my direction, one of these crack shots beside me will blow your useless heads off. Even you, Josie-with-one-eye. If any of you attempt to escape, you will be cut apart with bayonets before you take three strides. Now get set."

The soldier behind Josie lowered his bayonet and placed his hands on her shoulders. His counterpart on the other side of the stage did the same to Richie.

"Go!"

The soldier attempted to shove Josie, but she was already in motion. Richie stumbled forward, his face showing sudden alarm at her countenance.

Zane said, "Wow. Look at little Josie go," his words punctuated by a theatrical laugh. But the sound never reached Josie's ears. Her mind heard Cara's screams and saw the faces of the terrified kids being gunned down at the bonfire on the pier. This was for them. Richie took two tentative steps. Josie hiked up the right side of her dress.

Zane said, "Uh, what's that?"

Richie's eyes locked on the black shaft in her hand. Instead of running, he wriggled in a panic, as if he could somehow shake out of the handcuffs.

Josie pressed the small silver button. The blade shot from the shaft like a chameleon's tongue.

Richie cried, "Wait!" three years too late for a bargain. Josie inverted the knife and hit him at full speed, ramming the blade into his throat right to the hilt.

"Guess what," she spit. "This is *your* knife."

Possessed by rage, she plowed her palm sideways into the knife handle, carving a swath through Richie's throat. She yanked it out, and a spray of arterial blood fanned across her face. She brought the knife down again, not hearing her own scream, into his chest, then withdrew it and plunged it into him again. He tipped face-forward to the stage, performing his own one-man reenactment of The Fall, but with more twisting and writhing and lots and lots of blood.

Ronan howled, "Fucking whore!" and broke free from his captors. Jorge, doing a poor job of refereeing, stood stunned in frozen shock and reacted too late to stop Josie from grabbing his rifle. He clutched at the air, tilting forward, and caught the butt end from Josie in his teeth, suffering worse damage than he had inflicted on her back in the cell.

Ronan bore down on her, a powerful form in motion even encumbered by handcuffs. From her knees, she heaved the bayonet forward as a battering ram, sinking it into her would-be attacker's crotch. He staggered backward and tripped over Richie's corpse. Josie stood and pressed her weight onto the rifle, forcing the bayonet deeper into Ronan's flesh. He opened his mouth as if to beg, but before he could make a sound, she squeezed the trigger. Simultaneous to the deafening bang, the weapon propelled backward, slipping between her arm and her flank and flying into the curtains.

Ronan lay on the stage, his eyes betraying confusion, legs bent at impossible angles around a red circle of shredded meat and organs. Josie kneeled beside him, retrieved her switchblade, and moved her face close to his. She inverted the blade. "You don't remember me, do you?"

He gazed at her, pleading and lost.

"You raped and killed my sister, and you shot me. You should have made sure I was dead." She raised the knife over his right eye. "This is for Cara."

She pushed down with all her weight.

When Ronan's fingers stopped clawing at the stage floor, Josie let off the blade. She turned her palms up. Blood lined the spaces between her fingers, goopy like oil. Josie Revelle truly, finally, had become one with the darkness.

She twisted around, saw Carter with his jaw hanging open as he stared at a stranger. The soldiers, in unison, remembered their roles far too late. They raised their rifles, and she covered her face.

"Stop!"

The soldiers, confused, stood down. Zane sauntered onto the stage. He clapped. "You are quite the destructive little monster, Josie. No one fools me, yet you fooled me. I wondered how a petite little willow such as yourself could survive all this time and deal with shithead snipers and wreck a thousand-ton freight train, and now I know. You are Satan's own daughter."

Josie crawled back, leaving the knife protruding from Ronan's eye socket, its purpose fulfilled.

"That was a most entertaining spectacle," Zane said. His voice then rose a dozen decibels. "However, I am sorely disappointed at the clusterfuck that took place around you, Josie, while all that was going on. I am not the least bit happy at the pathetic showing of my warriors, standing there like slack-jawed morons, watching an eighty-five-pound girl blow the balls off of a two-hundred-pound killing machine."

He stepped up to one of his bodyguards and pressed his forehead against the boy's. "What just happened is a catastrophic failure on your part. At least go stand there and guard her, you moron."

Zane pointed to Carter. "Take the Pink Panther back to his cell. We'll deal with him later."

Josie avoided looking at her friend for a moment, then turned to him once more. She mouthed, "I'm sorry." She was sorry that she could have gotten them both shot for what she did, for not giving Carter a choice. She was sorry for disgusting him and making him ashamed of her and for not being Josie anymore, because whoever Josie Revelle may have been before, she no longer existed.

The four soldiers guarding Carter couldn't drag him out fast enough.

Zane made a circle around the carnage and walked with determined strides toward Jorge, who remained on the ground feeling his broken teeth and mangled, swelling lips from Josie's strike. "Get up."

The boy rolled to his knees and then stood, wobbling in place.

"I see from your insignia that you were in charge of apprehending and guarding the prisoners. Is that correct?"

The boy nodded, his eyes tearing.

"Then it was your responsibility to search her to make sure she did not pull a goddamn switchblade knife from her snatch, wasn't it?"

The boy nodded again, holding his mouth and crying. Josie forgot the cruel soldier who butt-ended her with a rifle and instead saw a confused, brainwashed little boy.

Zane motioned for his other bodyguard. "Shoot him."

The bodyguard's eyes turned to saucers.

Zane inhaled and let out a long, slow breath. He pointed at Jorge. "Don't make me give a different order. Shoot. Him."

Josie covered her head with her hands in an attempt to block sight and sound. She still felt the concussion of the shot in her chest and the tremor beneath her when Jorge's limp body hit the stage.

"Get her cleaned up and bring her to my office," Zane ordered. "I want to see her alone."

# CHAPTER 38

**4:32 p.m.**

Grace watched Shawnika pace across the cell, stop, stare at Melvin, and then pace some more, her eyes and mouth big and crazy like one of those Japanese masks from International Day at school. Grace could almost hear the gears grinding behind that face. Shawnika's brother might be alive. Josie and Carter might be dead. No way to process those conflicting thoughts without making a Japanese-mask face.

*Damn it! I didn't save these people so they could get executed.* She popped up from the bench and marched to the bars dividing prisoner from soldier.

"Listen Melvin, or whatever your name is. Josie and Carter are our friends. You let us out of here right now! I've been through too much crap today to stand here like a chicken in a coop."

Melvin stared straight ahead.

"When my brother-in-law, Tucker, finds out what happened to me, he's going to come in here and tear you all to pieces. He's as big as a tractor and mean as a bull." It was worth a shot.

Melvin stared straight ahead.

"And another thing," Grace started to say, but she cut herself off when the jail door opened. In shuffled Carter, wearing the vacant gaze of some other kind of mask, accompanied by four guards and Cristobal, who also seemed jarred. Melvin stepped to the controls. The click of the latch echoed off the hard surfaces, and the door slid open. The guards shoved Carter into the cell, and the door closed. The whir of the electronics reminded Grace of landing gear retracting into a jet's underbelly.

Cristobal and the soldiers gathered, and a murmur arose from their huddle, a break in the discipline Grace saw before. Then the public-address speakers crackled to life. "*Attention. This is Emperor Zane,*" the voice said. The sound of it was warm and strangely inviting, like the narrator of a children's story. "*I have a very special announcement. Something you've all been waiting for has come at last. Please join us for an assembly in exactly two hours in the main hall. The moment of joy is at hand. Rejoice!*"

The soldiers shuffled and jerked like caged chickens. Carter stared at the PA speaker mounted on the wall, his lip curled in contempt. Cristobal said, "You heard Zane," and the guards, including Melvin, charged from the room, bursting with nervous excitement.

Shawnika hugged Carter. "What happened?"

"They shot Josie."

Grace's heart began to pound. *We're all going to die.*

Carter lowered himself to the bench. "They had rifles pointed at her. They dragged me out of the room, and then I heard the shot. That guy...the one on the speakers...He's like Osama bin Laden or something, only a white kid. Totally fucking psycho."

Shawnika plunked beside him. "Did you *see* her get shot?"

Carter gazed at the floor. "I fucking loved her, Shawnika." She placed her arm around him and laid her head on his shoulder. Grace felt her eyes well up.

"What did you see, Carter?" Shawnika said. "Maybe she is okay."

"Dude. She went fucking apeshit. They took us to this theater annex on the other side of the building, and those two snipers that chased us yesterday were there. That dictator motherfucker, *Zane*, wanted us to fight them, like in a death match. Josie busted out her knife, stabbed that one sniper right in the neck, then she curb stomped that dick that hit her before, then she shot that other sniper in the fucking balls. It was the most badass, motherfucking thing I've ever seen in my life. It was like a movie."

Shawnika lifted his chin and looked him in the eye. "If there's anyone you know who can find a way to survive, it's Josie. We gotta have hope."

Grace didn't know much about Josie, but she could tell by looking at her that the girl would stare the devil in the eye and not blink. If they shot her like Carter said, she probably spit blood on them before she—

Grace cocked her head toward the cell door. The lock never clicked when those soldiers closed it a minute ago.

Shawnika comforted Carter. "I know she found a way."

Grace strode to the cell door, gripped the bars, and shoved it open. "Why don't we go find out for ourselves?"

# CHAPTER 39

**5:37 p.m.**

Josie watched the blood-tinted water circle the drain and turn clear. Then more drops would run down, turning the water red again.

Four young girls, with faces that looked well fed but got little sun, watched Josie shower from across the locker room, guns aimed at the floor but poised to raise and shoot within a moment. Earlier, three still-younger girls had undone her cornrows, otherwise ignoring her and all the blood but giggling to themselves.

Josie shampooed. More red in the suds.

She felt her fingers massaging the shampoo into her scalp. A killer's fingers. The fingers that squeezed that rifle trigger and blew apart Ronan's pelvis. The fingers that cut his eye out so he would know what it was like, except that he was already in shock and scared stupid. She avenged Cara all right.

Cara. Still dead.

\*\*\*

*It's her. It's fucking her.*

273

Zane stared at the painting of the angel from his dad's study, now hanging in his own office. This angel and Josie-the-half-pint-psychopath were identical. The same willowy frame. The same small lips and triangle nose. The same single eye, deep and enigmatic and haunted.

*It's about time she showed up.*

Zane glanced at the clock and smoothed his uniform. He had ditched the Roman emperor outfit for a military ensemble. Patches and bars and all that. He'd saved it for tonight, except he hadn't known tonight was going to be tonight until he'd seen Josie the Monster enter stage left about forty-five minutes ago.

A knock sounded. Cristobal's knock, always the same pattern, this time bringing Josie with him as instructed. "Enter," Zane said, facing away. He waited to turn around until the dramatic tension reached at its full height. Three, two, one: pivot.

Holy shit. With her wavy blond hair down, Josie the Monster had become Josie the Angel. Angel of Death, perhaps, but she looked rather remarkable in the layered chiffon gown nearly identical to the one in the painting.

"Well now," he said. "You look quite lovely."

She reacted in a way he had not expected. A furrow of the brow. Fingers forming claws, poised to strike like a cat's paw.

She thought he had brought her here for sex. Yuck.

"Don't worry; I have no interest in or intention of touching you. I actually wanted to know if you fancy the theater?"

She did not respond.

"You can talk to me," he said. "If I were going to shoot you, it would have happened already. So, do you fancy the theater?"

"Do I *like* it, you mean?"

"Yes. Do you like acting, being on stage, the lights, the music, and so on?"

"That was my first time before."

Zane rubbed his chin, feeling like a Broadway producer. That might have been his calling if not for all this apocalypse business. "Hmmm. I'm afraid people are going to say you're hard to work with."

No response.

"That was a joke."

Nothing. Time for a different tack. "Cristobal. Leave the room a moment."

Cristobal frowned and exited. Zane's personal advisor knew the request was all part of the show, but the poor kid just didn't understand performance art.

Once the door closed, Zane said, "That kid is a flipping genius with electronics and finding out how to make things work. I couldn't do any of this without him. He's my Albert Speer. I wanted him to be my Goebbels, but it turns out I have to be my own Goebbels. Though I don't suppose you know who any of those people are."

A pause. "Not really."

"Anyway, Josie. Give me an honest answer. What are your thoughts on God and the second coming of Christ and all that?"

"It's not my thing."

"What if I tried to talk you into it?"

"You'd waste your time."

He liked her honesty. He also didn't want her to get too comfortable speaking plainly to him. Time for a subtle reminder. "I thought you might say that," he said. He reached into the drawer and removed a small pistol, placed it in his black holster, and made a show of wobbling it around and judging it inadequate. He smiled at Josie, put the peashooter back in the drawer, and removed the .357 Magnum, the weapon intended all along. The

Mother of All Hand Cannons went into the holster with gravitas. He stepped from behind the desk, came around, and sat on the front edge.

"It's just not my thing," she repeated. Good response. Not combative, but not wavering. She was clever.

"That's why I never bring anyone into the compound over the age of nine. If I get them early, I can educate them my way. I used to be set up in an old run-down theater about fifteen minutes down the road—by car—with a bunch of guys my age, but they were too hard to control. That's why I can't have you and your friends here in my snazzy new complex. You're too old and set in your ways.

"See, I've crafted myself into a messianic figure—a Jesus of sorts. My people really look up to me. The thing is, I've been promising them that the Lord would come and save all of us for three years now, and some of these kids are getting on for eleven and twelve. I'm starting to lose them. That's where you come in."

Josie the Monster's one eye fell onto the angel painting behind Zane's desk. Clever. Clever. Clever.

"Yes, you are dressed the same way as that angel behind me. I almost shit my tunic when I saw you walk onto that stage before. I was dumb enough to push it into the back of my mind and was ready to laugh at you for bitch-slapping that handcuffed kid around, but then you didn't bitch-slap him, did you? No; you cut his fucking throat. I took that as a sign. As sign that we should work together."

"You want me to walk around and tell everybody I'm 'the Lord'?"

"Not exactly. We're going to put on a little show in about an hour. You, me, and Cristobal. It actually isn't a little show, it's a big show. We'll be in the arena, not the theater. You're going to come in with all kinds of light and sparkles, tell everyone you're the Lord and that you will return in ten years to save everyone, and that they need to be patient. Then we set off a smoke pot, and you're gone down a trap door. I've been telling them the picture behind me is the Lord for over two years. They'll buy it."

Josie turned and strolled to Zane's bookshelf. She tilted her head and began scanning the titles. "What happens after ten years and no one shows up to save them?"

"By then, they'll either realize that I already saved them, or I'll have the East Coast powered back up and they won't need to be saved because we're all drinking Coke and Pepsi again." *And I'll execute any of the little shits who have a problem with it.*

Josie removed a book on Josef Stalin. "My friend Shawnika likes to read biographies."

"Yes. I didn't appreciate Stalin at first, but I've learned a lot about leadership from him. Speaking of your friends—and this is the part where I tell you what's in it for you—if you agree to do this, I will set them free. Tonight."

Josie was now reading the back cover of the Charles Manson biography. "You can force me to do it anyway."

"Yeah, but I need you to sell it. Besides, I get the feeling that threats don't scare you that much. Despite what you think, I'd rather work a deal than use force."

"You'll set them free, and you'll give them water and food to travel with?"

"I will. After your performance, but if you chicken out, the deal is off. You know what, though? Within a couple of years, they will be surprised to find the lights back on and the roads cleared. You've just seen a few soldiers so far, but I've got lots and lots of kids working on lots of projects. We aren't on generators here. This is real power from a real power plant we got running a few months ago." He bounced up from the desk ledge, took the book from her hand, and turned her to face him. "And I want you to be part of it. Truthfully, your friends have to go, but I think I can offer enough to make it worth your while to cooperate. After you do your little performance tonight, I'll give you a chance to say good-bye."

"I won't need to say good-bye."

Josie, always full of surprises. "Why not?"

"Because I'm not one of them anymore. I'm one of you."

"Excellent!" Zane gave her a half smile, the kind he always employed on closing the deal. "Now promise you won't say anything to anyone about our plan."

She nodded, and then he raised his voice without breaking eye contact. "Cristobal!"

The door opened, and Cristobal slid back into the office. Zane left Josie at the bookcase and went to his Minister of Everything. He nudged Cristobal in the other direction so the girl could not read their lips, because that was something a clever girl like Josie might do.

"Okay. She's in. Get her outfitted with the wings. And go with the gold flash pot. It'll look cool with her hair when it goes up. She won't scream, will she?"

"I'll pack in some extra powder. She'll be a ball of flames before she knows what hit her. Then we'll lower the floor, hit the music, and they won't even know she burned."

Zane patted him on the back. He admired clever people like Josie, but he liked watching them die even more. "The execution?"

"Her friends? Yeah, that's easy enough. They'll be below the platform so she won't see it. Only the audience will."

Zane spun around and smiled at Josie. "Apologies for the hush-hush over here. Trade secrets!" She responded with an unenthusiastic shrug. She would have been useful in another life. *Shrewd without being all that bright,* Zane thought with a touch of lament.

Back to Cristobal: "I want hoods on the executioners. Flames. Torture. Real medieval, fire-and-brimstone shit."

"Won't that confuse the audience? Angels and executions."

Cristobal was the opposite of Josie: Super intelligent but not the least bit cunning. Zane exhaled his impatience. "If the little brats *know* the execution is real, they'll accept the 'Lord' bit as real too. Why do I have to explain the psychology of theatrics to you over and—"

A soldier stuck his head into Zane's office without knocking. A stupid soldier with a death wish.

"Sir. Emperor. May I speak with you please?"

Zane shoved the soldier into the outer office before he could catch sight of Josie. "Are you fucking insane coming into my office without being summoned?" At once, he saw the urgency in his eyes. "Wait here."

Zane slipped back into his office. "Cristobal, get her ready."

Cristobal whispered into his ear. "What about the kids who saw her already?"

So many loose ends. "Kill them."

Back in the reception office, he found the soldier trembling with fear.

"Well, say it already."

"Sir. The prisoners escaped."

*What the fuck. Is this chick in my office giving off chaos waves?* "How? Never mind. I don't care how. They're either outside the building or they went to the theater. If they're outside, they can't get past the barricade. If they went to the theater...fuck it. Bring them to me alive."

# VORKOV

Zane composed himself and returned to the office, where Cristobal and Josie were engaged in a staring contest. Zane whispered to Cristobal about burning Josie's friends at the stake and impaling their heads on it afterward.

# CHAPTER 40

**7:18 p.m.**

After three years with no electricity, trying to sneak around hallways bathed in florescent light was like trying to hide on a football field during the Super Bowl. Grace's golden yellow Easter dress didn't help.

"I almost miss crawling around in the subway," Carter whispered.

Shawnika trailed close behind him. "I don't."

Aside from the one time they slipped into a restroom to avoid a group of kids pushing around two pint-sized construction vehicles on wheeled platforms, they had found the corridors empty. Whatever that big announcement was about before, Grace didn't know, but it seemed to involve everyone in the complex.

"Found it!" Carter said, sprinting ahead. He pressed the service elevator's button. The doors opened, and the girls piled in behind him.

Automatic doors. The last time automatic doors opened for Grace, a tsunami of flame and smoke had just engulfed her mother's body and she was running beside her brother with a toddler in her arms.

"If they see us," Grace said, "Let's all take off in different directions."

Shawnika watched the floor numbers change. "I think we should stick together."

"For what? I've seen this guy in action," Carter said. "We escape or he kills us, so we're better off splitting up. I'm going to do what Josie would do: take as many of those fuckers with me as I can."

Shawnika stretched out her long, lean arms. Scabs covered the knuckles on her right hand. "I told myself no more violence. Shit."

*I'm glad you're on my team*, Grace thought.

The service elevator door opened to the backstage area. The trio ducked out and made for the shadows cast by the heavy curtains and all the sets and equipment, survivors seeking refuge in the forgotten spaces between here and there.

Carter led the way as they squeezed and squirmed their way toward the stage. He motioned for the girls to stop and pointed. Through the gap in the curtains, over Shawnika's shoulder, Grace saw two sheet-covered bodies on platform hand trucks. Judging from their size, she guessed they were older boys, not a thirteen-year-old girl. Several young children, ignoring the fresh corpses, swept wet mops over the bloody stage. An orange cone marked a hole in the floor, perhaps where Josie blew one of those now-dead boy's private parts off, as Carter had reported.

Carter and Shawnika, with hopeful eyes, nodded in silent agreement. Carter offered Grace a thumbs-up sign. *So Josie is still alive, but that doesn't mean—*

Shawnika stood and parted the curtain. "Hi kids. Don't be scared. My name's Shawnika. I'm very friendly."

The children froze.

"I'm not going to hurt you. I just want to ask you a question. Is it okay if I come over there?"

One of the girls nodded. Shawnika tiptoed onto the stage and into the spotlights. "Do you know where our friend Josie went? She has blond hair in cornrows and is wearing in a blue dress."

"No, but you're in trouble."

"Why?"

"Because of them."

Four soldiers marched from the shadows to surround Shawnika. As Carter charged in, Grace could only stare at the blur of Shawnika's fists dropping one attacker after another. Within a moment, though, another dozen boys with rifles had swarmed the stage, pinning Shawnika and Carter to the floor. What happened after that, Grace did not know, for she turned and fled. As she approached the elevator, the orange light went on and the bell chimed. She darted left, following a red emergency exit sign. She burst through the door, into darkness, just making out the stairs in front of her. She reached for the rail, ready to vault herself down to the landing below, when two hands clutched her shoulders and yanked her backward into the corner. She struggled to free herself, but his powerful arms wrapped around her like a snake.

As one of the hands slid up and covered her mouth. "Shhh," her abductor said. "I know where your friend is."

# CHAPTER 41

**9:12 p.m.**

Zane exhaled. *Don't disappoint me, Cristobal.*

He stood in the tunnel, in the dark, four soldiers in front of him, four behind, and one on each side. The buzz in the arena resonated down through the architecture supporting the seating risers above. Zane patted down his uniform once more, wiping the sweat from his palms. The moment had finally come. His moment.

The house lights dimmed. Fanfare exploded from ceiling-mounted loudspeakers. The center lane, extending from the tunnel to the stage at the other end of the arena, became an avenue of light as search beams along each side sprang to life. Zane nudged his soldiers, and the group marched forward in unison. He hoped like hell the power station could sustain all this current.

The fanfare by John Williams came from the soundtrack to *Superman: The Movie.* None of the kids in the building had a clue.

As Zane stepped out from under the awning into full view, the crowd of four thousand kids broke protocol and roared. Zane didn't mind. He pumped his fists over his head.

Maybe Cristobal had overdone it with the smoke machines. The shit was everywhere. Still, the light beams shooting toward the ceiling seventy feet above looked even more badass than Zane had imagined. This gag came right from Adolf Hitler's playbook. Hitler, the first rock star.

He continued his triumphant march down the center of the floor where thousands of kids stood on each side, half filling the lower tier. How amazing if it were full? Next year, maybe. He had too much work to do to get caught up in glory seeking.

Zane reached the stage some two hundred feet across the arena floor from the tunnel. His soldiers waited at the edge, turning to face the crowd while Zane ascended the steps. White spotlights poured on him. He turned and pumped his fist again. More cheers. Then he displayed his palms, and silence fell.

No microphone. Shit. Oh well. His mood remained high. They were only fifteen minutes behind schedule. Not bad for a few hours' notice and with having to recapture Josie the Monster's costars.

He glanced to his left and motioned to the kids just out of sight. From behind the speaker towers they came, using pallet jacks to deliver a rather nasty device of Zane's own design. Two of these devices, actually: steel industrial vats cut down to twelve inches tall, each with a welded-in iron fence pole jutting up from the center. Great for tether-ball, except the vats were full of coals soaked in kerosene, which made them rather better for burning someone at the stake. Zane had been looking for an excuse to use this contraption for months.

Ha! Those punks were going to die screaming.

The kids deposited the makeshift fire pits over the X's Cristobal had marked on the floor. Next, two Spydercranes, one from each side of the stage, drove out. From their hooks hung ropes, one terminating at the wrists of a black girl and the other a white boy. He could have sworn someone said there were three of them, not two. Ah well. Let Cristobal worry about the details.

The boy, a gag stuffed into his mouth, glared as Zane passed, causing him to lose focus for a second. No one glared at Zane. Ever. No matter; a truly *Grand Guignol* spectacle awaited the audience, and this fool's charred head would be decorating the top of the barricade soon enough.

Who doesn't love theater?

Zane made his way to the spiral staircase along the side of the elaborate stage set, left over from some entertainment spectacle that was to have been performed back on June 10 three and a half years ago. He began his climb to the theme from *Raiders of the Lost Ark*.

Halfway up the stairs, he paused for a look down at the miniature cranes. Was the boom long enough to get that black girl off the ground? She'd be hanging from her arms. Did Cristobal account for the extra sixteen or so inches? If audiences only knew how much planning went into public executions. The logistics!

**9:18 p.m.**

Shawnika tried wrestling free, but she couldn't get any leverage with her hands up over her head. That and the little crane kept backing up and moving forward to get into position, yanking her around. The drivers were trying to park them side by side under the big platform over their heads. Sweat ran into her eyes as the gag in her mouth sapped moisture from her tongue.

Shallow tubs sat on the stage in front of her. With spotlights blinding her, she couldn't figure out what the tubs were for. Were they full of rocks?

The crane moved, yanking her forward. The smell hit her: Kerosene.

*Oh God.* They were going to burn her alive.

She tilted her head toward to see Carter. He caught her glance and shook his head, his eyes dim with despair.

She thought of her feet burning. Of the heat melting the soles of her shoes. Of her skin peeling away and the flesh turning black and the bones showing. How long before she went numb and left this place and this noise and these lights and this Earth and found peace at last? How long would she suffer?

She twisted around. The crazy bastard psycho finished his climb, and she couldn't see him anymore. She sure heard him.

"Welcome…"

His voice boomed from the speakers, swelling to fill the arena. The crowd hushed again.

"Thank you, everyone, my people, for your continued loyalty. I love you all!"

The fools cheered.

"You have been patient, and you have worked hard. Without you, we would not have been able to move into this building, the safest, most secure place in all the world. Without you, we would not have grown crops and raised animals. Without you, we would not have restored the water and resparked the electricity. You came to me as innocent children, and now you are the vanguard of humanity."

Carter began to jerk up and down, accomplishing nothing but abrading the skin where the rope pinched it.

"I give you my protection and my wisdom and my love. But I must ask you to do more. I ask you to serve me still so we can bring not just this building back to life, but the whole city. It will take time, but you will be delivered unto salvation!"

Riotous cheers shook the stage.

"I am not just here to talk. No. It has happened, as I foretold. I have made contact with The One."

A thousand gasps went up.

"I was a fool. I, who have talked of her coming for so long, did not recognize her before my own silly human eyes. I thought I was protecting you from darkness. But she showed me the light. She is here. Tonight. The Lord has returned."

As the arena exploded with cheers, Shawnika locked eyes with Carter. She swore he smiled under that gag. A smile that said, *Josie.*

"In honor of her arrival," said the psycho on the platform over their heads. "We prepare the animal sacrifice."

The soldiers guarding them shot looks at each other, confused. One shrugged. Then, hurrying from the darkness beyond the speaker towers came two boys, each carrying a battle ax in one hand and a fiery torch in the other. They wore red executioner hoods.

Shawnika heard the whirring of the hoist behind her before she felt anything. Then the tug came and the rope crushed her hands together, and then she was dangling two feet above the stage, her arms ready to tear out of their sockets.

**9:21 p.m.**

"Get your hands off my chest."

Cristobal, standing behind Josie, fiddled with the angel wings. "I'm not interested in your distressingly small chest." He stepped back, eyed the prop, and then made an adjustment.

"What happened to your sling? I thought I gave your arm a boo-boo."

Cristobal jerked the wing harness tight and attached the hooks down the back. A stab of pain jolted Josie's damaged ribcage as he latched each one. "I got better."

She shook her head. These people were a bunch of phonies trying to trick each other all the time. "Who has angel wings just lying around?"

"Zane collects theatrical costumes. Don't worry. It'll look real to the audience."

Josie peered up through the hole above her. Somewhere up there, Zane continued delivering his speech, though it sounded like a bunch of muffled echoes down here on this gangway hidden inside the platform. From this vantage point, she only saw a lighting truss directly above with colored spotlights and rigging ropes attached to the truss frame.

"You remember your lines?"

"Yeah. Why are these wings, like, forty pounds?"

Cristobal turned her around. "That's the explosive."

She knew it. "Dick."

"Relax. It's just so you don't try anything funny. You go up there, say your lines like you mean them, and then come back to the drop floor. You behave, I lower you, and I remove the explosive." He detached a small rectangular device from his belt. "Zane has so many cool toys. Like this remote detonator, for example. I turn this switch, press this red button, and you go up in flames. It's radio frequency, which means I don't need to see you to kill you."

Josie figured they would shoot her afterward. But no, they planned to blow her up. "You let my friends go. Tonight. That's the deal."

"As soon as this show is over, I'll personally unlock the cell and walk them outside the barricade. But if you do something foolish, your friends die. That's pretty simple."

Zane said something about The Lord.

"Oh shit," Cristobal said. He flipped a switch on an automation box mounted to the gangway's handrail, and the lights dimmed above them. Then he fidgeted with the device once more, and, from silence, a note swelled, sounding halfway between a flute and a woman's voice. Cristobal repositioned Josie so she would face the audience. He leaned up to her ear. "I'll be watching you from the control booth. You best pray I don't screw up and press the red button by mistake."

With that, he stepped away, and the floor began to rise. As her head poked above the opening to the platform, a golden light, bright as sunlight, fell into her shoulders. A chill ran through her as the cavernous arena revealed itself.

**9:23 p.m.**

Warm blood tricked down Shawnika's arms from the rope cutting into her wrists. With much jerking and clumsiness, the cranes moved her and Carter into position over the foot-tall vat while other children guided the ropes into a notch at the top of each pole. Then the hoist whirred and lowered them so their toes nearly touched the tops of the kerosene-drenched charcoal. The executioners took their places, one on her left, the other on Carter's right, their ax blades at attention and the torches held forward. They glanced at each other through almond-shaped cutouts in their hoods, then up toward the platform.

Carter began to jerk his head from side to side, rubbing his face against his arms. Shawnika wished she could signal him not to panic. She didn't want his last moments to be spent in terror.

**9:24 p.m.**

After a sufficient dramatic pause as the gasps in the arena faded, Josie took slow, long strides to the microphone. To her right, Zane kneeled in pretend supplication with his arm outstretched and his head bowed. By the time she reached the mic, he had disappeared into her blind spot.

The crowd below stood frozen, gazing upon her with reverence, yet the vast hall crackled with nervous energy. Below, the main stage sat in darkness, the orange fire of two torches piercing the darkness.

"People of the empire," she said, her voice booming across the vast space and bouncing back, startling her. *Keep going*, she told herself. "I am the Lord. I know you have waited for me so patiently and for so long. One day I will return in glory, but only when you have followed Emperor Zane and rebuilt the city. When that time comes, you will be rewarded beyond your imagination. If you ever have doubts or you lose your faith, remember...you are the chosen ones!"

Not the exact script Zane gave her, but she thought her ad libs came out better. Good enough to satisfy the crazy dictator and, she hoped, free Shawnika, Carter, and Grace.

She tilted her head, angelic and graceful, toward Zane. She tried to read him. Would he really set them free? He gestured with his eyes and an almost imperceptible nod: Get back to the drop floor. She took a breath, deep and long, one last taste of life before they took it from her. She took the mic and ad-libbed once more. "Bless you," she said. "My son."

Josie returned to the drop floor, facing away from the audience. To the side, hidden from the crowd by curtains, Cristobal watched from the control booth. He made a circle in the air with his finger, indicating she should turn the other way.

Then, from below, a voice cried out, slicing the silence. "Josie!" Carter.

Cristobal held up the RF remote, placed his thumb over the button, and mouthed the words, "Sorry. I lied."

Josie smiled. He did not know something she knew: Grace had entered the control booth from behind and was lining him up for a tackle. She charged. Their bodies collided and Cristobal fell forward, the detonator flying out of his hand. Josie's one eye widened enough for two. The device spun, button up, button down, button up, button down. It plummeted toward the platform button up, button down. It landed button up, flipped, and landed button up again.

Grace and Cristobal began to grapple, but Josie had already turned away on another mission.

She strode toward Zane, whose face bore the sudden, baffled countenance of someone not used to things going awry. She reached under the gown he had given her, withdrew the small pistol she had tied to her thigh, and pointed it at his face. "You should have locked your desk drawer, dipshit."

He laughed. "You little fucking monster. You are incredible."

"All you had to do was let my friends go and I would have done whatever you wanted. Hector warned me about guys like you."

Zane's hand shot across his chest and ripped the .357 Magnum revolver from its holster and pointed the barrel at her forehead. "I don't think you're going to shoot me, Josie. After you did those two idiots before, you looked pretty sick with yourself. I don't think you have another murder in you."

"Let my friends go."

"Okay." Zane leaned toward the microphone. "Execute the animals!"

Josie had one more in her. She squeezed the trigger. The gun clicked.

Zane shrugged. "I took the bullets out, silly monster." He took aim once more at her forehead. "I want you to hear your friends scream before I shoot you. Parting gift. EXECUTE THEM!"

**9:26 p.m.**

Shawnika locked eyes with Carter, trying to say, *it's just you and me here. Just look at me for a minute and then we will know peace.* Carter, his gag hanging loose, gazed back apologetically. "We tried," he mouthed.

The executioners raised their torches, wound up...and whipped them at the soldiers guarding the stage. In unison, they turned and chopped the ropes holding Shawnika and Carter. Shawnika dropped into the coals and tumbled out of the vat just as the torch came flying back at her. She rolled away as the fuel ignited, sending a jet of flame up fifteen feet.

The executioners threw down the axes and withdrew automatic pistols from behind their belts, turning and aiming them at the group of startled soldiers charging the stage. Commands of "Drop your weapon!" were exchanged between loyalists and traitors.

Shawnika crawled behind the crane. Carter had already freed himself and began working on her bonds. "How did you?"

"My superpower," he said. "I can squirm out of anything. I didn't live this long 'cause of my looks."

The crane driver, making the mistake of trying to restrain Shawnika after Carter untied her right hand, soon found himself staring at the ceiling and sporting a broken nose.

Meanwhile, the soldiers aimed their bayonets at the executioners, and the executioners aimed their pistols at the soldiers. 9:26 became 9:27, and the murmur working its way through the crowd turned to alarm and confusion and cries.

## 9:27 p.m.

Zane held Josie by the throat, pressing the handgun to her forehead, his confident stare betrayed by welling anger. Without taking his eyes from her, he said into the mic, "I don't hear anyone dying down there." He peaked over the edge of the platform.

Josie squirmed her head to the side and bit his thumb, grabbing for his gun hand as he howled. A shot boomed past her into the curtains, missing her by inches. She rammed her head into his chest, trying to knock him back. His eyes blazed with fury, and he threw her to the platform.

"What the fuck is going on down there?" Zane said. "Kill those two idiots!" Then he stepped up to Josie and aimed the .357 at her chest. "Good night, Monster."

Josie closed her eye and hoped the next thing she saw would be Cara. She had one final thing to say: "You forgot one idiot."

"What?"

She heard a thump. She opened her eye.

Not Cara. Grace. Swinging from a rigging rope.

Grace let go of the rope and dropped three feet, landing with a muscular *thunk* onto the platform. Zane, gripping his ribs where her feet had struck him, grabbed Grace by the arm and dragged her to the ledge. She leaned back to fight the motion, but her feet slid. Zane placed a hand on her hip and began to push. "Sayonara."

Josie squeezed the trigger hard on the .357 that had skittered from Zane's grip when Grace kicked him. The recoil threw her backward, pain jackhammering through her ribs when she smacked down.

Zane staggered and turned, inches from the ledge, staring at the undersized girl lying crumpled on the floor with his gun in her hand. He sucked for oxygen in choppy breaths, trying to fill a punctured lung that could take no air.

Josie climbed to one knee, her own breathing labored. One angel wing, limp and broken, hung crookedly. "Carter!"

A voice echoed from the stage below. "Yo!"

Josie raised the gun. Grace covered her eyes. "Heads up!"

She unleashed a second round into the emperor's chest.

The force of the shot knocked Zane away from the platform. He seemed to hover for a half second, throwing out a defiant fist and then plunging, sending up a plume of sparks when his body plowed into the flaming stake below and impaled itself.

A sharp popping noise crackled through the auditorium when the lighting rig overhead shorted out, followed by a hot smoke and sparks shooting down like burning rain.

Taking advantage of the screams and confusion, Josie tossed the gun and crawled to Cristobal's detonator, fumbling to remove the battery cover. She accessed the compartment and pried out the nine-volt Duracell that stood between her and death. She glanced at Cristobal's unconscious form draped over the mixer and then sent the detonator flying over the edge of the platform.

Grace stood dumbstruck, glaring at Josie with a mix of awe and alarm.

Josie tugged her arm. "Grace. You're going to get shot standing there. Let's go."

Grace followed her to the staircase. "I'm just sick of mean people, you know?"

Josie nodded. "Me too."

# CHAPTER 42

The soldiers, the would-be executioners, Carter, and Shawnika stared as the body of Zane Barzán slid down the pole and sank into the fiery coals. His dictator uniform, perhaps made without fire safety in mind, went up like flash paper. The soldiers laid down their rifles. One of the executioners removed his hood. "That smells bad."

Melvin Tubbs.

Shawnika turned to the other hooded figure. *Please…*

He ripped off his hood and threw it onto the fire. She placed her hands on the side of his face. So tall. Almost her height now. But not quite.

"Sorry I couldn't free you sooner, Sis. We had a plan."

She squeezed Tre hard, like she used to, but he didn't complain this time. "I found you."

"I found *you*."

Shawnika looked him up and down. "What the hell did they feed up here? You grew a foot and a half."

Before he could answer, a rustling motion startled them. Shawnika whirled, ready to defend her brother from anyone or anything that intended to take him away again. She smiled. Carter had lifted Josie off the ground and was spinning her.

"Easy, big boy," Josie said. "I'm wearing a bomb."

Melvin went to work at once, using a pocketknife to cut away the harness.

Grace completed her descent from the platform, peered at Zane's burning corpse, and covered her nose. "Should we say a few words, maybe?"

"How about, 'Burn, motherfucker," Josie said.

Shawnika couldn't wait anymore. "Josie! I want you to meet someone." She shoved Tre forward. "My brother."

Josie came to his chin. "You got kidnapped? How?"

"I kinda had a growth spurt recently."

Grace spread her arms out and pushed the group away from the stage. "Maybe we should get the heck out of here?"

Melvin said, "I'll handle it," and tossed the angel wings onto the coals. With the soldiers having abandoned their posts, the rest of the group ducked behind the speaker towers. Melvin climbed the spiral staircase leading to the platform. The makeshift flash pot inside the angel wings went off with a crack, sending up a mushroom of fire and sparks that drew the focus of the crowd.

Melvin tapped the mic. Nothing. He cupped his hands around his mouth.

"Uh, hey everybody. There's been an accident. You don't have to be scared or anything. No one is in trouble. Just go back to your barracks or wherever you belong for the night. Tomorrow, do what you normally do, and we'll figure it out. Okay? Just go on and get out of here. Guards. Make sure nobody gets trampled, right?"

Shawnika listened, trying to remember that chubby little kid she rescued from the snowstorm almost three years ago. Tre wrapped a strong hand around her arm and said, "Come on. Let's go. He's got this."

In the hallway leading from the stage to the dressing rooms, Shawnika hugged Josie. "Carter told me you wasted those snipers by yourself."

Josie pulled away. "We have to get you some bandages for those wrists."

Shawnika rolled her forearms over under the light. The skin was rubbed off, but nothing time wouldn't fix. "You had to do it, Josie. Kill those shooters. It was you or them."

Josie gazed toward the wall, that one green eye blocking access again. "The problem is I enjoyed it. I wanted blood."

Carter stepped between them, threw his arms around Josie, and kissed her. "I love you!"

Josie pushed him away. "Can someone tie him back up please?"

Melvin appeared. "Hey, Shawnika. Sorry it got kind of close there."

Shawnika didn't care how close or how far. She had her brother again. "Guys, that there is Josie, Carter, and Grace. This is Melvin, and this handsome boy is my baby brother, Tre."

Grace said, "I know. Tre and I met already. We had an intimate moment in a darkened stairway."

"Say what?"

Tre tried to explain. "Melvin told me you guys were captured. He tried to let you escape."

"I left the cage unlocked, but you guys *had* to go rescue your friend."

"Emperor Zane gave the order to ambush you at the theater. I wanted to head you off, but I was too late 'cause you were already caught. Then I ran into Grace, and we made a plan to save you."

"Oh shit," Melvin said. "Those two kids are still tied up in the closet."

Shawnika refrained from scolding him for cussing.

"That's why we were late," Tre said. "We had to kidnap a couple of executioners and borrow their clothes."

*What the hell kind of place is this?* "So that fool trained children to be executioners?"

"You have no idea how fucked up that guy was. Me and Melvin was going to kill him ourselves."

"Tre Williams! Where'd you learn to cuss like that?"

Grace said, "So what do we do now? My plane is crashed."

Melvin gestured into the space behind him. "You can stay here."

Josie stepped back. "You know what? If you could hook me up with a flashlight and a bottle of water and point me to the nearest exit, I'm gonna take off."

Shawnika took her by the arm. "Why?"

"I guess I kind of got used to no electricity. And there's too many people here."

Truth is, Shawnika didn't like all these florescent lights and concrete hallways that much herself. "Winter is coming."

Josie shrugged. "I'll figure it out."

Shawnika stomped her foot. "I don't want you to be alone."

"I've always been alone."

Shawnika wished she knew what Josie hid behind that sweet face. Whatever it was, it hurt her. "You have us."

Carter said, "Well, fuck it. I'm going with Josie."

Grace's eyes darted from face to face.

A cry escaped from Shawnika's lips. She just got her old family back and was losing her new one. She turned to Tre. "Tell them to stay!"

Tre, once so childlike at ten, now seemed so much older than twelve. "I'm not sure I want to stay here, either. It was bad under Zane, but now it's going to fall apart."

Shawnika hardly knew what to make of the changes in her brother. "So what about it, Josie? Do you mind some tagalongs?"

She could have sworn a smile was working its way onto Josie's face.

"As long as I get to keep this angel gown. I like it."

Grace said, "Speaking of which, can I get out of this stupid Easter dress?"

Carter took a gander at himself. "My jogging suit is kind of singed."

"That's my jogging suit," Shawnika reminded him.

Tre and Melvin exchanged a glance. Tre said, "There's a wardrobe room in the theater like you ain't seen. You can walk out of here dressed like ninja turtles if you want."

# CHAPTER 43

Josie nibbled a corn muffin, watching the sun's rays fan out over the trees yonder, just past the concrete barricade surrounding the complex. No doubt the arena roof would have provided a better view than here atop the theater, but she couldn't figure out how to get up to it.

She heard rustling and turned. A seagull had landed beside her, bobbing its head with curiosity. Josie broke off a piece of muffin and offered it. The bird plucked it away. "Leave the finger, huh?"

The bird flew off.

Josie had woken an hour earlier and snuck outside. No guards attempted to restrain her. No soldiers circled the perimeter. She wondered how long before Zane's grand empire would be forgotten.

Muffin consumed, she brushed the crumbs from the front of her hockey jersey. She'd found it in the wardrobe room below, believing the rich green matched well with the soft blue and green chiffon of her gown. A blue whale's tale made up the logo on the front. Underneath the garment she sported a goalie's chest protector to support her aching ribs, and beneath the gown she wore hard plastic shin pads. In case she had to jump off any more moving trains.

She downed a second muffin, chased it with bottled water, and brushed herself off all over again. The morning sun, sitting on the horizon like a giant coin, turned the space around her into gold, no need for Cristobal's special effects and music.

Cristobal. They'd made him sleep in the jail cell. He'd survive.

Voices echoed up from below, poking a hole in the morning calm. Josie peered over the edge of the roof. Shawnika, hands on hips, stood beside Carter.

"Where the hell did she go?"

"Maybe she found a tunnel."

"She wouldn't just run off."

That kind of stuff.

Josie let out a slow breath and stood, wincing at the pain in her leg. She'd probably cracked the bone. What else was new? She retreated to the roof-access door and made her way down to ground level.

Her two friends were still discussing her whereabouts as she slinked up behind them.

"Gotcha!"

Shawnika let out a squawk and turned. "Girl, you give people fits. We thought you ditched us."

Carter, dressed as a Russian Cossack, said, "Cool! Where'd you get the Hartford Whalers jersey?"

"In a trunk of sports stuff."

A group of kids appeared in the parking lot, among them Grace, Tre, and Melvin.

"You really gonna leave?" Melvin said.

Tre shook his hand. "I wanna be with my sister, man. You sure you don't want to come?"

"Me and some other kids think we can keep this place going, only without all the chopped-off heads and everything."

Shawnika hugged Melvin. "Good luck, Mel. Remember: Absolute power corrupts absolutely. You saw what happened here."

Melvin gave it a minute. Tre broke the silence. "She reads a lot of books. Just agree so you don't get a lecture."

"I think I know what she means."

The sticky sound of tires rolling over damp asphalt made Josie turn. A big black SUV pulled up. The driver, barely tall enough to see over the steering wheel, cut the engine and got out.

"That's Zane's Caddy," Melvin said. "He said it has bulletproof glass and doors. You guys might need that."

Carter and Tre high-fived. "Sweet!"

"It's got a full tank, but when you run out, that's your problem. There's water and food in the back, and a couple blankets, and I put some handguns in a box with some ammo."

Carter said, "I'm driving!"

Grace swiped the keys from the driver's hand and twirled them just beyond Carter's reach. "I'm driving."

The five of them piled into the Cadillac, Grace behind the wheel, Carter in the passenger seat. Josie sat in the back with Shawnika and Tre. Grace turned the key, and the engine roared to life. Carter said, "You sure you can handle this thing?"

"I can fly a plane, ride a horse, run a tractor, drive a motorcycle, race a go-cart, and four-wheel in an ATV. And snowmobile. I can drive a car."

"Yeah, okay," Carter said. "But pull over *before* you run out of gas this time."

Grace studied the gear shifter a moment and then set it to drive. She waved to Melvin, gave it a bit too much gas, and then eased off. Two boys, soldiers until last night, turned a manual crank that opened the metal gate built into the barricade. The SUV passed through and into the parking lot for the arena. Grace circled left, pulling up to the wreckage of the Piper.

"Good-bye," she said, blowing a kiss toward the mangled aircraft.

Next, she made for the exit of the parking lot. Josie leaned back, imagining they were on a family vacation. But this vacation would not have amusement park rides and pizza and cotton candy. It would have dead bodies and cruel people and hunger and cold and dirt.

Grace held her foot on the brake, the SUV sticking halfway into the street. "Where are we going?"

Shawnika said, "Josie was talking about a farm or a beach a couple days ago." Josie felt a soft squeeze from Shawnika's hand on hers. "Did you make up your mind yet? Where are we going?"

To Josie, gazing through the window at an empty world of crumbling buildings, rotting cars, and clocks without purpose, this debris-strewn avenue seemed no different from any other. It went somewhere or nowhere.

"Home."

# ACKNOWLEDGMENTS

I owe a debt of gratitude to the following people: Candace Johnson for her editorial guidance; An Guk Hwang for stepping up to the plate and hitting a homer off the first pitch; Lauren Lebano, the first person to read what was then a seven-page scrap of an idea, who then followed through with invaluable advice; Janna G. Noelle for being my favorite sounding board; all the supportive folks I've met on WordPress and Twitter who offer encouragement and laughs; Monique Happy and everyone at Winlock Press because this wouldn't be happening without them; and, of course, to Sunny and Ethan for putting up with me.

And to you for reading!

# ABOUT THE AUTHOR

Alex Vorkov is a veteran copywriter, blogger, and editor whose fiction resides in the realm of the dark, the fantastical, and the delightfully gruesome.

When he's not writing post-apocalyptic and horror novels, he's composing songs and banging around on the drums and guitar.

Alex lives near New York City.

KING ARTHUR AND THE KNIGHTS OF THE ROUND TABLE HAVE BEEN REBORN TO SAVE THE WORLD FROM THE CLUTCHES OF MORGANA WHILE SHE PROPELS OUR MODERN WORLD INTO THE MIDDLE AGES.

Morgana's first attack came in a red fog that wiped out all modern technology. The entire planet was pushed back into the middle ages. The world descended into chaos.

But hope is not yet lost— King Arthur, Merlin, and the Knights of the Round Table have been reborn.

PERMUTED
PRESS

# THE ULTIMATE PREPPER'S ADVENTURE.
# THE JOURNEY BEGINS HERE!

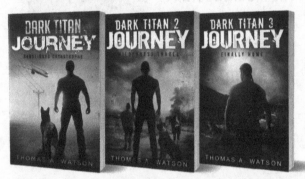

EAN 9781682611654  $9.99     EAN 9781618687371  $9.99     EAN 9781618687395  $9.99

The long-predicted Coronal Mass Ejection
has finally hit the Earth, virtually destroying
civilization. Nathan Owens has been prepping
for a disaster like this for years, but now he's
a thousand miles away from his family and
his refuge. He'll have to employ all his hard-won
survivalist skills to save his current community,
before he begins his long journey through
doomsday to get back home.

# THE MORNINGSTAR STRAIN HAS BEEN LET LOOSE—IS THERE ANY WAY TO STOP IT?

**EAN** 9781618686497  $16.00

An industrial accident unleashes some of the Morningstar Strain. The doctor who discovered the strain and her assistant will have to fight their way through Sprinters and Shamblers to save themselves, the vaccine, and the base. Then they discover that it wasn't an accident at all—somebody inside the facility did it on purpose. The war with the RSA and the infected is far from over.

This is the fourth book in Z.A. Recht's The Morningstar Strain series, written by Brad Munson.

PERMUTED
PRESS

WE CAN'T GUARANTEE
THIS GUIDE WILL SAVE
YOUR LIFE. BUT WE CAN
GUARANTEE IT WILL
KEEP YOU SMILING
WHILE THE LIVING
DEAD ARE CHOWING
DOWN ON YOU.

**EAN** 9781618686695   $9.99

This is the only tool you
need to survive the zombie apocalypse.

OK, that's not really true. But when the SHTF, you're
going to want a survival guide that's not just geared
toward day-to-day survival. You'll need one that
addresses the essential skills for true nourishment of
the human spirit. Living through the end of the
world isn't worth a damn unless you can enjoy
yourself in any way you want. (Except, of course, for
anything having to do with abuse. We could never
condone such things. At least the publisher's
lawyers say we can't.)

PERMUTED
PRESS